D0754277

KALYNA

a novel by
Pam Clark

KALYNA

a novel by
Pam Clark

Stonehouse Publishing
www.stonehousepublishing.ca
Alberta, Canada

Copyright © 2016 by Pam Clark
All rights reserved. No part of this publication may be used without prior written consent of the publisher.

Stonehouse Publishing Inc is an independent publishing house, incorporated in 2014.

Cover design and layout by Janet King
Cover Photo: *Girl from Volhynia*
Photographer: Maria Mishurina
Photographer in Ukrainian language: Марія Мішуріна
Printed in Canada

National Library of Canada Cataloguing in Publication Data
Clark, Pam
Kalyna
Novel
ISBN: 978-0-9866494-1-7 (paperback)
Second Edition

I would like to dedicate this book to Tony, Hanna and Emily for their gift of time.

PART I: WATER

"Hope is the thing with feathers that perches in the soul and sings the tunes without the words and never stops at all."

Emily Dickinson

Chapter One

The woman lying beside Katja wept. Each tear pooled upon the straw pillow, her sobs shaking the bedstead. Katja shivered and rolled over. Comfort would only come for Aya with sleep. Katja lay silently, willing the stream of dreams to wash over her bedmate.

Nights on the ship had been unbearable since they had left Antwerp. The Arcadia had docked and all passengers were ordered not to disembark. The ship lulled in the lapping water for hours as the crew took on hundreds of barrels of cement as ballast to steady the ship on its Atlantic journey. Passengers were locked into the third level of the ship, the stench already building, the heat stifling. Aya had tried to subdue her husband, but he was overtaken with the feverish desire to get off, to be on land once more. He had caused such a ruckus, pulling away from her, telling her he couldn't stay on the ship a moment longer. He banged on the locked door of their third level hold and bellowed. The crew acted quickly, unlocking the door, taking him by the arms and pulling him up the stairs. Aya followed, her skirt billowing, her arms reaching for him.

"No, no," she cried into the air. She was forced back down the stairs and pushed back into the room. The lock clicked.

"Too late, Miss," the crew mate said through the door. "He's not coming on this trip. Too unruly. Too unpredictable. Can't have that on the open ocean." Aya doubled over in sadness, and when she lifted her face to her fellow passengers her complexion was white, stricken with grief and fear. She pushed her way to the porthole, peering out for one last glimpse of her husband. She saw him there and banged on the porthole. "Pasha," she cried out.

Katja had watched this scene with horror. It was like watching someone lose a limb; Aya's husband torn from her and heaped on shore. Katja had gone to Aya then, and instinctively embraced her in her woven shawl. Aya looked through Katja, her eyes glassy, hollow, shocked and filled with such longing that Katja thought this woman may never be whole again.

Katja lay in the darkness, her back curled to Aya, wanting to reach out to her but cocooning like a fearful child, the damp sheet veiled over her. Katja cupped her growing belly in her hands and breathed deeply. If she listened carefully, in between the soft sobs of Aya she could hear the rhythmic breathing of Wasyl, or she imagined it, high in the bunks above. She closed her eyes to bring him beside her, to the iron bedstead, while the ship pitched and rolled.

Katja awoke to Wasyl's caress, his rough fingertips feather light on her forehead, twirling the curls which sprung out from her crown like wild corkscrews. His face was peaceful. He had slept well, he said.

"And you?"

He always asked about her. And what to say? Katja felt as though she had not slept at all these past four nights, the weight of her worry added layer upon layer to her fatigue with each passing day on the steamship. The stench of the sleeping quarters enveloped her like a cloud of fog, a plague of sorrow. How to sleep?

"Yes," she said. "Thank you." She chastised herself for this daily lie to her new husband, but it was the only one. She told herself it would be the only one.

"They have opened up the deck, Katja. Let's go breathe the fresh air of freedom." Wasyl sounded so earnest. It seemed only Wasyl saw the ray of hope among the hundreds of peasant immigrants abandoning all they had known and feared in their home country to begin this new struggle.

When the ship left Hamburg, Katja had taken stock of her fellow passengers, her countrymen, the Galicians. Men, women, and children snaking their way up the gangplank, heads down, shoulders slumped, hearts aching. Katja kept her eyes forward, her husband's strong hand guiding her, clutching her meagre bundles tightly. Katja remembered his smile, the same smile he gave her each morning; the only one out of so many somber faces, as if only he knew the secret of their journey. The rest of the passengers boarding were expressionless, even their eyes silent.

Their country had been at war for Katja's entire life, borders capitulated with each invasion: Poland, then Romania, then Russia. Her country had always been in transition, the very name Ukraine meant borderland, with the boundaries of her beloved country fluid and ephemeral. Countries invaded and Galicia fought back, and her people died.

To pass the endlessness of the nights on the S.S. Arcadia, Katja would conjure up images of the idyllic Galician countryside, its prairie grasses swaying marigold yellow and canary green. Her childhood memories filled her with a sense of belonging and she would feel herself relax, lulling herself to a sleep state. Only the tightness in her chest would wake her, choking her. And there were Aya's sobs.

With the land owners in control, Katja's family had nothing, even her family home belonged to them, the outsiders, and her father was powerless against their insurgence. Katja worked for the enemy, fist to mouth, working the fields every day that once belonged to her ancestors. With each scoop of the soil, she felt the fury of her father, his father, and her forebears. Her family heritage was at once tied to and ripped from the land. So many Galicians felt trampled by their homeland, their spirits buried in the very earth they hoed and turned each day. Still, they worked the earth envisioning the day it would rightfully return to them.

Katja and her mother, Anna, took the harvest to the Drobomil market every Saturday morning in the summer months. There was always something to sell: radishes, potatoes, carrots. The profits of their sales were split in half with the landowner, but at least it was something.

It was a sunny day in early September, she remembered. Katja had been kneeling beside Anna, their moth-eaten blanket laid before them strewn with potatoes, turnips and fresh beets from the landowner's plot. Anna had called out to passersby,

"Fresh vegetables for the finest stews, the finest soups, the finest meals!" Heads would turn to size up Anna in her kerchief, Katja in her babushka, and the blanket with dirt coming up through holes like worms in the garden, but the shoppers did not stop. Only Wasyl. He heard Anna's voice and felt his stomach rumble. He wanted soup, he wanted the finest soup. Perhaps, this vendor at the market had soup for him.

He walked toward the ladies kneeling, their heads down as they rearranged their produce, their kerchiefs bobbing at him. He scanned their blanket, eyes searching. There was no soup anywhere, he must have misheard, but there were fresh vegetables. Pausing before them he wiped the sweat off his forehead creating a streak of black, leftover from his day in the coal mine. He took off his hat and bowed to Anna. When she looked up she smiled brightly at this young customer, her blue eyes shining.

"Hello, Sir! Fresh vegetables today?"

"I would really like some cold beet soup!" Wasyl laughed easily.

Anna laughed back, "Perhaps this could be arranged, for a price."

At this, Katja looked up from arranging the vegetables and smiled. This man had made her mother laugh, which was a great sign.

Wasyl's eyes met hers, shining with life, bravado, and mischief, and he wore that black streak on his forehead like a badge of heroism. She looked away, overcome with shyness.

"You work? You have money?" Anna persisted.

"Yes, Miss, I do and I do." Wasyl answered Anna, but kept his eyes on Katja. She was striking, her blond hair tucked under her babushka, golden ringlets springing loosely from her blue scarf like spring flowers bursting with freedom.

"How much for soup?" Wasyl asked gently.

"How much you have?" Anna answered, unsure of a price.

"I have grivna. I can pay what you ask."

"Just one moment."

Her mother turned her back to Wasyl. "Katja, what do we do? How much for him to come and have soup?"

Katja stole a sideways glance at the gentleman before them. "You mean come to our house, mama?"

"Yes, the landlord will never know and I do make the best borscht."

Katja laughed with her mother. She glanced over her shoulder. The man was still there looking around patiently, respecting their privacy.

"I think we should ask him to pay what he thinks is fair."

"Yes. What is fair, very good idea," her mother nodded. "And we keep this secret, you and me."

Turning back to Wasyl, she stood up on her toes to be eye to eye with the stranger.

"I will go home now and make soup for you. My daughter, Katja, will stay here and bring you to our home in one hour. You will pay what is fair." She turned and winked at Katja.

Katja. Her name was Katja. Wasyl rolled the name in his mind over and over.

"I will stay here in the market until Katja," he nodded to her, "says it is time to come. You are most kind and I will be most fair in my payment to you." Wasyl had almost one hundred grivna in his pocket from his weekly work at the coal mine. He had never had so much currency and needed to save some for lodging and for food for the rest of the week. *How much?* he pondered. He wanted to win them over. He wanted to win Katja.

Wasyl had hovered near her stall engaging in small talk, asking about her life and taking the opportunity to tell her about the coal mine, which had just opened. Drobomil was experiencing a surge of village life these days as many farmers sought higher paying jobs in the stoneware factories and the coal mine, the dull and danger-ous work an escape from the oppressive serfdom in the fields. Wasyl had been one of these young men who had left his family farm, escaping from under the thumb of the Russian landowners, yearn-ing for independence. And now, he had found that freedom and wondered if he had found love as well.

* * *

Katja's legs felt like blunt pieces of ancient wood as she swung them over the thin mattress on the bedstead, Wasyl's voice urging her on. "Yes, yes, that's it."

Her feet had gone numb in the woven sandals she didn't dare take off at night for fear they would reappear on another's feet by daylight. Wasyl stood in front of her, his tanned arms outstretched like a father to a child. She shook her head, determined to over-come the stiffness in her legs. She pushed herself off the mattress, embracing Wasyl.

She could feel Aya's eyes on them. She whispered to Wasyl, who nodded.

"Miss Aya," he began. "Will you join us for a stroll above deck? The weather has cleared and the sun beckons us."

Wasyl's gaze was met with blank eyes; Aya's spirit was broken. He thought he caught just a slight movement of her head before she turned her back to them returning to fetal position. Wasyl sighed and whispered to Katja. "She'll come around. It is too soon."

The soles of Wasyl's well-worn boots slipped in the ocean spray as they emerged from below deck. Katja steadied him and he smiled at her softly. Wasyl held her close, his arm around her tiny waist, clutching her like a rag doll at his side. Katja swayed with the rhythm of the waves and he whispered in her ear to look forward and concentrate on the horizon.

"I'm here, Katja, right beside you."

Her legs grew sturdier as they strolled, the muscles awakening with each step. Katja glowed inside, memories pulsing life through her despite the bracing gusts that prevailed on the deck of the ship. Wasyl held her shoulder as they walked silently side-by-side, each lost in their own thoughts.

Katja remembered the sun beating down on them at the village fair later that summer, the 'pleasure wheel' that had spun them wildly, and Wasyl's proposal. The ride transformed her, sent her braids flying out from her kerchief, freeing them and her heart at the same time. Wasyl had proposed that day and she had shouted "Yes!" into the wind as the giant wheel descended on its roundabout journey. Without hesitation, and with a full heart.

She regarded her husband admiringly, immersed in his warmth. His eyes were busily searching the watery horizon.

Wasyl was mesmerized by the promise of land of his own, in the 'last best West ' of the country across the Atlantic named Kanada. Talk in the coal mine in Drobomil was that many of his countrymen had already settled there, where cool streams teemed with fresh fish and the land produced wheat the colour of the sun. He had made up his mind to journey there even before he had met lovely Katja.

"We will have a new community, a new family," he had told her.

"I have a community and a family here," she had answered.

Yet she had come, leaving her mother and father; she their only child now with child herself.

Wasyl touched her shoulder and felt protectiveness surge within him.

"You feel better today, yes?"

"Yes, thank you. Aya has stopped coughing too," she answered. "Only her tears consume her now."

Aya had not left her bunk since the moored nights in Antwerp and had developed a high fever and a cough which quickly spread to Katja. Those feverish nights Wasyl would sit on the rough-hewn planks beside her bed and stroke her damp forehead, brushing away the wisps of curl, urging them back to the tight crown braid she wore. Wasyl often thought this plaited braid resembled a halo on his lovely Katja, so innocent at only eighteen years of age. He would sing her the lullaby, *Oi Khodyt Son Kolo Vikon*, ending with the line, "Sleep, sleep, my little falcon; Sleep, sleep, my little dove." and tell her that their own dream was coming true. "Is this a dream?" she would ask, in her fever.

Wasyl would only climb up to his bunk with the other men when the crew members slapped their batons menacingly and spoke harshly, "Separate! Separate!" They would hound him and the other husbands and sons forced to leave the women's quarters.

"I'll see you in the morning," Wasyl assured Katja each night and she would smile weakly, knowing he would always be there for her. She would roll over, turning to Aya whose sad eyes glistened even in the dark, puddles of loneliness and longing.

This morning he watched her sleeping so peacefully, waiting for her eyes to flutter with the officer's booming voice announcing the opening of the top deck. He playfully urged her awake with a kiss on her cheek. She smiled, life coming back to her now that her fever had broken.

On deck, Wasyl scanned the horizon, knowing they were one day closer to land and imagined their new life in Kanada. This Kanada had free land; the posters in his village had advertised "Free Land for Millions". He and Katja and their unborn child would homestead and make their life here in this new country. Life and freedom would prevail.

Katja steadied her balance with each step forward on the drenched deck. The expanse of saltwater slapped and chomped at the side of the ship.

"Wasyl, where are we now?"

"This is the English Channel, Katja. This is the way to the Atlantic waters which will take us to Kanada." Katja scanned the indigo sea before her. The waves rocked the Arcadia impatiently, churning and urging the ship forward. Katja held the railing before her, feeling queasy and completely adrift. She turned to face Wasyl and focused on the stillness within him. His dark eyes shone with the reflection of the sun and she thought she had never seen him so at ease.

"How long must we journey?"

"Ten days if the weather holds, give or take." He glanced at the aquamarine sky, streaked with striations of white cloud, as if to procure the answer. He was uncertain, only estimating the duration, but he needed to tell Katja something. She trusted him, her family trusted him. He searched his memory for what he had heard in the market before they left. "It should be ten days more. We should arrive by May 1st," he said with conviction.

"May 1st," Katja repeated. "The promise of spring and new beginnings."

"New beginnings and time to plant a harvest," Wasyl said, smiling.

Wasyl had sold Katja on Kanada the moment he assured her they would have land of their own, free from oppression. It would belong to them. She had begged her mother and father to come with them. They had agreed initially, seeking the dream of freedom for themselves, but then recanted, her mother's pale eyes scanning her homestead. "I could never leave, Katja. I am too old to start again. But you, you are young and you must go." With great tenderness, she had cupped Katja's face in her rough, calloused hands. "Go in the hands of God."

Katja turned her gaze back to the deep blue of the ocean and imagined what lay below its menacing surface. Wasyl had told her there were whales in the ocean, giant friendly fish, that would twirl and leap out of the water in the waves. Where were those whales now? How did they know which direction to go? How did the water speak to them? The vastness of the ocean seemed to envelop and suffocate her. Light-headed, she steadied herself on the railing. No whales. No coast line. No direction.

Chapter Two

Calm weather held, yet the days passed slowly on the ship. Men played cards below deck and women tended to their children. Seasickness was rampant and many passengers remained bed ridden for days at a time. The third level of the ship was exclusively for the immigrants; below them was only livestock, the ballast, and excrement. Katja and Wasyl spent every possible moment on the top deck, breathing in the healing sea air. The smells below deck churned Katja's stomach, and the cures for the sickness nauseated her; onions and whiskey were passed and shared to calm the vomiting around her. Only on the top deck did she feel she could truly breathe.

"We've got to keep up our strength. Fresh sea air is good for the baby," Wasyl said.

Katja nodded and pulled her babushka tighter around her chin as they emerged on deck. Three other couples stood huddled on the port side of the ship. Otherwise, they were alone; mere ghosts floating among the busy crew tending to their ropes and sails. Today the wind blew colder and stronger. Dark grey clouds threatened. Katja shivered in the breeze, her thin cotton dress and crocheted shawl no match for the ocean winds.

"Here, take this," Wasyl offered his tattered woollen jacket. "I have my vest and you have baby."

Katja was grateful for his kind and generous nature. This is what she was attracted to back home. She felt tired and empty inside, so exhausted by the prolonged journey which seemed to be so many days now. How many had it been? Nine? She yearned for land and for this to be over. She was forgetting what home looked like. She forced herself to recall but it all seemed a blur to her. She tried closing her eyes and could just make out the Kalyna bushes surrounding Mama's house.

"Let's walk," Wasyl urged. "We'll stay warmer if we walk." The comforting image faded.

Katja wrapped herself in the woollen jacket, still warm from Wasyl's pulsing heart. She leaned into Wasyl and felt his chest rise and tense next to her. The captain's shout startled them both. "All passengers must go below! Now!"

The crew men were herding up the passengers on deck like cattle, prodding them toward the metal ladder to their cells below. Wasyl could see the waves had risen now, the dark clouds had descended. A storm was clearly brewing, and he knew they must return below as quickly as possible.

"We must do as they say, Katja. It's for our own safety."

Katja nodded and followed her husband back down the ladder. The third level reeked from the stench of life. It suffocated Katja and she cupped her mouth in an effort to prevent herself from vomiting. The ship heaved and she fell to the side of the doorway. Wasyl reached out to her.

"I'm going to be sick," she whispered.

"I'm right beside you."

Wasyl guided Katja to her cot and told her to sit down. It was safest for her. Passengers were still coming in the hold and the ship shifted heavily again in the rolling waves. Wasyl took Katja's hand in his to calm them both as he heard the seamen shut and lock the hatches of the third level door. The crew had only done this one time before, in Antwerp. Locking them in.

"It's for our safety in the storm," Wasyl assured Katja's questioning eyes. "We are safe here."

Katja lay back on the cot, Wasyl at her side. Her stomach churned with each loll of the ship. It was easier to lie down and focus on Wasyl's face. She felt Aya move closer beside her. She reached out her hand and Aya clutched it.

"What's happening?" Aya's tremulous voice whispered.

"We are okay, Aya." Katja stroked her trembling hand. "Vsi peryadky. Sey."

Grey metal surrounded them with one porthole to witness the crashing mountains of waves against the Arcadia, plummeting her sides and filling her upper deck. Wasyl hummed the lullaby, though he knew no one would sleep now. Shrill voices, crying babies, and hushing mothers surrounded Wasyl and Katja. Wasyl tried to focus on the human sounds to block out the haunting screams of the storming winds above. He stroked Katja's wild curls. How thankful he had been when she had agreed to leave her family for this new land. How brave she was and how trusting of him. "Dear Katja. Vy smilyvi."

She smiled weakly at her love. "I trust you. Ya doviryaayutobi," she managed.

She had always trusted him and he, in turn, had felt this assurance and responsibility for her. He smiled to himself, remembering one of their first afternoons together in Drobomil when he had urged her to the stage of the magic show at the travelling fair. Trust in him had prevailed and, at his urging, she had held out her hand to the magician they called Malnik the Magnificent.

"Do you remember Malnik?" he asked, "And the dove?" Katja's eyelids squeezed shut and he knew her eyes were there again, in the magician's tent. "Remember, how you trusted me, how you had such courage, just like that dove?" He could still see Katja's face up on that stage regarding him with a look of foreboding. He had smiled confidently and nodded to her, channelling courage.

Malnik the Magnificent had handed Katja a snowy white silk scarf, waved his magic wand and poof! the scarf had become a dove released from captivity, wings flapping in unison with the audience's applause. Katja's eyes had tracked the dove in wonder. At first it hovered, then soared to the top of the canvas peak searching for freedom. Katja's eyes had flashed with surprise then boldness. She clapped her hands in loud and joyous applause as the dove changed direction and found the tent opening, emerging and becoming only a speck in the sky. The audience applauded in sync with Katja, their conductor, and all her fears had dissipated.

Wasyl willed her the same courage now, the same confidence. He watched her eyelids flutter and startle, tracking the sounds of the storm. 'Let her feel safe,' he prayed.

Katja listened to Wasyl's calming voice intently, trying to match her breathing with the rhythmic cadence of his voice. She cupped her belly protectively and circled it, spiralling, focusing her energy and trying to calm the churning within her. Katja had balked at going to the fair at all on that summer's day. Surely it was a waste of money, so frivolous and extravagant, when she knew Wasyl was saving for land of his own. Wasyl had been pragmatic. "The money had already been spent, the fair was to be enjoyed with great pleasure," he said.

He had waved the tickets for the rides in the air as soon as they entered the gate. Her senses were overwhelmed by the sights, sounds, and smells of the fair; the food, the crowds, the rides, contraptions made of wood and metal, magical rides that turned and twisted and twirled, carrying fairgoers shrieking with excitement and fear.

Katja had hesitated before getting in the open metal cart with four rickety wheels on the Russian Mountain ride. They boarded on a flat train platform, but up ahead she could see the waves of the track take form. Now, she imagined herself back on the Russian Mountain ride at the village fair with Wasyl. She saw his head flung back, his wild eyes smiling at the thrill and speed of it all. Her hands had gripped the bar in front of them, then slipped with her nervous perspiration. Wasyl had clasped her hand in his and replaced them on the bar, as one. They would ride this out together. She had descended the ride a new woman, transformed by its speed and exhilaration.

"You liked it?" Wasyl shouted at her.

"I loved it!" she beamed.

The crammed train they had taken from Rava to Antwerp had been different altogether. Rows upon rows of peasants with blankets made into makeshift duffels, overflowing with meagre personal belongings and bits of food. The scent of woollen jackets, mothballs; knitted shawls, greys, browns, and black; the colours of emigrants; the hues and odours of the earth. Hundreds of people clustering like flies, risking their lives for a better life. Leaving their land for another, ready to be claimed as their own. A land of blue sky, yellow grain, and red maple leaves. Drawn by the poster urging emigrants to make the 'last best ' their home, the train leaving Rava was filled with hope and palpable trepidation. She had stepped on that train, Wasyl in the lead, his wild eyes smiling. Wasyl had found one empty seat.

"Sit, sit, Katja," he said. "Rest yourself and the baby." Always the baby. The baby that was their gift on their wedding night.

In her dreams, Katja saw her baby boy. She felt certain she was having a boy. She saw the black eyes of her husband in her son. She stroked his soft blond curls, her gift to her child. This baby would be born in the new country, the new land. He would be Kanadian. Her chosen name for him was Olek, protector of mankind. He would be just like his father.

Wasyl was grateful that Katja had drifted off. Her left hand still gripped Aya, who lay silently staring at him over the rise and fall of Katja's belly. He smiled gently at her. She smiled back. "We will be on land soon," he whispered. Aya nodded. Her eyes misted. And then what would happen to her? Wasyl didn't know, but they would disembark together. She mustn't be left alone in the new land, he and Katja had decided.

He looked up at the men's bunks and nodded to a fellow passenger named Ivan. Ivan was travelling alone and Wasyl had befriended him in Antwerp, the same time Aya and Katja had met. Ivan was huddled on his bunk, his face pale and gaunt and his tattered blanket wrapped around him like a cocoon. Wasyl confirmed that Katja was indeed asleep with an unrequited kiss, then climbed up the ladder separating the bedsteads to his bunk beside Ivan.

"You okay?"

"Yes. Feel chilled, is all."

Wasyl knew Ivan was afraid. Truth be told, he was terrified himself. At times, he wanted to turn this ship right around and head back to Drobomil, back to Katja's parents and his own family farm or even the coal mine. Then he would remember the depth of their poverty and the turmoil of their homeland and know he needed to do this for his wife and baby, for all of them to have a more independent and free life. But he knew fear and he understood the look in Ivan's eyes just now.

"Hey, where you headed when we arrive in Quebec?"

Ivan's eyes darted. He had not thought of this, only of escaping the terrible conditions of life as a peasant farmer. He lived life day by day as his mother had taught him. "Won't be disappointed then," she had told him.

"Don't rightly know just yet. Go where there is work, suppose. You?"

"The last best West! Just like the posters said. We're getting on a train and heading west to a place where horses run wild and grain grows wilder still." He paused to see Ivan's reaction to this collection of poetic images.

"Yeah, how far is this place?"

"Don't know for sure. A train ride away. But we've come this far, haven't we? The poster said the government wants people to settle the land. Gives you 160 acres for free and you have freedom!"

Wasyl's effort had worked its charm and Ivan loosened the blanket from around his neck, warming up to the idea of land and his own house and freedom.

"Work?"

"You're your own boss out there, farming the land; and there's probably work in the mines." Wasyl was reaching here. He had no idea if there were mines. He had no idea what else he would do for money, except be as self-sufficient as he could on his farm, and farm the land and sell his grain to the wheat board. That's how he would make a good, honest living. He had brought money to change to Canadian currency when he arrived. Until then, he didn't even know how much it was worth.

"This storm is pretty bad, huh?" Ivan said.

"Yes, but it will pass," Wasyl encouraged. "When we wake up, it will be over."

Chapter Three

Katja woke to quiet and still waters, the hum of the ship's engine and the muffled whispers of passengers around her. The hold was grey, and the air stiff and thick with sweat and excrement. She pulled her shawl over her nose and mouth and breathed in the earthen smell of her farm; of her mama, Anna. Anna had crocheted the shawl specially for this journey so that Katja would have a reminder of home. Anna had dyed the wool herself with beet and berry juice, entwining the burgundy and blue strands to form a kaleidoscope of colour. Katja breathed in again. What was her mama doing just now? Katja rolled over on her back and rested her hands on her baby boy. Now, she would be the mama and the beautiful life growing inside her needed her to be healthy, strong, and happy.

There was the occasional rustle among the whispers, but sleep had still overcome most of the passengers around her. She was a stranger to them and yet they all shared the same dream. It was unspoken but they all wore the halo of hope. She blinked sleep from her eyes, sensing the dawn was not yet nigh. She knew Wasyl would be at her side when she awoke again. She spiralled a design on her belly and thought she felt movement, like a flutter, like a butterfly's kiss inside her.

Wasyl lay awake listening to Ivan's erratic breathing beside him. The storm had passed, he knew, and by all accounts they were nearer to Kanada than before. It was April 28th and they should be nearing land today. According to his tattered map, the journey of the Arcadia went through the narrow Strait of Belle Isle in between Labrador and Newfoundland. This strait opened into the mouth of the Gulf of the Saint Lawrence, the mighty river to carry them to their first stop in Kanada, called Quebec. He knew the worst of the Atlantic voyage was behind them. What tidal currents could be here in this narrow strait? No more harm was to come to them.

He heard the latch of the passenger hold open and crewmen with oil lanterns entered, swinging their light alarms. The scraping of metal roused him.

"We need all passengers on deck. Captain says now! We are ice-bound and need everyone on deck!" The words echoed off the walls of the ship and continued, relentlessly.

"Ice-bound, deck, now!"

Wasyl shook Ivan awake. "C'mon, Ivan. We need to help out."

In his dream-like state, blanket wrapped tightly about his shoulders, Ivan climbed down the ladder to the floor level of the bedsteads. Babies cried, woken and jostled, as one by one, passengers were ushered through the door leading up the ladder onto the top deck. Wasyl found Katja among the empty faces and clutched her hand. It was cold as ice.

"It will all be okay," he promised. "Ice is good, no? It means shallow water and shallow water means land."

Katja blinked away the cobwebs in her mind. She reached for Aya, but Aya curled away from her.

"No," she mumbled. "No, I can't."

Katja shuffled her feet and nodded at Wasyl, but was not really hearing him. She felt the veil of fear suffocating her again.

"Katja, we've almost made it! You can do this."

On the bridge, there was a cacophony of shouts, cries, and whistles. Wasyl kept hold of Katja and his eyes darted about, searching for the captain. He nudged and pushed his way to the side of the ship where Katja would have room to breathe. He knew they must be in the strait. The railing of the ship blended into the striated ice floes surrounding the port side. The floes surrounding them were beautiful, glimmering white in the dawn's eerie light; reflective and powerful, locking the ship in place. They were little growlers, chips off icebergs that had floated into the strait and nestled around the ship while it had cruised slowly during the storm. Like puzzle pieces, the ice floes packed into each other with ease, hugging the Arcadia in a death like grip and immobilizing her completely. The whistle again.

"Attention!" The Captain's voice boomed. "We need your help. We are ice-bound and we need your assistance to dislodge our ship."

Over his voice, there was a grinding as ice floes scraped the sides of the Arcadia, screeching their discontent about the forthcoming plan.

"When I whistle, we need all passengers to come to port side," He gestured left. "Then I will whistle again. That means you come starboard—to the right side and we will steer her out of the ice floe, breaking the bastards. We will repeat until we've broken free of this prison! Will you help us?"

Wasyl and others shouted their agreement with the plan. Wasyl and Katja could see the ice, thick and ridged, bobbing at the sides, just challenging them to break free. Wasyl said, "We haven't come this far to be caught in ice."

Katja nodded silently, praying it would all be over soon. The sun had risen and she felt warmed by Wasyl's hands, orange in the awakening light.

"Hold on now, Katja. Stay with me!" Wasyl seemed energized by this challenge and he squeezed Katja's hand tighter. The whistle was shrill. Katja held on tightly to the railing as the ship swayed to the left. A throng of bodies pressed into Wasyl who pressed into her and she felt her torso crushing against the railing. She used all her strength to protect her bulging tummy from any pressure, forcing herself away from the railing and back into Wasyl's chest. The whistle again. This time, Wasyl pulled her under the sail starboard and they were on the outside of the crowd.

Grinding, scraping and swaying, the ship lurched forward, thundering, full throttle. The whistle again. Wasyl let others push past him to the railing this time, knowing the outside, closer to the centre, was better for Katja. The sway of the ship caught her off balance and she slipped in his arms. She had grown so thin these last few days, like a paper doll. The whistle again! Starboard again and this time; the screech was mournful, chirring, ululating that seemed to go on for minutes as the Arcadia streamed her way free of the fierce bergs.

The captain's manoeuvres had worked; the Arcadia was free. There was a loud cheer from the passengers. The Captain whistled three times, his thanks, Wasyl guessed, and descended the stairs.

"Now what?" Katja managed to speak. She had not uttered a word this last hour on the bridge. Other passengers trudged past the couple, many returning to the third level and sleep.

"I don't think I can sleep again, Katja," Wasyl answered. "Look there."

Katja glanced in the direction of Wasyl's nod. A flash of light startled her.

"What is it?"

"It's a lighthouse warning us of the cliffs, of the rocks on the shore! On the land!" Wasyl was bubbling over with excitement. He strained his eyes to see the shoreline, the coast of his new home country. He scooped up Katja and twirled her around and around on the bridge as if they were ballroom dancing. "We are here! Our new land! We are in Kanada!"

Chapter Four

Two more days passed before the Arcadia docked at the port of Montreal. The St. Lawrence Seaway had guided the ship with a gentle hand to the shoreline where trading ships competed for berths with the passenger liners and fishing trawlers. The ships jostled for position closest to the dock where thick hemp ropes would moor the Arcadia, hugging her to the shore after her long journey. Crew members scrambled with the mooring winches, turning the lines and winding the ropes taut around. Passengers milled about on the bridge of the great ship, chittering and chattering like seagulls, anxious to touch solid ground once again.

Wasyl was dressed in his finest woollen jacket, his sweater vest and hat, feeling emboldened as he breathed in the air of this new land. Katja's shawl enveloped her bony shoulders and softened her willowy frame. The ship had arrived a day early. They were here. Kanada. Katja scanned the bustling port, the fishing nets, hawser lines, and boat bumpers lining the docks. How long ago docking at Antwerp seemed to her now, a world away. The air smelled fresher here somehow; cleaner and freer. She looked directly at Aya, who was red-eyed and swollen from all the tears.

"Please come with us," Katja urged. "My husband knows where we can stay. We want you to be safe."

Aya was silent, but nodded. She would follow.

"Time to leave, Katja," Wasyl urged quietly. He glanced about on deck for Ivan. Passengers clustered in a constellate and Wasyl's eyes searched for the grey blanket. These last few days, he had come to think of Ivan as a younger brother and had offered him a place to stay with them when they got to Edmonton. He had not told Katja about Ivan yet. He was concerned that she would think they were taking on another mouth to feed, which they were, but this young man had endeared himself to Wasyl and Wasyl felt compelled to ensure Ivan found his way to a better life out West. He had told Ivan he could stay with them as long as he wanted until he got up on his feet. Wasyl also thought how valuable Ivan's strength would be in clearing the land, building the soddy, and setting up the garden for their new homestead. And now as he walked side by side with Katja, he sensed they also had Aya. What would become of Aya?

Katja took one last look at the ship, her heart beating with excitement as she walked down the gangway to the wooden dock. She smiled at Aya, about five passengers behind. She squeezed her shawl tightly feeling her mama's hug, her red kerchief flapping loosely against the fresh breeze and, trembling, stepped onto this new land. Katja held the railing to steady herself, wanting to make this first landfall on her own, independent of Wasyl. Wasyl followed close behind her, in deep conversation with a young unshaven man cocooned in a moth-eaten, tattered blanket. The young man stared at her every time she turned around and she felt his eyes boring a hole in the back of her head.

The long line of emigrants shuffled slowly snaking their way like Hydra to the immigration officers' table where they would present their passports, provide their personal information, and be officially entered as immigrants to Kanada.

"We will be registered landed immigrants," Wasyl had told her.

Katja held her passport in her hand and met the officer's eyes. He asked her to remove her babushka and asked her name, birthdate, and occupation. He recorded this information in a ledger with handwriting and lots of numbers. With great authority, he stamped the passport, nodded sharply to her, and gestured her on. Katja walked a little ahead then stopped and waited, watching as Wasyl did the same, stating his occupation as farmer, and then the two of them descended onto the street. Here the line burst into clusters like fireworks, as the feeling of freedom overcame the crowd.

"Katja," Wasyl gestured. "Please wait a minute. I need talk to you." They turned to wait for Aya and Ivan who was fumbling with his passport under the tattered blanket. Aya was slowly making her way to them, pausing with each step as if the land before her might crumble. Ivan was just approaching the entry table. The immigration officer had asked him to remove his blanket and when he caught up to Wasyl and Katja, he replaced it with a flourish like a Spanish bullfighter. He and Aya reached the couple at the same time. Katja instinctively reached out and took Aya's arm to support her.

"This is Ivan. I met him on the ship, next bunk over. I've encouraged him to stay with us awhile 'til we all get our bearings." Katja nodded politely at Ivan who removed his hat, revealing wavy brown curls and soft hazel eyes. He looked so young to her, younger than even her eighteen years.

"Hello Ivan. I am Katja."

"Hello Missus."

"And this is Aya. Her husband…"

"I know about her husband. Terrible thing. Hello Missus." Ivan regarded her shyly.

"Wasyl, Aya will stay with us as long as she needs to, yes?"

She gestured to Aya, whose eyes were downcast, not raising them even to greet the immigration officers, her very will to live seemingly wiped away in Antwerp.

Wasyl nodded. The foursome walked slowly on the cobblestones, relishing each step on the solid earth beneath their soles. Wasyl held a map of Old Montreal and was peering at it to find the church that Father Michaelchuk had circled for him. That was their salvation. He would ask the Sisters of Mercy to watch over Aya until her husband arrived on another ship. They would know how to get word to him that Aya was here in Montreal, safe and waiting; waiting for him.

Wasyl unfolded the tiny hand-drawn map revealing veins of white from time, and moisture from their voyage. The street names were blurred. Wasyl peered closely to find the church.

"Maybe I can help," Ivan said, taking the unfolded map in his hands.

I knew he would help us, Wasyl thought to himself and he linked Katja's arm in his.

Ivan stopped. "I think it's back this way," he turned and faced the way they had just come. Turning west, the view of the port left them breathless. The sun was just beginning to descend, the St. Lawrence shimmering with dusk's light.

"We have to double back and then go down this street." Ivan turned the map to show Wasyl.

Wasyl leaned over and decoded the smudged letters, identifying the street as Catherine Street on the map. He winked at Katja and she smiled.

Everything felt right just now, the European architecture, wood, rock, and brick, and the familiar cobblestones. Her step felt light and lively as they made their way in the failing light of day. She clutched Aya close to her, willing her friend to find inner strength in this new land.

Catherine Street was crowded with stalls and merchants with fresh fish and market goods. The smells of the baked breads and sweets made Wasyl's mouth water and he motioned for Ivan, Katja, and Aya to follow him to a stall. Wasyl reached into his worn front pocket to find his grivna. Would this currency work here?

"One loaf, please," he said.

"Show me your money," the gruff voice demanded.

"I have grivna. You take?"

"No, no, you need Canadian money. Go away!"

Wasyl shrugged his shoulders and glanced optimistically at Katja. "Maybe at the church we will eat something?"

Ivan traced Catherine Street with his finger. "It should be right here," he said. "The map says the church is right here."

Four heads looked left, then right past the market stalls to the side buildings. There was no cupola in sight, no ornate spire to indicate a Greek Catholic Church. "Over here, I think," Ivan motioned to a towering wooden door. Just above the door frame was a copper plate with the name Saints Martyrs Canadiens engraved upon it. Ivan squinted at the letters and shrugged.

"Not sure. What do you think, Wasyl?"

"Let's go in and ask," Wasyl suggested.

The men removed their hats as they knocked softly on the grand door.

A padlock was unhinged and the door was opened by a woman dressed in a nun's habit.

"Bonjour, vous êtes les visiteurs d'Ukraine?" Wasyl recognized the word Ukraine and nodded.

"Yes, Ukraine."

"I think she asked us if we were from Ukraine," he whispered to Katja.

"Oui, Oui, entrez-vous, s'il vous plait."

The nun stepped back and waved her arm sweepingly in welcome. The hallway was brightly lit and led to a large room lined with cots. Katja hesitated and stumbled when she saw the beds and rows of people in the cots with their sacks and bundles by their sides. She squeezed Aya's hand in hers. Crying children and musty odours filled the room and Katja was transported back to the ship and their hold for just an instant. She grabbed Wasyl's elbow with her free hand instinctively, her eyes wide. She wanted to leave, now!

"It is only for tonight," Wasyl assured her. Tomorrow, they would take the train out West.

The nun seemed to float among the cots, her feet propelled by an invisible force under her gown, until she came to four empty ones. "Voici!"

Ivan immediately settled into one and Wasyl followed. Katja waited for Aya to select one. Wasyl motioned with his chin for Katja to put down her meagre bundle and settle beside him.

She felt the weight of her exhaustion and exhaled as the well-worn straw mattress sagged beneath her. She looked directly at the sister.

"Eat?" she touched her mouth.

Wasyl stood up immediately. He made an eating motion to the nun.

"Is there anything to eat? Any food? My wife is with baby. I have grivna." With this, he reached into his pockets to show her the coins.

"Non, non," the nun gestured to the money. "Un moment, s'il vous plait."

She turned away, her gown swirling like a cape around her in a flurry. Katja settled herself on the cot, putting her aching legs up to release the blood flow to her swelling feet. She didn't dare take off her sandals, fearing she would not get them back on again. She reached out to Aya, who clutched her hand in return. They lay down together silent, mute in their friendship borne out of sadness and loss.

"Thank you," Aya whispered to Katja. "You give me hope, Katja."

Katja smiled weakly. She glanced around at the cots. How many others had laid their weary heads here?

Ivan sat still, perched like a meerkat, surveying the room. He watched intently as the nun spoke to another sister near the door. There was a great deal of nodding, then the nun who had greeted them returned.

"Vite, vite," she encouraged them.

"She wants us to follow her," Ivan translated the urgency in her voice to Wasyl, Aya, and Katja.

"Come."

The swinging door revealed an odiferous paradise where the smell of freshly baked bread filled their senses.

"Restez-vous ici," the sister motioned to the long wooden bench, solid and strong, facing a table of plenty. Crusty bread and soft, white cheese washed down with fresh water and cold, frothy milk. Nothing had ever tasted so good to Wasyl as this food from Kanada. Their empty bellies filled quickly as they ate in complete silence. The nun stood stoically beside them, hands folded and eyes closed in prayer.

Wasyl reminded the others, "We should pray and give thanks for this food and this shelter."

They bowed their heads and Wasyl spoke quietly, whispering thanks. He stood and reached for the nun's hand. She simply bowed and smiled a soft smile at him and then at Katja.

"Pour le bebe."

Katja smiled.

"Yes, for the baby, thank you! Spasybi!"

Chapter Five

"Bonsoir," the sister's voice rang out to the sleepless, homeless, and penniless in her care. She dimmed the lights and, catching Katja's eye, put her hands in prayer position and cocked her head. Katja could only hope that sleep would come to her. Her senses seemed on high alert, blocking out Ivan's snores and focusing on Wasyl's regular breathing; reminding her of the rolling waves of yesterday.

On the cot beside her, Aya lay on her back, eyes open. She rolled over to face Katja.

"Tomorrow, you will go?" she whispered to Katja.

"Yes."

"Then tomorrow I will send message to my husband."

"Wasyl will help. He will ask the nuns. They will know what to do."

Aya nodded. "You saved me, Katja."

"I think we have saved each other, Aya. Try to sleep now."

Katja closed her eyes and tried to block out the sounds from the cobbled streets outside. Boots scuffed and heels clacked on the stones outside the church basement window and Katja could see silhouettes of legs passing by. She could feel her pulse racing with the rhythms of this new city. Somewhere in her state of exhaustion, she slept.

The metal heels of the black leather boots clicked on the cobblestones, scuffing dirt and leaving a trail of cloudy, grey dust in their wake. With their rifles held taut at their sides, and their arms stiff like steel rods, they marched. Soldiers, police, or uniformed men, she couldn't make them out exactly. Still, they marched. In unison, four in a row, like synchronized wind-up toys whose springs go on endlessly. They stared forward, seemingly unaware of the wide-eyed innocents kneeling in fear and desperation as they passed, coughing up their dust, showing their deference and respect. The heels ever powerful, clicking. Black: the colour of control, of fear, of death. Those boots, she could see those boots; coming for her, for Wasyl, and for her baby. Those black boots.

Katja awoke with a start. There was a horn sounding, from the port. A ship coming in to dock in the dark of night. Warning others. She imagined the passengers, weak and sleep deprived, stumbling off into this city unknown. She felt a sudden urge to get up and run to that ship and get on and scream to the captain to take her home; she desperately wanted to go home, she needed to go home. Katja wiped her brow, clammy and cool, and breathed deeply releasing the flutter of life within her. Remember this night, she told herself. Remember. A flashlight bounced on the sidewalk outside the church basement window; a policeman on patrol. This was a place of safety. She was safe here. Safe.

PART II: EARTH

"How does the Meadowflower its bloom unfold? Because the lovely little flower is free down to its root, and in that freedom, bold."

William Wordsworth

Chapter Six

The dry prairie breeze fluttered the baby quilt; its frayed edges trailing tendrils like spiderwebs ripped apart by the thoughtless wind. It was Monday and Katja was hanging out the wash to dry in the heat of the mid-morning sun. She had strung a piece of hemp string from the hinge on the east window sill to the one remaining tree on their plot, a dying aspen, solitary, weak, and withered, but still strong enough to hold the line.

"Perfect for firewood," Wasyl would say each time he passed by that tree, but he never cut it down. One day maybe, but for now, that tree symbolized strength and perseverance to Katja here in the elements. She saw it as a survivor on the prairie, so trammelled by brush and grasses that they had not seen it until they had managed to clear the land. Immediately, Katja had been struck by this tree, appearing as if from nowhere; on its own, like her. Her tree, her line, her wash. Wasyl understood these things without saying, and so the tree stayed rooted.

Olek ran between her legs, breaking the silence of the moment and tickling her knees with his fuzzy locks. She laughed and rumpled his hair. He stared at her adoringly.

"Catch me if you can!"

She lunged for him playfully as he bibbed and bobbed behind Wasyl's wet pant legs and peeked out from her cotton apron hanging on the line.

"Let's play hide-and-seek, Mama," he begged.

Katja nodded. "You hide, Olek, and I will find you!"

He was the spitting image of Wasyl, except for the bluest eyes from her. Olek had been born early that first autumn on the land, three years ago now. Katja lifted her hand from the laundry basket to cool her forehead, warm in the sun. Three years. So long ago, it seemed.

She counted loudly enough for Olek to hear, "One, two , three... ready or not, here I come."

This was Olek's favourite game and he took pride in his hiding places, hardly making a peep. They had been playing since he was old enough to walk, then run, then hide. Katja loved playing with him, laughing with childhood wonder of her own all over again.

Katja tip-toed around the perimeter of the white-washed walls of her house, the house that Wasyl had built just before Olek was born. Until then, they had lived in their soddy made the first week on their land in Edna-Star. Layered with bricks of grass and earth to insulate the aspen branches and protect them from the November winds that swept over the fields like an icy hurricane, cutting into their flesh with frosted icicles. The soddy was now their root cellar; nothing ever wasted.

Wasyl had spoken of expanding the house in the three years since, of adding on another room for her newborn, Pavla, but Katja loved it as it was. The lime-wash white was so pure and clean, and reminded her of her mother's house in Drobomil. The kalyna bushes surrounded the house to the south. She had seen their blossoms the Spring they'd first arrived. A good sign. A sign of luck. A reminder of home. The kalyna bushes were a sign of hope to the Ukrainian people and were a symbol of strength and survival. Katja had grown up eating them; sour but full of vitamins, her mama would say. Only the strong people ate the kalyna berries. Many aspects of this new land reminded Katja of the old country. The rolling landscape, a grassy river waving and winding its way among the stunted fir trees, had welcomed her to Edna-Star. It had felt like coming home.

She could hear Olek giggling now, his sweet voice muffled as he covered his mouth to drown out the sounds.

"Boo! Found you!"

She reached for him and scooped him up in her arms, twirling around. Her dear boy, so full of life just like his father.

Setting him down lightly, like a helium balloon that would float away the very next second, she said, "Time to feed the chickens, my little Olek."

And he was off, cap tilted slightly to the left, his right overall strap hanging off his shoulder and his shoelace untied and dragging in the dry dirt, as he skipped his way to the pen.

She glanced at the direction of the July sun, sensing time passing. Pavla would awaken from her morning nap very soon and she would need feeding. Katja gathered her wooden pegs, picked up her woven basket and felt the baby blanket. Almost dry. How quickly the earth warmed up each day. She glanced at the pen again, taking in Olek's joy once more as he pounced and tried to capture the chickens.

"Olek, I'm going inside. Leave them alone, won't you?" She laughed, knowing that game of chase would last a long time.

Katja felt enormous pride every time she opened her door. It was made of solid birch wood that shut out the heat and kept them cool in the summer and warm in the winter months. Katja was thankful every time she entered her home, remembering their first shelter after arriving from Montreal.

The train that brought them to Edna-Star from Montreal had passed through fields of rolling of green, wound through desolate rocky outcrops and thick forested areas, and finally flowed through the prairie landscape. This land of Kanada had became more wild and rugged with each passing mile until the fields of prairie gold appeared. The wheat glowed, radiating the promise of a new life in a land that could have been a picture postcard of her Drobomil settlement. They looked so alike at first glance.

The Canadian Pacific Railway passenger train stopped at Strathcona Station, on the south side of the City of Edmonton. The station master had waved the passengers off here, saying that this was the last stop for two days and everyone had to disembark.

Wasyl had taken complete charge, asking the conductor himself for directions to the Dominion office. Wasyl, Katja, and Ivan walked in together and joined the line of immigrants, bundles of belongings and registration papers in hand. The office was small and stifling even in May. There was one tiny window behind the clerk, offering a slight, respite flow of fresh air. The officious government clerk sat at his desk, with a pile of papers on the right side and a large wooden stamp on the left. His glasses kept slipping down his face, from the heat Katja supposed. He held his white handkerchief in one hand dapping at his forehead while the other held the stamp. The slight breeze from the open window fluttered the enlarged map of Dominion Lands on his desk, and he rose to close it, ignoring the inaudible message the crowd before him sent to please keep it open. Katja felt herself gagging. Every breath she took seemed to dry out her mouth more. She felt like she was on fire.

"I must go outside for fresh air, Wasyl. I must stand in the shade."

Wasyl nodded and looked at Ivan.

"I will go with her," he offered.

"Yes, thank you. Come back in fifteen minutes, Ivan. You will need to sign for your own land."

Wasyl held their place in line, while Ivan steadied Katja and led her down the wooden steps to the shaded side of the office building.

"Sit if you like, Missus," Ivan offered.

Katja swirled her skirt about her as she collapsed in the cool grass, green and moist here in the shade. She felt awkward here with Ivan. He was meant to protect her, she knew, in this strange city, but he was practically a stranger to her. He sat down beside her, equally uncomfortable in their proximity, and broke the silence between them.

"I want to thank you, Missus."

"For what?"

"For including me. For taking me on and bringing me here with you and Wasyl."

"We're not there yet, Ivan." Katja stopped. She could hear the negativity creeping in her tone and knew it was her discomfort. She blinked it away. "My husband is a good and kind man. You can trust him completely."

"I want you to know he can trust me too. You can trust me, Missus."

"Thank you, Ivan."

"I best be going in now."

Katja sat silent, alone, and wondered about trust. She twisted the blades of grass between her fingers. How trust entwines and entangles people in a state of friendship and how quickly it can melt away. Her own country trusted Mother Russia, the landowners who said the farmers would still work the land and receive pay. But their words twisted with time and the pay was meagre. Poverty was the price of this trust. Galicia's strength, her land, had been stolen and the trust broken.

And what of Aya? Katja coughed out the dryness in her parched throat. Had Aya made contact with her husband? What of their trust?

Wasyl seemed to be taking a long time. She wondered if she had the strength to go back inside. Of course, the land would be in her husband's name, not hers, so there really was no need. She patted her forehead with her fraying handkerchief and didn't see the pink rubber ball rolling on the grass next to her. A small child with wild, unkempt, curly red hair tip-toed on the damp grass in his bare feet. Katja looked up at him like he was an apparition, a ghost from her village in Galicia. The ball was at her knee, too close for the child to comfortably take it from her.

"My ball, Missus?"

"Your ball, Sir." She rolled it about two metres away. "There you go."

The impish boy laughed, carefree, and picked up the ball and ran around the building to his waiting friends to continue their game.

All human encounters are built on trust, Katja thought. She rose, smoothed her skirt, and walked back to the energy-draining Dominion building. She carried a palm-sized rock in her left hand.

Wasyl and Ivan were next in line to be seen by the clerk. Wasyl smiled at Katja and welcomed the breeze the open door brought.

"I wanted to be beside you, Wasyl."

"This is good."

"Next," the clerk called out.

Wasyl, Katja, and Ivan strode to the official's desk.

"Please sit."

There were two chairs and Ivan stood behind so that Wasyl and Katja could claim their land first.

"Kind sir," Katja charmed, handing the rock to the official. "May you please open the window? This rock will hold your papers."

"Of course," the official nodded. "Thank you."

He placed the rock on his papers, the land deeds he was to disperse, and gratefully lifted up the window, releasing the heat which intermingled with the breeze. There was an collective sigh of relief amongst those in the line-up.

"We are landed immigrants, here to acquire land for our homestead," Wasyl stated confidently.

"Yes, yes, as advertised. The Dominion offers you this homestead with the provision that you must reside on the land for at least half of the year, and you must clear and cultivate at least two acres of your homestead within the first three years. Then you will be granted full patent. Do you understand?"

Wasyl nodded.

"The land has been divided up into quarter sections." At this, the official took off Katja's rock and lifted the top sheet off.

The clerk turned the map to the Federchuks. He adjusted his glasses to see more clearly. "This will be your land," he pointed to an area on the small map that had a box around it.

"All the land in the Star area has been slashed and subdivided. Land is distributed in parcels so your friend there will have the section beside you." He nodded towards Ivan. "You'll be close to town here and there is fresh water running through the property." He looked at Katja. "Mighty nice parcel, if I do say so myself."

Wasyl squeezed Katja's hand. They settled the minimal payment with the official and rose from their seats. "We will wait outside," Wasyl whispered to Ivan.

Ivan took their place. When he received his map, he held it in his hands like it was a piece of gold; a treasure to behold. He looked up only once at the official to say, "Thank you, Sir. You have made my dreams come true." He folded up the map into sixteenths and fit it tightly in his pocket, patting it for good measure.

"We're landowners now," Ivan could hardly contain his excitement as he emerged from the office. "If Mama could see me now."

It had been so easy, too easy it seemed, to acquire their land.

Their optimism was unbridled during supper at the Strathcona Hotel that night. Katja laughed easily and Wasyl thought he had never seen her so happy.

Katja woke alone the next morning in the small hotel room. She stretched out to touch Wasyl, feeling only the stiff cotton sheet, cool to her fingertips. She rose slowly and walked to the second storey window. Gazing at Main Street, bustling with its horses and buggies, she adjusted her skirt. When she looked up again, she recognized his hat first; Wasyl sat patiently in the driver's seat, Ivan at his side, parked outside the hotel door, a beautiful brown horse harnessed expertly to the open wagon. Wasyl held the reins on the horse so proficiently, as if he had done it many times before. She waved to him and shouted, "Good morning!"

He had been waiting for her to emerge and appear at the window and now he took off his battered, dusty, brown hat, held it over his heart, and smiled up at her in the second floor window.

"Looking for a ride, ma'am?"

The horse tossed its head impatiently and Katja grabbed her blanket, scooped up all of her belongings, and walked carefully down the narrow wooden staircase. She nodded her thanks to the front desk clerk before she burst through the hotel door.

"Yes, I am."

Ivan stepped down off the passenger side of the wooden seat, took Katja's duffel and belongings to store in the back, and offered her his hand to help boost herself up. She had been on the Russian Mountain ride, thought Katja. *How hard could this be?* She scooped up her cotton skirt and petticoat and climbed aboard. Ivan got up next to her and scooted to the back of the wagon, where he wrapped his worn blanket around his pencil-thin shoulder blades. Wasyl smiled, full of confidence, and with a click of his tongue the second leg of their journey began.

Very quickly, the ride turned treacherous as they made their way through wild lands. The open prairie grasses were peaceful, but were no place for a homestead. They needed wood, water, and some grassland for crops. They needed to go to the interior lands, off the beaten path. Ivan took out his Dominion Map every hour those whole two days of travel.

"It looks to be about 40 miles," he estimated using his fingers on the map, measuring the distance to Edna-Star. It was as though he guarded his job as navigator with his life. He had a compass which he carried in his trouser pocket. It was tied to his belt loop with a piece of potato-sack hemp that had been braided and knotted to be sturdy through the elements. He kept the map folded up so tiny in that same pocket.

Edna-Star was their destination; a bloc settlement for new Ukrainian immigrants where neighbours were separated by distance, but bonded by language and culture. The clerk at Dominion Lands had told Wasyl the settlement had a church and was well established, with dirt roads and pathways between homesteads. Their homestead would be about five miles beyond the village. Katja imagined their settlement with a farmers' market and children playing in the streets. She thought it would be just like Drobomil. They would make the trip over two days, Wasyl explained, on account of their newly acquired horse; a brown gelding, young and energetic.

A meandering creek dancing with fresh perch proved to be the perfect locale to break camp. Sleeping under the big sky that first night, Wasyl fell asleep holding Katja's hand tightly in his. His last words to her before he drifted off were, "We did it."

Katja lay awake, alert to the sounds of the night encircling her. Her thoughts spiralled; the water rushing by, the icebergs capturing the ship, Ivan's snores, dear Aya. She tried to quiet her mind, soothed only by the thoughts of her new baby.

The second day of the journey, their horse was exhausted. He trudged through the mud wells and stumbled on the tree roots criss-crossing the trail. When they came to a rushing stream whose current thundered down the boulders, the horse balked, reared, and backed up dangerously. The wagon jackknifed and hit a rut, then a tree, and the back board snapped off. The sharp sound of the break startled the horse, arching his neck back. His eyes flashed in fear.

"Whoa, now," Wasyl's voice was calm and controlled. "Take these." He handed the reins to Katja. She held them gingerly, trepidatiously, watching Wasyl slowly climbing down from the seat, calmly approaching the horse's side, stroking and whispering to him. Ivan hopped off the opposite side to inspect the damage to the wagon.

"Looks okay back here," Ivan reported. He stooped to pick up the board that had been dislodged on impact and tossed it in the back with their duffels and few belongings.

Wasyl motioned to Ivan to walk with him and together they led the skittish horse across the stream bed to the other side. Crossing the creek, aptly named Beaver Creek for the dams they encountered, Wasyl and Ivan settled the horse and released the harness from the wagon hitch, giving him free range on the grasses.

"It's only about two more miles to the village and then five beyond that to the land parcel. Perhaps we went too far yesterday; perhaps we were too eager." Wasyl muttered to himself.

He needed to talk through each step methodically. They had come this far. He looked at his exhausted horse, at Ivan's hunched back as he kneeled stream-side splashing water on his face and neck, and at Katja, patiently waiting for his word. He walked back to the wagon and inspected the damage, then came to Katja's side and offered his hand.

"Let's rest a while here, Katja."

They shared some bread leftover from the hotel and sat in the soft swaying grasses. Midday light streamed down on them and Katja closed her eyes and raised her face until it was directly pointed to the sun like a sunflower. She felt so alive and free. Somehow, sleep had come to her in the night and she felt rested and refreshed. The Beaver Hills rolled along the horizon and she could see the land level off and it reminded her of her beloved country. They were almost home.

After a spell, the horse raised his head, drank from the stream and then walked slowly to the front of the wagon and waited.

"All ready to go?" Wasyl asked the horse.

Katja raised her eyebrows at him and laughed.

"Well, he looks it, doesn't he?" Wasyl chuckled back.

Wasyl put the reins and harness back on the gelding and hitched the horse to the wagon.

"It's the final stretch," he announced.

Wasyl chatted as they trundled on, his optimism brimming over about the house he would build, the crops they would grow, and Katja's own garden; their own land. When he caught sight of the copper cupola glinting in the sun, a beacon as bright as that of the Belle Isle Strait lighthouse that had first welcomed them to the new land, he grew speechless. Silence filled the space between them as

they entered the clearing onto the dusty main road running astride
the railroad tracks. They had arrived.

Chapter Seven

Katja's eyes darted back and forth at the buildings and the dusty road. There was no spirited market alive with people and vegetables. No children were playing. In fact, the street was quite deserted. One shopkeeper was leaning on the wooden railing outside his Hudson's Bay tuck shop and nodded to Wasyl. Wasyl tipped his hat to the man. Robert Benton had seen many of these new folks come through here and knew that the farmers would be back to town for some staple goods when the time came. Best to be welcoming now.

"There is no one here." Katja murmured, "Where is everyone?"

Wasyl knew Katja was expecting a life similar to Drobomil and he too had expectations, for what else did they have but their previous life to compare this to?

There would be greater isolation at first, he anticipated, but this would subside as more land was settled and the bloc settlement continued to grow. The Dominion Land clerk had confirmed this with his land grant.

"Katja, there are many of us, just like in Drobomil. We just live farther apart. That is the government's declaration. They want dispersed settlement. We will meet people. We will come to the church on Sunday and meet others just like us." He nodded to the cupola. "It is a reminder of home, no?"

Katja glanced sideways at Ivan whose eyes were downturned. Was he to be her only other adult to converse with? Katja desperately wanted to have a female friend here who could guide her and understand the pregnancy and just be her confidante. Too much to ask, she feared, at this moment. She tried to hide her disappointment as she pursed her lips forcing them into a half-smile at Wasyl.

"Yes, Wasyl. It does look like home."

The rocky road began to narrow as they passed stakes planted pointedly in the ashen soil at the side. Their land was identified by a red stake and a perfectly slashed line in the grasses by Dominion Surveyors. N50, E 44 was their marker and it matched the surveyor's map Ivan held in his hands. This was to become the Federchuk Family homestead. Wasyl leaned over Katja and handed Ivan the reins. He leapt off the wagon seat and examined the stake, comparing it to the map.

"This is it," he confirmed. "We'll need to go by foot to clear the branches. The wagon won't fit through this tangle otherwise." He knelt down just past the stake. "Looks like a trail was made here at one time." The Old Indian trail to the creek had stood the test of time and now remained as a guide for the new settlers.

Wasyl returned to Ivan and Katja. He nodded at Ivan who handed the reins to Katja, jumped down and strode to the back of the wagon.

"We'll need knives to do the job, Ivan. Got one?"

Wasyl retrieved his knife from his duffel. It was not long, but it was sharp, and it would slash the brambles into a makeshift pathway leading to the fresh water noted on the surveyor's map. It had been his father's.

"There is an overgrown trail that way." Wasyl pointed. "I think it must lead to the stream the clerk told us about."

Ivan pulled out his map and examined it with a trained eye.

"Yes, it leads us due East."

"Katja, we'll go first. We need you to follow slowly behind."

Katja nodded. Her stomach rumbled and she felt an overwhelming feeling of hopelessness. How would they get to the creek through this tangle?

Compass in hand, they started out, Ivan and Wasyl slashing and scooping up branches, clearing the way for Katja, the horse, and the wagon. The trail had already been established and was cleared in some parts more than others, but the pines and firs intertwined and the horse hesitated, cringing at the scratchy needles on his legs and belly. Wasyl took hold of the harness and urged the gelding on and Ivan took the lead breaking the trail. Once again, Wasyl was thankful Ivan was there with them.

When they finally caught sight of the rippling clear water stream, Wasyl took the reins from Katja and helped her down. He handed the reins to Ivan who unharnessed the horse to let him drink freely from the stream. Wasyl seemed to be in a hypnotic state, walking away from them deep in thought; measuring, surveying, imagining. Katja waited patiently by the horse and wagon. She spied what looked like kalyna bushes immediately to the south and felt her eyes mist up. Her family home in Drobomil. "Only the strong eat the berries," her mother's voice came back to her.

"We will build here," Wasyl announced.

Ivan rose from creek side, water dripping down his face and neck, streaking his blue shirt. He regarded Wasyl's land with a prospector's lens. Yes, this was a good spot for Wasyl.

"This plot is close to fresh water, sheltered from the North winds by the forest, and we have a valley to the west for planting."

Wasyl walked with Ivan, talking quietly.

"Yes, this is it, Katja!"

Katja clapped her hands and felt hope return inside of her. There was not much of a clearing yet, but she closed her eyes and lifted her face to the welcoming sky and imagined her home. She could see the house near the stream, the fence for some animals, the valley beyond green with potato leaves, and the kalyna bush with white blossoms. Yes, anything was possible. The baby's kick brought Katja back to the overgrown frontier land she stood upon.

Chapter Eight

Her eyes fell immediately upon the dried berries on a blossom-laden low bush, similar to her country's kalyna. Last season's growth gone wild here in these untouched brambling woods, she unfurled her apron like a bowl to put the tiny berries in.

"How do you know these are okay to eat?" Wasyl asked her protectively, coming by her side.

"These berries are Kanada's kalyna. Besides, I watched the horse eat them yesterday and he's just fine. I'll be fine."

She tasted one, a little hardened by freezing, but sweet, sour, and tasty all the same.

"Here, want one?"

Wasyl reached out. *They did resemble kalyna berries*, he thought.

"They are perfect," he said.

Ivan watched them as he tied up the horse to an old weather stripped tree near the creek. The limb of the tree extended straight out like an arrow and Wasyl took this as a sign.

"We will build our first shelter here," he said facing where the branch pointed.

Ivan and Wasyl worked tirelessly gathering twigs and fallen branches, deadfall, for their temporary shelter; a zemlyanka made from the earth. Soon, a mound of collected building material lay near that tree.

"This is only a start," Wasyl noted. He looked at Katja, her apron quite full of berries now, thought of their baby, and repeated, "It's only the beginning." He was overcome, and turned and knelt beside the creek, its clear droplets mingling with his tears.

That night Ivan slept under the stars tending the fire, his roll became his bedding. Wasyl and Katja slept in the wagon, clear of the morning dew and ground moisture. She fell asleep counting the stars in the sky against a palette of ebony. Her hands ached from picking berries and gathering building materials and she longed for oil to massage into her scratchy wounds, intersecting each other like crimson mazes.

They awoke with the sun. Katja felt as though spiderwebs had crept up her arms and filled her mind. Groggily, she surveyed the scene. Ivan was tending the fire they had kept burning all night Wasyl was walking the land, hands on hips, talking to himself; creating a list in his mind of the numerous items he needed to purchase in town.

"Remember the shop we saw? I will go there to buy tools to build our home."

Wasyl nodded at Ivan. "You will stay and keep the fire going, yes?"

Ivan understood Wasyl's unspoken concern about leaving Katja. He understood that the lighter the wagon, the better it was for the gelding, so he answered with conviction.

"Yes, I will stay and do some fishing to build up our store of food."

Katja smiled. At least she wouldn't be alone.

Wasyl returned from the village with a pitchfork, saw, shovel, and wheelbarrow. The shopkeeper, Mr. Benton had explained that these were the tools that were purchased the most by the settlers. These were the instruments to construct their zemlyanka.

Day by day, Ivan and Wasyl cleared the base of a one-room dugout facing south, away from the creek. Their pile of small twigs had grown into an overflowing mass of willow and aspen branches, and even thin sapling trunks from the abundant poplar forest. Wasyl and Ivan constructed this first abode using the age-old folk form of their forebears, their focus on providing immediate and effective shelter. Poles lined the outside of the hut designing the vertical house. The men had trenched around the floor of the house and as Wasyl set up each towering branch, some just starting to bud, Ivan would follow with the shovel and the pail of water and mud it in place. The sides of the shelter were at forty-five degree angles, like a lean-to, forming a peaked roof, a tangle of branches; wooden tentacles reaching for the sky. The entrance was a space of about twenty inches, just large enough for them to squeeze in, but narrow enough to keep wild animals out.

They had not encountered anything wild yet, but the shopkeeper in town, Mr. Benton, had warned Wasyl about the deer, bison, and bears who wandered about the land. Wasyl had returned from town on his second trip with a rifle, for protection he said.

Ivan had fashioned a fishing rod from a poplar twig and his hemp twine and had caught two perch these last three days. Katja had cooked them over their open fire and added the tiny crimson berries before she served them. The meals were nourishing and fresh and melted in her mouth. The land was sustaining them for now.

She watched admiringly as Ivan and Wasyl added mud slabs to the sides of the logs; weather-proofing it, they said.

"How can I help?"

"You can get us some water to mix into the earth in this wheelbarrow," Wasyl suggested.

Katja scooped up her dress, weathered and worn by days of travel, trekking, and working in the dusty earth. She gathered her ocean-coloured shawl around her shoulders, feeling her mother's strength embrace her.

"You can do it!" the voice inside her urged.

The wheelbarrow trundled down the footpath Wasyl had cut to the stream. She took the cooking pot and began to scoop one, two, then three potfuls into the wheelbarrow's basin. As she rose, a movement across the stream caught her eye. There was a shadow of something rustling amongst the branches; brown, large, moving.

"Wasyl!" she called out and the animal stopped, startled and stilled by the shrillness of her voice.

Wasyl came running with the shovel ready to strike.

"There," Katja whispered, barely audible.

The grand elk with its rack of antlers was camouflaged amidst the tree trunks. Katja had never seen an animal quite like this one.

"Isn't he beautiful?" Katja murmured, lost in the moment.

"Yes, he is," Wasyl agreed, making direct eye contact with the animal. He thought of running back for the rifle for just a second, but was held captive by the elk's majesty. Ivan was rushing down the pathway now, rifle in hand, ready to shoot.

"What is it, Missus?" he called out.

At Ivan's shout, the elk broke free of Wasyl and Katja's gaze and trotted farther into the woods. "We have to be careful," Wasyl said. "I'll take the water now and let's head back up together."

* * *

Katja felt shy with Wasyl as she undressed in the corner of their dugout, the fresh poplar and wet earth scents filling the air. She knew Ivan was just outside tending the fire, the rifle at his side. She tried to hide it, but she felt as nervous as she had been on her wedding night. Her braid unravelled as she ran her fingers through its curl springing back to life and shrouding her in its softness. She hugged her shawl around her shoulders and climbed adeptly into the blankets on their dug-out floor. Wasyl smiled at her, his black eyes flashing, amused by her modesty and humbled by her beauty. He stroked her curls and twirled them in his finger. "Our home," he said. "Welcome to our home." Katja felt tears well up inside of her at the pride in his voice and she was swept up in his arms, the warmth of his body bathing her. His calloused hand stroked her bare belly lightly caressing the baby and moved lower. She relaxed with his gentleness and snuggled into his bare chest feeling his heart beat and wondering at his tenderness.

The next day, Wasyl was gone from the zemlyanka by the time Katja awoke. The hut was dark inside, a testament to the fine job of mudding the men had done. Only a sliver of light shone through the entrance, cradling and cajoling her. She rolled herself over in the frigid morning air and reached for her clothing. She could smell the fire and when she emerged from the hut Ivan and Wasyl were deep in conversation, each straddling a poplar log they'd fashioned as seats.

"Good morning," Katja said quietly, so as not to disturb.

Wasyl rose, came over to her, took her by the shoulders and kissed her lightly on the cheek.

"How did you sleep, my little dove?"

"Well, and you?"

"The best in a long, long time," Wasyl answered and he squeezed her hands tenderly.

He looked directly into her blue eyes.

"Ivan wants to begin to build his hut today. We would have to head over East according the Dominion Map. We're not sure when the inspectors will be coming 'round to check on the building requirement so he figures the earlier in the season he begins, the better."

"I understand," Katja acknowledged. "I will pick more berries to bring for the day."

"It would be a long day, Katja. I think you should stay here."

"On my own?"

No! Katja wanted to shout. No, I don't know where I am and no, I don't want to be on my own in this wild land. But she held her feelings deep inside.

"Whatever you think is the best thing to do, Wasyl, I will do. I trust your decision."

"I think you should stay, Katja. I will come back midday to check on you and let you know our progress. Ivan says he won't need a hut as big as ours and now that we're experienced..." his voice trailed off.

He had a nagging feeling that he shouldn't leave Katja, but knew this would only be the first of many necessary separations when he worked the fields or went to town.

"I'll be back soon, I promise."

Katja unconsciously lowered her eyes. The soil here was black, rich with minerals, and would be excellent for planting. She saw the yellow grasses, crushed down from the snow, just springing back to life. She took a deep breath and looked up again.

"I will continue to thatch the grasses for our roof, Wasyl. Rain will come soon and we must be prepared."

Wasyl smiled at her effort to be independent, but it could not hide her trembling hands and he held them firmly.

"I'll be back soon, I promise."

He nodded to Ivan who tipped his hat to Katja. They untied the horse, hitched him up, and loaded the tools into the wagon, even the rifle. Wasyl returned to Katja.

"Take this knife to cut any stubborn grasses."
She closed her eyes as they embraced.

Chapter Nine

Katja watched as the wagon reeled and rocked through the bushes, heading back to the main path that led to the village. This was where the markings on the map connected at the cross-roads and she could just see Ivan unfolding that map now and setting his compass for East.

There were few berries left on the bush nearest their hut, and Katja needed to pick more, which would mean straying a bit farther from the camp. The fire was the first priority. We must always keep it burning, for now. Wasyl's words rang in her head. Katja scrambled through the brush and scooped up fallen twigs and smaller branches that she could bundle to use throughout the day, leaving the logs Wasyl and Ivan had cut for the nighttime. The grasses were dry already, the winter snows having melted months ago, but they still retained winter moisture that would make them flexible for weaving. First the fire, then the roof, she reminded herself. Then the berries.

Carefully pushing away the grasses, seeking out small twigs for kindling, Katja opened her apron using it as a bucket. She knelt down crunching something under her weight. She slid over and cleared away the top layer to reveal a grassy nest, carefully hidden, a safe haven for three whole eggs. The one that had cracked had spread across the tiny nest. What kind of bird's eggs were these, she wondered? So tiny and speckled. She examined the nest so lovingly thatched and thought of her own thatched work for the roof ahead. She scooped up the eggs and balanced them amongst the kindling in her apron as she rose to head back to the fire.

The full breakfast satisfied her and she found herself less on high alert and more at ease in her surroundings. The twittering of sparrows and flickers comforted her, as she used Wasyl's knife to cut and gather the dried grasses. When she had a large pile, she would rest with a palm-full, separating them into three bunches. Braiding the grasses together in a tight thatch and layering the bound bundles would make their roof waterproof. Her mother had taught Katja this technique in the old country and it was an annual task for the two women of the house. Katja was so engrossed in her work that she almost didn't hear him approaching.

There was one medical doctor for the district north east of Edmonton and the doctor worked out of the village, Edna-Star. Dr. Edward Smith was an Englishman who had immigrated to Canada as a child with his family. The Smiths had settled in the city of Edmonton and Edward's father, also a doctor, had immediately set up a successful family practice. Edward was the eldest child and had always been an avid learner who excelled in the Sciences.

He was doted on by his mother and learned to flatter and fawn over her in order to ensure he got his way. When he had graduated from the University of Alberta's Faculty of Medicine in their first graduating class, his mother had insisted on a photograph of only the two of them, he in his brand new grey woollen suit, bought by his mother of course, and she in her silk wraparound dress, imported directly from China. Elizabeth had broken up with him shortly after she saw this photograph hanging in the front entryway of the Smith household.

"Don't you see how she controls you, Edward? You'll never be free of her until you leave here."

Elizabeth had walked out of the house then and had not returned his phone calls for two weeks after his graduation. *So that is love and how it ends*, Edward had thought to himself. He had cared deeply for Elizabeth and she had been his first sexual partner, hushed in his parent's basement when he knew they were in their port-wrought slumber upstairs. Elizabeth was older than he was, working as a clerk in the courts, and had met him through his father's practice. There had been immediate sexual attraction between them, and the undeniable connection only strengthened their bond and then this; this shunning, this dismissal of his very being, and all over a photograph. He'd looked at the photograph critically. His mother was turned directly to him, her head lifted like a lover awaiting a kiss, staring admiringly at him, her hand on his heart, while he stood tall and proud for the camera.

When his father told him he had arranged a residency for Edward at his practice, Edward took him aside privately and explained he would like to leave Edmonton, for the time being anyway. He had read in the Edmonton Gazette about an opportunity in the Ukrainian bloc settlement not forty miles from Edmonton.

"I will be close, Father, but will be able to stand on my own and develop my own practice." As Edward said this, he felt melancholic at the memory of Elizabeth nuzzling his neck. Maybe now she would come back to him.

The eldest Dr. Smith had nodded, in admiration at his boy who seemed to have grown up overnight. He could not, however, have anticipated his wife's nightly weeping over the next seven days as Edward packed up his boxes and prepared to leave on the train. When Edward finally left it was without fanfare. Mother, Father, and sister Fran seeing him off at Strathcona Station, heads held high all around and pecks on the cheek for good luck.

He had been struck by the rugged beauty of the land as the train entered the village of Edna-Star. The rolling hills with their trio of greens exulted in him a memory of springtime past; perhaps in his childhood England, but he couldn't be sure.

Dr. Edward Smith was fine-featured, fair-haired, and very fashionable. As soon as he stepped foot on the bloc settlement soil, he distinguished himself from everyone else who lived there. His very being seemed to float off the train. Heads turned and tongues wagged at the finely-dressed English doctor who had just arrived in town.

Edward was raised believing that how you present yourself is how others will perceive you. A simple thing, it seems, but perspective alters in an outside environment. So, it was in this belief that Edward made rounds to the new immigrants' homesteads wearing a three-piece suit every day. Dr. Smith could have been visiting the Prime Minister at 10 Downing Street in London, he was so dapperly dressed and elegantly composed on this very day when he met Katja. He trotted into her camp area on a blazing Belgian with a royal air, and Katja felt his presence before she saw him.

"Whoa there, Milly," he directed his horse.

Dr. Smith tipped his felt topper to Katja and bowed his head.

"Good day, Ma'am."

Katja set down the braidings abruptly, startled to face this visitor. She stood up quickly, awkwardly smoothing her apron over her belly and wiping her hands down. "Hello," she said to the stranger.

Dr. Smith dismounted.

"If I may introduce myself, I am Dr. Smith, chief physician of the area. The shopkeeper, Mr. Benton, told me you and your husband had come through a few days back now and that you were with child. I thought it prudent to come out and introduce myself to you."

With this lavish introduction, Dr. Smith outstretched his hand to Katja. She rubbed her right hand in her apron again and lifted it gingerly to him.

"Hello. Pleased to meet you. I am Katja. My husband is Wasyl Federchuk."

The touch of Katja's hand sent shivers through his body. It had been four weeks now without Elizabeth. He yearned for her. He shook the memory away and stared at Katja's hand in his. It was soft and white like the petals on the spring kalyna blossoms. Dr. Smith noticed Katja's blond curls peeking out of her babushka playfully, framing her face. She couldn't be more than eighteen years, by his account.

"How far along are you now?" he asked, releasing her tender hand.

"Four months. The baby will come at harvest time." Katja twirled her loose curls nervously wishing Wasyl were here.

"You are eating well?" he asked doubtfully.

"Yes, very well." Katja thought about asking him about the berries and what bird had left those eggs for her to nourish her baby, but she didn't want to seem unintelligent so kept her questions tucked inside.

"And your husband?"

Dr. Smith's striking blue eyes darted about the camp, hovering over the zemlyanka which showed remarkable care and workmanship.

"I'd like to meet him too."

Katja found herself staring at the doctor's blue eyes then at his perfect teeth. Her hand went instinctively up to her own to hide her teeth, yellowed from the days without care.

"He is tending to our neighbour and will be back shortly."

At this, Katja glanced at the sky. Yes the sun was almost directly overhead, it was midday.

"Neighbour, which way?" Dr. Smith asked.

"East," Katja pointed.

"Ah, well, maybe next time," the doctor sighed. "Miss Katja, I'd like to check in on you every few weeks or so and see how you're feeling. We want that baby of yours to be born healthy now, don't we?"

Katja marvelled at how debonair this man was. She had never seen a gentleman dressed so finely, with hair slicked back, and a horse with a braided mane and a name, Milly. And here he was, straight from the cultivated English countryside to the untamed wilds of her new homestead, like an apparition.

"Yes, thank you. And thank you for visiting. I will tell my husband you came by."

"Good day to you then, Miss Katja." Dr. Smith twirled his hat back on his head like a showman. He wanted to take Katja's hand again, but felt it imprudent. He would have to fight the urge to bring it to his lips so he could kiss her fingertips.

"Good day, Dr. Smith," Katja mirrored his formality.

She suddenly felt like laughing at his dramatic flair, so out of place here on their homestead.

"Let's go, Milly," he urged.

Milly obediently backed up and made a perfect one-hundred-and-eighty degree half-circle, like a horse in the circus, and they trotted back through the brambles.

Katja did laugh then, a wild girlish guffaw to release her nervousness and to unleash her pent-up tension.

Branches scraping the wooden sides of a wagon gave Katja pause. She looked up in wonder at who would be her next visitor. Wasyl's windswept face smiled broadly as he approached, like a beacon of light shining out of the pathway. She waved wildly.

"I met the good doctor coming down the path," Wasyl said as he dismounted and took off the harness and hitch. "He said he stopped by to introduce himself to you, what with the baby coming and all."

With these words, Wasyl wrapped himself around Katja. She was safe. They had weathered this first separation.

"Let's go inside, out of the sun."

Ivan's hut was coming along, slow and steady, Wasyl told her. There was plenty of poplar on his land and the trench was dug and the front entrance poles set with caked mud. The same stream runs through his property, Wasyl told her.

"He chose a plot just on the property line so he is close, should we need each other."

Katja marvelled at Wasyl's kindness and brotherliness. He had left three brothers in Galicia and she was suddenly very glad that Ivan was here, with them, a part of their new family. Wasyl said they would send word to the old country soon, to let everyone know they were safe and had shelter.

"I told Ivan I would return shortly and we will work on until the sun sets. He will sleep here again tonight and maybe tomorrow until we are finished. Then, we will help each other prepare the fields for seeding."

Wasyl's voice was so tender when he spoke of Ivan, filled with such caring and protectiveness.

Katja remembered the tiny speckled eggs she had found. "I found eggs this morning, Wasyl. Tiny ones this big." She held her fingers into a tiny circle.

"Ah, they must have been fresh quail eggs," Wasyl remarked. "This land will sustain us." He paused and held her close. She could barely hear his whisper. "We belong here, Katja. I feel it inside me."

Chapter Ten

The Russo-Orthodox church in the village stood prominently on the prairie landscape. Its cupola rose to the sky and it was the largest building in Edna-Star. Ivan, Wasyl, and Katja sat together in the front seat of the wagon. They surveyed the consecrated grounds and saw the bell tower set back from the church. The bells were ringing, calling them for service.

It was their first time to meet other homesteaders like themselves. So far, Wasyl had only met the shopkeeper, and he and Katja had both had met Dr. Smith. Katja was eager to meet other women from home; from the old country. She desperately missed the company of her mother and the companionship of her sisters; the way they understood each other and laughed at the same things.

Her shirt and skirt had come clean as she'd scrubbed them in the flowing stream, and only her apron still had stains of life remaining. Leaving the apron at home this Sunday morning freed her. She wanted to make a good first impression and show her respect to the church. She glanced down at her worn boots, scuffed by their month's journey across land and sea along with her kneeling to collect the grasses for the roof. She hoped no one would notice and judge her harshly.

The priest welcomed them at the door with a dignified bow. Ivan and Wasyl removed their hats and the trio made their way in. The dark wooden pews and golden altar transported them to their church in Drobomil. Wasyl led the way to the third pew on the right side. They slid in together, nervously bumping the pew in front of them. A radiant smile peeked around, eyes shining just beneath the brim of a frilly blue bonnet.

"Hello," a soft voice voice whispered, looking directly at Katja.

"Hello," Katja whispered back. Could her prayers have been an-swered so quickly?

The young woman turned back once more and whispered, "I will introduce myself after," she said and winked.

How lively, Katja thought and her heart lifted with possibility.

She glanced at other members of the congregation, smiling, and caught sight of Dr. Smith, sitting just opposite them. His blue eyes shone as brightly indoors she noted, as he nodded his greeting si-lently to her. Gently, she nudged Wasyl and he nodded back at the doctor. Ivan stared straight ahead at the brown curls on the lady in front of them. They curved exactly around her earlobes like a halo. They sprung with life, just like her.

An austere woman dressed in dead-rat brown rose from the front pew to take her place at the piano at the front of the church. The processional hymn. As the priest entered from the back of the church and strode to his place at the pulpit, the congregation stood and bowed their heads. Katja felt shy all of a sudden, keeping her eyes down; a feeling swept over her of being a stranger in this house of God.

The priest spoke in Ukrainian to his congregation, blessing his flock as part of the invocation. Wasyl, Ivan, and Katja followed the others' lead and sat down as the priest began recitation of the litany, his prayers for the people. Eyes closed, heads bowed, hands clasped dutifully in laps, they prayed.

"For peace from above and peace for the whole world, let us pray.

For all people to lead wise, honest, and truthful lives, let us pray.

For the security of our nation, our motherland, our home, let us pray.

For a spirt of knowledge and understanding for all people, let us pray.

For seasonable weather for abundance of fruits from the earth, let us pray.

For those abroad who may be sick and suffering, let us pray."

Wasyl squeezed his eyes tightly and prayed with all his heart. He prayed for his parents and brothers and those he had left behind in Drobomil, in the deep mine, in poverty. He prayed for Katja to find friendship here in this new land; for Ivan to find his own way with his homestead; for the fields, not yet cleared and tilled, to yield good harvests of rye and hemp and root vegetables; for a warm spring to bring sunshine and warmth to his family; for his unborn child to be born healthy; and for peace and prosperity in his new country Kanada. He prayed with his heart and repeated the priest's every word on his own tongue.

"Dear Father, hear my prayers."

As they exited the church, the priest was waiting. Wasyl reached out his hand and introduced himself, Katja, and Ivan to the priest. The priest cupped Wasyl's hand in his and read the man's face. Wasyl was a hard worker, a man with a lust for land, for freedom; for his dream. He was a leader of the people.

"Welcome to Edna-Star, Mr. Federchuk. To you, and your family." He nodded to Ivan and Katja. "Ours is a growing parish and settlement and you will be very happy here."

The priest's calm demeanour washed over Wasyl, still mesmerized by the litany, as he stepped through the church doors renewed in spirit and energy. He felt cleansed by the sunlight flooding the grounds.

Outside, small clusters of people gathered talking quietly, exchanging greetings and sharing news. Katja would come to know just how important these exchanges were each week, as the bloc settlement of Edna-Star spread out one hundred miles in each direction. She soon learned that she and Wasyl were one of the lucky homesteaders with land so close to the amenities of the village. The power of luck.

"Hello again," the enchanting smile was back. "I'm Mary, Mary Onyschuk."

Katja reached out her hand.

"So nice to meet you. My name is Katja Federchuk." Katja curtsied as her mother had taught her.

It was only the second time Katja had introduced herself with her married name, the first being when they had disembarked from the S.S.Arcadia. It sounded perfect.

She turned to introduce her husband and Ivan. Ivan stared at Mary, starstruck, his eyes glassy, smiling shyly. He reached out his hand before Katja could say anything.

"I am Ivan. Ivan Kelemchuk."

"Pleased to make your acquaintance," Mary smiled delicately.

"This is my husband, Wasyl." Katja gestured towards Wasyl.

"Pleased to meet you."

Introductions underfoot, Mary asked Wasyl if she might introduce Katja to more of the women from the congregation. Wasyl nodded and gave an encouraging wink and smile to Katja.

He watched the two women stride together, Mary holding Katja's arm like an old school chum, laughing easily, pulling her toward a group of women standing beside the church entrance where Katja was enveloped in their fold.

"Well, Ivan, looks like I have lost my wife for the time being. What do you say we meet some of the others?"

Ivan nodded, breaking his yearning eyes from Mary.

"She's beautiful, no?" Ivan said directly to Wasyl.

Wasyl was not surprised by Ivan's declaration. Mary had fine features, a dimple on her right cheek and burning brown eyes that crinkled when she laughed, which was often. She exuded happiness. Wasyl knew Ivan's look. He had experienced that rush of euphoria when he had first laid eyes on Katja at the market place in Drobomil.

"You like her?" Wasyl asked gently.

"Yes."

Ivan's eyes dropped slowly to the ground as if he had said too much.

Wasyl put his arm around Ivan.

"We'll ask Katja about her. And now, we meet the men."

They walked to a group of farmers laughing together, who immediately welcomed Wasyl and Ivan into their circle. Wasyl noticed that Dr. Smith was standing apart, smoking a thin cigarette and watching the proceedings like an unattached observer; a fly on the wall.

Chapter Eleven

Mary was clearly a ringleader among the women folk, the only child of Josef and Sonja Onyschuk, who came with one of the first waves of settlers to come to Edna-Star at the turn of the century. Katja learned in the first few minutes of their conversation that Mary had been born Canadian, a source of pride to her. Mary conversed with confidence and introduced Katja to Marta and Olga, sisters and seamstresses; and Bettina, a francophone settler, who welcomed Katja with a hug and two kisses on her cheeks.

"Like in my country," she said. "You are welcome here."

Bettina took Katja by the arm and asked how she was settling in. Katja listened closely, Bettina's French accent still strong in her speech. Bettina and her husband Henri had settled in Edna-Star ten years ago, she told Katja. They had three children and Bettina immediately asked Katja how she was feeling in her pregnancy.

There was little room for pretentiousness on the prairie. Things were said that needed to be said and no words were spoken frivolously.

"I feel wonderful," Katja beamed to her new friends. "Our baby will be born in autumn."

The conversation shifted to family, to planting, and to the old country. Katja recognized the power of the group, the power of solidarity, of standing together and supporting each other in this new land. Bonded by experiences and dreams, the women formed a chain, each link strengthened by the next.

Mary's mother had passed away from tuberculosis when Mary was just twelve and it was then the women from the community rallied around her and her father, generously providing meals and support during their period of grieving. Even after her father had remarried, she felt it her duty to welcome all newcomers with the same genuine love and support shown to her. And now she had found Katja. She could tell Katja was shy and wondered if there was more underneath. Regardless, Mary had already decided they would be fast friends.

Katja left church that day with her heart full and her thoughts in the clouds. She thought it polite to wait to tell Wasyl all about her new friends until they were alone together and tried to sit patiently on the wagon seat. Ivan's heart was also full, and he fidgeted with his compass, tossing it from one hand to another, desperate to ask Katja about Mary. Only Wasyl felt completely at peace, his prayers bringing him solace in the service and in meeting others in the same boat as himself, fellow farmers readying themselves for the spring seeding.

Wasyl broke the silence of his two passengers. "Katja, tell us about Mary." Relieved to be asked, Katja bubbled over with information, spending the rest of the journey relaying all she had found out about Mary in that short time; how brave and generous she was, how she lived alone with her father and stepmother (the latter whom she had come to view as her mother) in the village of Edna-Star, and how she was born here in this settlement. Ivan sat at full attention, eating up every detail about Mary. Wasyl winked at him and he smiled appreciatively back.

Reflecting on their first two weeks on the homestead, Wasyl and Ivan walked around the Federchuk property. Time had been good to them; used well and productively. The Federchuk and Kelemchuk zemlyankas had been built and mudded, and the men had set up a small chicken pen built for their first five chickens, who ran madly about trying to escape through the chicken wire. Both the wood for the pen and the chickens had been bartered from Henri and Bettina Bourassa.

Ivan remained a constant at their camp each night though his own hut was now ready. Without a horse, the distance was just too great and he found valuable time was lost. He and Wasyl had agreed for him to stay at their camp as long as he needed. Wasyl had wondered at giving Ivan his horse for the evenings, but worried about Katja. He decided that the best way to help Ivan was to pay him for his work and give him pride of independence.

A private man by nature, Ivan spoke sparingly. It was at the evening campfire, when Katja had settled in the zemlyanka that the two men shared stories. Ivan was on the run, he explained. He had left his home to escape becoming a soldier, for Russia or the Austro-Hungarian army. Both armies were advancing in Galicia along the Carpathian Ridge. His mother didn't distinguish between them, he said.

"'Join either,' she told me. 'You will be paid.'"

Both sides needed young men and he would be provided a salary.

Ivan looked directly at Wasyl when he said. "I knew that I could never kill another man."

He was a coward, his mother had told him, and he made up his mind to escape Galicia and the war. He took off his hat and wiped his forehead down to his eyes, which were misting up.

"I left my mother, Wasyl. I should never have done that. I am her only son. I am a coward."

Each statement seemed to catch in his throat, his breaths shortened and staccato. Wasyl listened. Finally he spoke.

"We all have our reasons for leaving and we all have our reasons for living."

That night he lay beside Katja, his right hand caressing her breasts then belly. He made a silent wish for his unborn child to live in a world where peace and justice prevailed.

Ivan had shown himself to be an excellent marksman with the rifle and he had killed a white tailed deer two days prior. Together, he and Wasyl had skinned the animal and let it bleed out, hanging it between trees and willing the cougars to hunt in another area. Those two days he and Ivan had remained at camp, building the henhouse and taking Katja to town when they went to fetch the chickens from the Bourassa homestead.

Katja loved going to town. She enjoyed perusing the shelves of the small Hudson's Bay Shop with its array of household tools and dried goods such as flour and sugar. She savoured the sweet smells of exotic spices from across another ocean called the Pacific, she learned from the shopkeeper's wife, Arlene Benton. But she especially loved to be in the shop when a child was there, usually a toddler, with their mother. At these times, she would unconsciously touch her protruding belly and try to imagine herself as a mother. She vowed to let her child hover over the penny candy and on occasion, she would buy him one as a treat; a token of love.

She hovered there herself on this day, mesmerized by the vibrant colours of the salt water taffy so delicately wrapped like individual presents. Wasyl and Ivan were on the other side of the store, in deep conversation with Mr. Benton about the variety and quality of seed available for spring planting. She didn't hear his footsteps, but suddenly Katja caught the scent of the ocean, a clean fresh scent that enveloped her in a cloud and when she turned, Dr. Smith stood beside her.

"Look good, don't they?" he nodded to the candy counter.

"Yes, I was just admiring the colours."

Dr. Smith waved Mrs. Benton over to the counter and ordered up five salt water taffies. He held them out on his palm toward Katja.

"For you," he offered.

Her fingertips sent shivers down his spine as she paused, then gingerly scooped up the sweets.

"Thank you, Dr. Smith, how very kind of you."

Wasyl approached and reached out his hand to Dr. Smith. "Hello, Sir."

Dr. Smith shook Wasyl's hand, then introduced himself to Ivan. Wasyl saw the taffies in Katja's hand, but said nothing.

Dr. Smith tipped his topper and said, "A good day to you all."

Katja spoke first, breaking the silence. "Was it wrong to take them?" She suddenly felt very small, like a child herself.

Wasyl smiled gently. "No, Katja. I only wish they were my gift to you," he answered.

Ivan shuffled his feet nervously, uncomfortable being privy to this moment of intimacy between Katja and Wasyl. Wasyl turned to acknowledge this and changed the subject.

"We found out that Red Fife and Marquis Wheat seed is aplenty and grows well here. There is a good market for the grains. That is what we will plant for our first harvest."

Katja was pleased to be speaking of something else. "Let's celebrate. Two for you! Two for you! And one for me."

She took off the taffy's paper wrapper and savoured the sour cherry flavour as it softened in her mouth. Wasyl laughed and immediately popped the yellow one in his mouth. Ivan looked worried.

Henri Bourassa's farm was a few miles west of Edna-Star. He had chickens to sell and Wasyl had bartered for five chickens, four hens, and one rooster in return for five days labour seeding the Bourassa fields. Katja and Anna had raised chickens in Drobomil and Wasyl knew this would keep Katja happy and occupied and give them fresh eggs daily. He encouraged Katja to pick out the five she wanted for her roost. Wasyl was grateful for Henri's mentorship as he would learn firsthand about the seeding process in this new land before breaking his own soil.

Henri and his wife Bettina were in their yard, tending to their vegetable garden at the side of the house as Wasyl, Katja, and Ivan approached in their wagon. The Bourassa farmhouse was gleaming white with lime wash, in harmony with the houses in the rest of the settlement. Someday, Katja thought, she would have a house like that.

"Before our baby is born." Wasyl had promised her.

Coming to town, they had passed other houses like the Bourassa's. The structures were unified in their south orientation, central chimneys, and size of two or three rooms. Katja valued this equanimity that bonded the settlers in their bloc community.

Henri and Bettina greeted them in French and urged them to follow them to the henhouse. There were scads of chickens whirling in the pen and Katja smiled at the plump hens atop their nests in the small henhouse to the left.

"These hens are my youngest and have plenty of livelihood left."

Henri pointed to the back corner where hens the colours of autumn bobbed for scattered corn at their feet. Henri went over and scooped one up. Katja reached out her hands and held the hen's body firmly, while ruffling the feathers to reveal red lobes at the side by its eyes. Red lobes meant brown eggs! This was good luck.

"Good! We want this one."

She handed the chicken back to Henri. Scouting out the roost-ers, she set her eyes on one that was speckled. It stood apart from the others and looked majestic with its crown of seven peaks. Also good luck! Its tail plume was black and white striped, and reminded Katja of a zebra. Yes, this was the rooster for her first flock.

"That one."

Amongst a flurry of feathers and squawks, Katja chose three more hens and helped Henri and Bettina gather the birds and put them in a ramshackle portable pen made of wood with chicken wire stretched around.

She and Wasyl thanked the Bourassas and Wasyl assured Henri he would be back to work the field when Henri was ready to seed.

Ivan had stayed in the wagon watching the proceedings with great interest. He admired Wasyl's easy nature and the manner in which he permitted Katja to make the decision. Ivan had come to regard Wasyl as an older brother and was thankful for his kindness and generosity. He knew Wasyl was not a rich man and yet, he would give Ivan grivna for work.

"To get on your feet," Wasyl had told him.

How would he ever repay this man for his support? When they piled into the wagon with him, Ivan smiled broadly.

"That was a good deal," he said.

Katja was surprised by this exchange as Ivan had always been so quiet.

"I think so," Wasyl acknowledged.

The chickens clucked their disapproval as the wagon jarred with each rut in the road.

Chapter Twelve

The sod-breaker, fanning mill, and harrow they had borrowed from the Bourassa farm were godsends for the seeding process which began the first week in June. Wasyl had been a quick learner on the Bourassa farm and, in return, Henri had agreed to loan him the tools necessary to break his own land. Through this brief apprenticeship, Wasyl had met other men, like himself, indebted to Henri. Together they had learned the best and most productive way to create furrows and use the harrow to rake up the mounds to create a softer soil for planting their wheat. Now in their tenth year on the land, the Bourassa family had farmed over sixty acres.

"Begin with one acre," Henri had advised. "Always begin with one."

Wasyl, Ivan, and Katja worked tirelessly, sandy soil seeping into their boots at the lifted soles, dusting their laces like brown snow. The dry soil blew behind Wasyl and the sod-breaker, showering Ivan who shielded his eyes as he used the harrow to break up the mounds into softer piles, as Wasyl had shown him. Katja pulled her bonnet down on her head, protecting her eyes as she walked behind the pair of them. Her eyes watered and her nostrils felt full of the silt; itchy and congested. She could see Wasyl coming back toward her in the next row, leather harness wrapped around his shoulders and his grey shirt caked with sweat; his hat tipped back on his head and the horses pulling the sod-breaker. His face was drawn in concentration, sheer determination. How she loved this man. How he took care of her and Ivan and the baby.

Wasyl and Ivan had bought their second horse from Mr. Bourassa too.

"He will teach your horse what to do in the field," Henri wisely advised.

The two horses pulled the sod-breaker in unison, synchronized in their step, save for the odd stumble on a clump of sod not yet softened. Wasyl took the lead of the three of them, and he was quite far ahead. He was on his second round now, snaking his way back and forth, creating furrow after furrow with the sod-breaker. It was a sharp pointed tool for cutting into the soil, with a gentle slope to twist and push away the clumps revealing a deep valley for planting. Ivan was second, hauling the harrow rake with its spiked teeth behind him to get rid of the clumps and smooth out the soil, readying it for seed. Katja followed, her canvas bag slung over her shoulder, seeding by hand; the Marquis Wheat highly refined and cleaned and treated for smut, the destructive fungus that killed a harvest before it began. Bettina had advised her against using the grain pickling process used by so many to wash the seed in a formaldehyde-water mixture.

"Non, non. Ce n'est pas bon pour vous et le bebe," she said in a motherly fashion. Heeding Bettina's warning, Katja and Wasyl borrowed their fanning mill to shake the seed through, cleaning it as best they could and filling the canvas sack to a weight Katja could comfortably carry.

Now in the middle of her second trimester, Katja felt a renewed energy with the sunny days and warmth of June upon them. This seeding signalled a turning point for her, part of the settling process that solidified their commitment to their new homeland. There was little time for Katja to mourn her life in Drobomil. She had written to her mother and younger sisters, explaining her daily life, the chickens, the zemylanka, Edna-Star's church, her friends. She assured them she was fine, healthy, and safe. Each week, she asked Mr. Benton if a letter had arrived at the post office for her.

"These things take time," he always told her. "Months sometimes."

Katja's letter home brimmed with optimism. She remained full of hope but listened nightly as Wasyl discussed his concerns with her, fears imbued through conversations with the other men after Sunday services. She sat at the pine table he built, her head in her hand, brow furrowed and gave him her full attention. Aside from irrigation and the threat of drought, they had to worry about grasshoppers and vermin eating their crops, and the possibility of smut or another disease still on the grains themselves. Sharing these fears had eased Wasyl and spread the weight of them. Although she understood very well that the course of life can take a tail spin, Katja felt assured they were on track and remained energized and sustained by this new land.

As she walked behind Ivan in the fields, the stillness of the air moved her. Dry, no breeze, spring heat. These were ideal conditions to plant, so the seed would settle into the freshly raked furrow, only to be tucked snugly in the earth by Wasyl's hoe.

This whole process took days, much longer than anticipated, and Ivan had resigned himself to not planting his field this first year. He was a stickler for detail and reminded Wasyl that they each had three years to clear and cultivate two acres of land to gain freehold title over their one hundred and sixty acres. Ivan knew they could not do this alone, and couldn't do it by hand. There had been talk in town of some of the men getting together to purchase a gas tractor, gang plow, and threshing machine. Both Ivan and Wasyl wanted to belong to that group, but knew time was not on their side. They had to make it through this first year, then, next year, they would explore more mechanized methods.

Ivan had remained at their camp for six weeks now, sleeping under the stars each night, without complaint. Katja knew that after seeding Wasyl planned to give him the new work horse to call his own. She, herself, had grown quite fond of Ivan. His silence spoke volumes, she came to know, especially when it came to Mary.

Ivan doted on Mary Onyschuk after each Sunday Service, walking with her and sitting together on the wooden bench in the consecrated grounds.

"Is he to be trusted?" Mary had whispered to her last Sunday.

Katja assured Mary that Ivan's intentions were genuine and sincere in every respect. Mary had then proceeded to share a secret she had kept hidden.

"Dr. Smith said he loved me too, and he has left," Mary shared.

"What? Where has he gone?" Katja asked, perturbed by the thought that he had just disappeared from their village.

"I don't know," Mary replied. "He left without any word; no note, no visit, no explanation before he left. We visited in secret in the garden behind our house. He said I was beautiful and that he loved me. I thought we would be married one day." Mary looked up at Katja's eyes, sky blue, sincere, and listening to her every word.

"Then, four weeks ago, he began to keep his distance, not coming round Father's house as much. Something changed, but I don't know what."

Katja shook her head sadly, commiserating with her friend's broken heart.

"Well, I don't know what to say about the doctor, but I can tell you that Ivan is as true and honest a man as they come," she stated firmly.

* * *

"Is Ivan to be trusted?" Katja asked Wasyl that night as they cud-dled in their hut.

"If you trust me, Mary can trust Ivan," Wasyl answered and smothered her with kisses.

Their intimate moments had altered as her pregnancy pro-gressed, but were always gentle and tender. Katja loved it best when she could straddle Wasyl and look deeply into his eyes, so lost in revelation. They were still newlyweds in her eyes and she was still learning about what pleased him, and he her. His body was firm and strong and when he held her tightly she felt like that rag doll on the ship so long ago, melting into his rock hard body, for support and pleasure.

Chapter Thirteen

Early in her ninth month, Katja soldiered on despite her feet swollen with the prairie heat, burning in her too-tight leather boots; soles worn and weathered.

"Only do what you can," Wasyl had urged her.

He had seen the black lines on his lovely young wife's eyes grow deeper each day as she slept fitfully on the hard dugout floor. He worried for her wellbeing and that of the baby as there was so much work to do everyday. Although Katja worked tirelessly, he noticed her slowing down and urged her to lie down when she needed.

"But the heat is too much for me in the hut," she would say, and would sit in the shade of the aspen, surrounded by a mushroom patch she would scour through, collecting the tender ones for supper. Always working.

She teased Wasyl about the hut, but didn't mean it, knowing that he was almost finished building their house. He had promised her they would have a house before the baby was born, and she had watched in admiration as he and Ivan had built the two-room house with its sloped roof and chimney inside, like the Bourassas and the other houses in the bloc. She could hardly wait to move in and use the fireplace and cook Wasyl a lovely meal with her harvest vegetables and bread! She knew she would still have a few months, before the snow would fly, to mud the house for extra insulation. She had already decided to wait to whitewash until Spring.

Katja supplemented their diet of mushrooms, berries, game birds, eggs, and fish with her traditional breads, baked skillfully over the open fire on a grate fashioned from scrap metal. In fact,

Katja had gained a reputation of being one of the best bread makers in the bloc community. Some Saturdays, she and Wasyl took extra loaves to town where Mrs. Benton paid good money for the baking, which she then resold. Katja knew it was her flock's eggs which gave her bread such richness and colour. Her versions of paska (babka bread with summer berries), kalach complete with the kolo, and her pampushki rolls were in high demand and reminded the settlers of the old country, Mrs. Benton told her.

Wasyl encouraged Katja to keep the money for herself.

"For a rainy day," he said.

She would tuck it in the periwinkle canister she kept hidden under her side of the bed, without counting it.

Katja loved caring for the chickens and in these few months her hens had tripled in number. Her flock was a kaleidoscope of colour, like a paint palette of a prairie sunset greeting her each morning. She took enormous pride in her daily work, from cooking, cleaning, and washing, to tending the vegetable garden. She had planted parsnips, corn, potatoes, cabbage, and onions this first year and already tiny green tendrils were peeking through the rich soil above the seed. Their original zemlyanka would become the summer kitchen and would store the harvest vegetables and any extra grain from the field harvest.

Katja found herself drawn to the water's edge, the stream's coolness comforting her. She would take the wheelbarrow down to the creek to fill it with water, and often sat on the grassy bank, the current curling around the rocks and streaming past, her eyes searching the brambles across the water for the elk once more. Feeling brazen one morning in September, she took off her ankle boots and her stockings and bobbed her feet in the stream, floating them on the rippled surface; the cool drops licking her toes and refreshing her swollen soles and ankles. She soaked her stockings and lay them on rocks to dry, then pulled them back on, still damp, cooling her feet as she squeezed them back in her lace-up boots. She lay back on the grassy shore and marvelled at the endless blue canvas above her. So much of this landscape reminded her of home. Had her mother received her letter yet, she wondered? She longed for news of her family.

As the midday sun beat down on her, Katja took off her bonnet and set it beside her. Lying back again, she circled her protruding belly, making a wish for Olek, as she did every day. Her eyes felt heavy and as her breathing slowed, she willed them to close. The sounds of the woodlands rose up in crescendo around her, starlings, chickadees, and buzzing black flies. Lulled by the natural melodies, the crack of twigs startled her.

Katja sat up, suddenly alert. Something was moving in the bulrushes beside her. There was a skirmish and a Trumpeter Swan family emerged, silently, stealthily, so as not to disturb their silent audience. Katja watched the majestic birds, mother and father, mates for life, and three grey feathered cygnets, trailing in between the protective parents. The adults' downy white feathers contrasted beautifully with their black beaks, shaped like diamonds from their eyes to their peaked tips. The family paddled away, carried by the stream's current and and Katja thought of her own family.

How long had she been resting here? *Wasyl would be worried*, she thought, so she tied up her boots loosely and gathered up her skirt. She felt dampness under her and touched the back of her dress. Wet. She thought she must have lay down too close to the water's edge and flapped her skirt in the air. *It will dry on the walk back to the hut*, she thought. She turned and heaved over with the pain low, deep in her abdomen. It stabbed her and made her double over. *The baby,* she thought. *It's coming.* She must get back to Wasyl. She stepped forward, slowly and trepidatiously, wanting to avoid that pain again. Maybe if she walked very slowly, it would subside.

Chapter Fourteen

It was Ivan who found Katja. He was on the hunt, tracking an elk that now stood directly beside the path to the stream, focusing intently on something, which lay before it on the path itself. Ivan saw only the elk's antlers as it high-tailed into the brambles before he caught sight of Katja. She lay limp on the pathway, her body aligned with the tree root under her. He dropped his rifle, knelt down to her still body, and listened. She was breathing but erratically.

"The baby," she murmured. "It is coming."

Ivan scooped her up and stumbled through the trodden pathway, shouting as he got nearer the homestead.

"Wasyl, I think the baby is coming! Wasyl!"

Wasyl met Ivan on the path and took Katja in his arms.

"The baby, Wasyl. It's coming." Katja's voice was barely audible above his thumping heart.

Wasyl choked back tears. He was not prepared. He lay Katja down in the hut rolling the soft blanket behind the small of her back.

"Ivan, you must get Mary. We need Mary."

Ivan nodded and rushed to the horses, not stopping to saddle up.

Wasyl left Katja's side only for a moment, scooping up some fresh water in the pot by the wash basin to bring to Katja.

"Have a drink, Katja. It is cold."

Wasyl held the small pot to her lips and she took a sip. Her eyes were still closed. There was the pain again and Katja recoiled her body in response, knees to her chest. Her eyes flew open. She gritted her teeth and Wasyl took her hand and she squeezed it with a grip that overpowered him.

"You need to undress," he said and helped her to remove her undergarments. He adjusted the blanket to keep her as comfortable as he could and counted down the minutes until Mary would arrive. He thought briefly about Dr. Smith, but no one knew where he was, and Mary would know what to do. She had to know. Wasyl's thoughts were a jumble and he took a deep breath to calm himself. Katja screamed and he knew the baby was very close.

Mary rode behind Ivan, her arms tight on his waist, her bonnet airborne, lifting off her head, the tie loosening with every stride. Ivan had flown into town and shouted at her house she must come, Katja needed her. She was down in a minute, with no seconds to spare. The baby was coming. She had promised Katja she'd be there, by her side. The brambles cut her face as Ivan heaved the horse forward with the reins, but she didn't feel them. She focused on holding on tightly as they screeched down the path.

"Wasyl," Katja whispered.

She was between contractions now and knew she had to sit up; to be in another position. Lying down didn't feel right to her.

"Yes, Katja."

"I need to be upright, Wasyl. Help me to the corner where I can sit up."

Wasyl curled his arms under her armpits, lifting her frail body to her feet. She shuffled her way, then buckled as another contraction hit her. Hearing her groan in such pain struck at the core of Wasyl's heart. He needed this to be over. Where was Mary? When Katja's body was calm once more, Wasyl helped her stumble to the corner of the shelter. Here she sat on her haunches, regaining her strength.

"Blankets, Wasyl, get blankets. Water, Wasyl, we need boiling water."

Wasyl recoiled back, afraid to leave her side. He scooped up the blankets and crumpled them under her buttocks, like a woollen nest. He squeezed her hand and told her he would be right back with the water. He hated to leave.

Mary hopped off the horse before Ivan had pulled on the reins. She stumbled forward and fell on her knees. Ivan jumped off and lifted her up and off.

"There, in the hut."

Mary raced into the hut to her friend's side.

"I'm here, Katja. I'm here."

Katja's eyes were closed, tears and droplets of sweat rolled down her face; beet red with pushing and the heaving pain.

"The baby, Mary. I need you to catch the baby," she managed.

Mary held her arms parallel to Katja.

"I am here, Katja. This is your time."

Wasyl remained in the hut, his eyes flooded with worry. When he heard the baby's first cry, his tears fell on the dirt floor. A baby boy, he heard Mary say as the mist shrouded him.

And he was named Olek, defender of mankind.

Chapter Fifteen

Wasyl awoke before Katja on the blessed Christmas morn. He slipped out of their cot and tended to the coals still burning in the fire. After a few prods, they erupted into a flaming explosion of warmth that filtered into the room. Katja stirred. Baby Olek lay beside her, cradled in her curled arm, her fingers entwined in his brown curly hair.

Wasyl tiptoed to his jacket hanging by the door and took out the wooden box from its inside pocket. He had wrapped it lightly in a crimson velvet ribbon Mrs. Benton had given him.

"For Katja," she had told him.

He placed the box on the wooden table and turned it just so, positioning the bow to face Katja when she awoke. He peeked out the lace curtains in the kitchen. It had snowed a sea of white in the night. Soft downy flakes caressed the grasses, transforming the yellow dips and crevasses a stark clean white. The water was boiled now and Wasyl sat down with his tea and waited.

He had longed to surprise Katja this Christmas with something special, something she would never buy for herself. When Mrs. Benton had shown him the tiny musical snuff boxes with their bell-chiming tunes, he had listened to each one, marvelling at the melodies and picking just the right one. Mrs. Benton had put on airs, calling them her "carillons de musique" feigning a French accent. Wasyl called them music boxes and when he wound them up, they played the first music besides the church organ that he had heard in his new country.

Music was an integral part of Ukrainian culture in the old country. Children learned folksongs and lullabies by heart and sung them at gatherings all through their lives. There was a saying in his family. "What do you get when you have two or more Federchuks together?" The answer, a choir. Singing and dancing.

He remembered dancing with Katja at their wedding in Drobomil. Following an elaborate ceremony at the church, their wedding celebration had been simple, held in Anna's yard with fields of flowers adorning the tables and his Katja. She had been radiant in her white dress with embroidered flowers, daisies in pale yellow, pink ,and cream, cinching in her tiny waist. She wore a halo of fresh wild flowers around her head and they had been stitched on her ribbons that intertwined with her locks of hair. And food! There was food everywhere and there was music. The troisti muzyki, three musicians, had played their first waltz and he had held Katja close, feeling the heat from her beating heart and they looked deeply into each other's soul, their love radiating. The violin, flute, and drum trio then sped up the pace with polkas that played on into the night, long after Katja and Wasyl had left.

Wasyl's memory faded with Olek's cries and hungry gasps, and he watched Katja pull him close to her bare breast. She gazed lovingly at this little being, her Canadian boy, growing so strong day by day. His first Christmas. Their first Christmas in the new country. Katja felt Wasyl's eyes upon her and smiled. The fire crackled playfully and radiated warmth in their home. Wasyl remained at the table, staring serenely at those he loved the most.

"Good morning," he said softly, coming over to nuzzle her neck and caress her back. "Merry Christmas, my love."

Such peace when Olek was feeding and such love between mother and child.

"I have something for you, dear Katja," he whispered excitedly.

"When you are ready."

After feeding Olek, Katja buttoned her dress and placed him in her sling tying him close to her chest. He looked at her with adoring eyes.

"Ready!" she sang.

She could see the wooden box carefully set on the table with the soft velvet ribbon. Wasyl handed it to her.

"For you, with all my love."

She untied the ribbon, then knotted it in her hair so it dangled just above Olek and he swung at it with his plump little fists.

"What is inside?" she asked playfully, shaking the box just a little.

It rattled side to side.

"Careful now. Open it." His tone softened. "It reminds me of our love, beautiful and everlasting."

Katja stared at Wasyl, wanting to savour this intimate moment. He rarely spoke so candidly, so openly about his love for her.

She unclasped the wooden lid revealing two dancers, a man and a woman, hands clasped in a waltzing embrace. She wound it up. The melody played. She had heard the lullaby before. Too La Roo La Roo La.

"Oh Wasyl," she gasped. "It's beautiful."

She set the music box down on the table and wound the handle to play the soft chiming music again. Wasyl smiled and reached out to her.

"May I have this dance, Miss," he asked.

"Always."

Olek gurgled happily, caught in his parents' embrace, as they swayed to the melody.

When the music slowed, then stopped, Katja whispered in his

ear. "I have something for you too."

She stole away to her side of the cot and lifted the blanket from under the bed. She pulled a fabric bundle out and brushed off the tiny straw bits from its hiding place.

"I made this for you."

Wasyl lifted the bundle from her, feeling its weight in his hands. He set it on the table and pulled back the cotton fabric to reveal a sheepskin woollen vest, in the Hutsul tradition, with fine embroidery along the seams in red and black. His eyes welled up thinking of all the time and fine detail work this entailed and wondered when did his Katja have time to do this. He looked at her, speechless. As if sensing his disbelief, Katja spoke first.

"Mrs. Benton ordered me the sheepskin wool for the vest, for warmth in the winter. Mary and I worked on the design and she helped me to stitch as well. Please tell me you like it."

Wasyl hugged her close. "I love it. It's too beautiful, Katja, like you." Wasyl felt as if his heart would burst. Nothing could take away their happiness.

PART III: FIRE

"Till the Autumn came and vanished, till the season of the rains, till the western world lay fettered in mid-winter crystal chains, still she listened for his coming, still she watched the distant plains..."

E.Pauline Johnson

Chapter Sixteen

Katja awoke in a cold sweat for the second time that night. She had been dreaming; only dreaming, she told herself. The house was quiet and still, save for the gentle hissing of the fire embers waiting to be stoked for the morning fire. She looked over at Olek, sleeping soundly on Wasyl's pillow and cuddled Pavla to her breast. Pavla had been born only days after Ivan and Mary married. Wasyl had joked with Katja that the polka music itself set Pavla on fire inside her and she was so excited to dance, she just had to be born.

Pavla had been very active inside of Katja, but was a peaceful baby, serene in every way. Happy to be carried about and coddled, Katja and Pavla would play with Olek in between their chores. Pavla squealed happily when Olek screamed in delight as Mama found him in their daily round of hide-and-seek.

The nightmares had begun as soon as Wasyl had been taken away. Those marching boots, outside the church window in Montreal haunted her, the memory so vivid, the incessant clacking sound of the heels upon the stone pebbles crushing her eardrums. The men in black boots had come to the bloc meeting in Edna-Star.

There had been many meetings before that darkest day. There had been warnings and hints of trouble to come, but Wasyl and Katja felt immune to it. They were law-abiding citizens in this free country, Wasyl had told her. Nothing could change that. Letters from the old country trickled in with news of the Russian advance upon Galicia. The divisions of loyalty were pronounced, regardless of borders. Anna wrote that men from Drobomil and other villages were divided in their loyalties, some enlisting with the Russians and others with the Austro-Hungarian Empire. The Austro-Hungarian army numbered in the millions, but was still smaller than the Russian Empire. This division was causing strife among the remaining citizens in each community and tensions were high. Anna had written that some young men signed up in hopes of Ukrainian independence at the end of the battles. The Great War had begun.

In Edna-Star, talk amongst the settlers was full of angst, agitation, and worry about their loved ones in the old country. When Wasyl had received word from his mother that his two brothers were fighting on the side of Austro-Hungary to defend Galicia's borders, he shared in that sense of helplessness and fear, of watching from afar; a mere observer.

Posters had gone up in town three days before the bloc meeting. Citizens needed to know what was coming. "We are not the enemy!" the headline on the poster cried out.

Wasyl and Katja came to the meeting with Olek in tow and Pavla clinging to Katja's shawl, her tiny fingers intertwined in the loops. The village hall was packed already and Wasyl scooped up Olek, for fear of losing him amongst the crowd. He led his family silently across the floor to where Ivan and Mary stood. The two men nodded to each other and Mary held out her arms to Olek who eagerly snuggled on her hip.

There was coughing up-front and a member of the Royal North West Mounted Police Force took the platform. He stood front and centre, his red jacket blazing fire, his black boots polished, and his eyes barely visible under the brim of his hat. Katja stared at the boots. The officer removed his hat and held it over his heart. He took a deep breath.

"On August 22, the Government of Canada enacted the War Measures Act. This Act is to protect our country in this time of war on European soil. Any citizen whose passport indicates a country of origin that is our enemy must register with authorities in Edmonton. You will be required to register as an enemy alien and your whereabouts will be tracked weekly by the postmaster here in your village."

With this declaration the young man paused, pointing his white gloved finger at Mr. Benton who stood sheepishly in the back corner of the hall.

"We will be monitoring immigrants who are seen as a threat to our security. All enemy aliens within the twenty mile zone of an urban centre must register and get identity papers. If you are found to be vagrant and without work, or you don't have your papers, you may be seized and held under this Act. This is a time of war."

With those final words, the officer nodded, put on his hat, and walked regally off the stage and through the crowd to a fellow officer and his waiting steed. The crowd was left speechless. Murmurings amongst neighbours grew and finally, someone at the back spoke.

Katja recognized the voice immediately and shot a look at Mary.

"Well, I'll be," she said. "He's back."

It was Dr. Smith, having returned from the city after his lengthy departure. An illness, some said; a woman, some hinted. His father's death, most agreed. Dr. Smith had been welcomed back into the community fold as a vital link to health and medicine. There had been no replacement found during his absence those months. When Edward Smith rose to speak, he was urged to the front of the hall, where the officer had stood only moments before.

Edward knew more details about this government policy from his time in Edmonton, and felt compelled to share what he knew with the common folks he worked with every day. He had been by his father's side when he'd passed away and his mother had begged him to stay. Elizabeth had come to the memorial service with her father, but he found her sexual boldness revolting. He found himself comparing her; thinking of Katja Federchuk, the shy new settler, and Mary Onyschuk, the courageous young woman he had thought he loved. He longed to be back in Edna-Star, from underneath his mother's watchful eye; back where he could breathe again. The community had welcomed him back with open arms and now he would return the favour.

"As you know, my country Britain and Russia are allies in this war against tyranny," he began.

There were murmurs in the crowd as many of the settlers saw Russia as the enemy, the exploiters of their homeland.

"Canada is a member of the British Commonwealth and so our mother country needs our support. Many of you have come from dire conditions, immigrated here for a better life, but come from the Austro-Hungarian enemy empire all the same. Our government is afraid."

"Afraid of what?" Dymytry Kolyk shouted out.

Others in the crowd concurred.

"Afraid of an uprising here. Afraid that people who subsist with so little and are unemployed will rise up against their nation." He added, "Even if it is their home nation now, they fear your loyalties will lie with the Old Country."

Edward took a moment to unfold an article he had kept from the Winnipeg Free Press.

"Budnuk a traitor!" the headline screamed.

There were audible gasps from the crowd.

Nykola Budnuk was the Ukrainian Catholic Bishop in the West and was responsible to parishes across the prairies. He had visited Edna-Star the Federchuk's first year on the land and blessed the community church they all worshipped in.

"What's it say?" Bohdan Sawchuk asked.

"Yes, read what it says!" the crowd chanted.

Dr. Smith took out his reading glasses and began.

"On July 25, 1914, when no country was yet at war, Nykola Budnuk raised his voice, encouraging Ukrainians to return home. Bishop Budnuk urged his fellow men, now free, to defend Galicia from the Russians, reminding the men to fight against the oppression they had lived under for so many years."

Wasyl felt fear wash over him as he thought of his two younger brothers, armed with rifles, low in trenches.

"However, on August 4th, Great Britain, our mother nation, declared she was at war with Austria-Hungary and was fighting on the same side as Russia. Shortly after, the Catholic Church and Bishop Budnuk rescinded the original letter. They sent a pastoral apology, printed in this very paper, urging that the original letter dated July 25, 1914 be disregarded. He encouraged all Canadians, whatever their country of origin, to perform their duty to their new motherland, Canada."

Here, Edward looked over his glasses out into the crowd, pausing for effect.

"The Manitoba Liberal Party has spoken out that damage has been done by Bishop Budnuk's first letter. They have accused Bishop Budnuk of disloyalty to Canada and sent this case for review to Prime Minister Borden. I hope this explains the situation more for you. We will stand together as a community and support each other, and we must follow what the officer said."

The crowd was speechless. This was a war of political and ethnic divisions and they had just been placed on the opposite side of their home country.

Edward stepped down from the podium and refolded the article. He had done his duty to the town folk. He needed them to know the undercurrent of the oncoming hostility, even if it went against his own father's wishes. In his last days, his father had asked him to stay in Edmonton; to take up his practice there. Young Dr. Smith knew that if he stayed he would be obligated to join the Dean of the Faculty of Medicine and many of his fellow students in the war effort on the front line.

He publicly announced his return to the village as his duty to the people of Edna-Star, but some nights after a few glasses of wine, Edward admitted to himself that he was a coward. That was why he was here and his classmates were at the front and that was the truth. He couldn't even stand up to his mother, he told himself in his drunken self-deprecation.

He put the folded piece of paper into his breast pocket of his vest and checked his gold-plated pocket-watch. Had he stayed in Edmonton he would have surely been called to service in the war, however, he had compelled the medical community to understand his call to service here in the rural communities surrounding Edmonton. He had used his highly-regarded position to convince the government authorities he could be very useful to them in his role.

He lobbied that there was a need for supervision of the process for maintaining the enemy alien records and while he trusted Mr. Benton, a fellow Brit, he kept that information to himself. He would be able to pass on anecdotal information should he see or hear anything untoward in his work in the communities, he told authorities. He would be able to know the undercurrent of any uprising before it could get off the ground. The authorities in Edmonton had agreed, in this culture of fear. Anything at all that was untoward or of a disloyal nature, Dr. Smith would pass on to them. They had agreed that a man in the field would be most valuable to them.

As he walked through the crowd, he stopped to smile at Mary and shook hands with Ivan. He had heard of their marriage from Mr. Benton upon his arrival back in town.

"You are a lucky man, Sir," he told Ivan.

Dr. Smith reached out to shake Wasyl's hand and looked lovingly at Pavla. "Surely, this is not the baby from before." He patted his stomach.

Katja laughed easily and nodded at Olek, still in Mary's arms. "This is Olek, defender of mankind."

"Now that is a powerful name and one the world needs right now," Dr. Smith said.

He reached out to shake Olek's hand. Shyly, Olek pulled away, smothering his face into Mary's neck and kerchief.

"Nice to meet you, Olek." With that he flipped his hat like a comical showman and it landed perfectly atop his head. Olek peeked back and Dr. Smith winked.

"Gotcha!" he said with a chuckle.

The group of them watched Edward Smith as he strode confidently out of the hall, his black leather shoes treading silently on the wooden boards, like a ghost.

"He can laugh," Ivan began, "He has nothing to fear."

He looked at Wasyl whose eyes were black fear and fury, focused on Olek and baby Pavla. There was movement all around them as the bloc community members left the hall, eyes downcast and hearts heavy.

Katja had so many questions. Her immediate reaction to the officer's words were disbelief. They had done nothing wrong. How could they be enemies of the country they had grown to love so much? She saw that same question in Wasyl's eyes as he looked at his children. She waited until Pavla was fed and asleep in her sling and Olek was tucked-in tightly to discuss the announcement in the hall.

"What did that officer mean Wasyl? What did he mean that men could be seized and held?" she asked.

"It means that their freedom can be taken away in this time of war," Wasyl explained. "We have nothing to fear, Katja." He looked deeply in her eyes. "Ivan and I will go to register in the city, and I will carry those identity papers until there is no longer a need. There is nothing to fear. We are safe here. This is our country too." With those words, Wasyl got up from the table. "I'm going to cut some wood."

Katja felt frustrated by her husband's stoicism. She wanted to shout and scream how this wasn't fair, that none of this was fair. They were Canadian citizens now and their children were born here. Why would they ever be thought of as enemies in their land of freedom? Instead, she kept all that bottled-up and tended to the fire, pushing the embers with more force than usual. She pushed away memories of the officers' marching boots.

Chapter Seventeen

Wasyl and Ivan left early the next morning for the Dominion Office in Edmonton. Wasyl remarked that it was just over fifteen months ago, they had received their land papers. Ivan sat slouched in the wagon, silent, eyes straight ahead. His stony stare worried Wasyl, but he respected each man for how they needed to be and patted his pocket for the third time, ensuring he had brought both his passport and his immigration papers.

The same officious clerk greeted them as the line of men snaked their way into the office. Wasyl saw the window was shut up tight, the air stifling and filled with the stench of sweat front the men.

"You know the rules now do you? "

The clerk continued his diligent stamping of the Identity papers for Wasyl and Ivan without looking up.

"You must keep these papers on your person at all times. Caught without them, you're subject to the law and can be interned."

He looked up and directly at Wasyl. "You understand, farmer?"

"Yes, Sir, we understand. We are law abiding citizens of Canada, Sir."

Ivan's continued silence on their return trip to their homesteads suffocated Wasyl as he urged the horses into a trot. He was eager to get home and get into his field, not one to miss a day's work when the harvest was so near. This had been a drier summer than last, and he wanted to ensure the harvest was in before any more sun burned up the fields.

"Hot day, isn't it?" Wasyl glanced at Ivan, hoping the small talk would draw his best friend out. "I will have to get into the fields right away."

"Wasyl." Ivan paused, collecting his thoughts. "Do you ever think about home?"

Wasyl didn't know where Ivan was going in this thought process. He paused. "Why are you worrying about that?" Wasyl asked him impatiently.

"No reason." He continued, "Just that I do think of home, of my family, of how I left." Ivan's voice cracked a little.

"Whoa now." Wasyl pulled up the reins and halted the buggy to look directly at his friend. "I'm listening."

"I need to tell someone, Wasyl. Sometimes, at night, I dream of my mother. She is sitting all alone by the San River. She begins wading off the shore, her apron floating, dancing in the current, farther and farther until her kerchief itself is underwater. She is drowning and calling out to me to save her, Wasyl. I reach into the air, but there is nothing."

Wasyl cinched the reins a little tighter in his hands, winding the leather straps around his palms calming the horses who were itching to get home to their fields. He looked directly at Ivan. He knew that Ivan had not heard from his mother since he had left. Mary had written four letters on behalf of Ivan, and all but one had been returned to sender. It was the unknown that was eating away at him now.

"You must have faith, Ivan. Your mother wanted a better life for you. That's why she scrimped and saved for you to escape. Remember, you told me?"

Tears ran down Ivan's face then. Wasyl was conveniently leaving out the part where he had told him that his mother had called him a coward.

"I am so angry at this country, Wasyl, calling us the enemy, making us register as such. I feel so helpless with this war. I feel I should fight for my country. I should go back home. And then Mary..."

"Yes, Mary. You must think of Mary, Ivan. Think of your new wife, your field to harvest, and focus on your freedom. Yes, we have these papers, but we are still free. Mr. Benton is on our side. We will get through this as with all things."

Ivan wiped his eyes with his sooty handkerchief. He felt exhausted.

"I have told Mary that if we can't make ends meet I'm going to get a job, Wasyl, in one of the mines, down south. I've told her, I need to support her and these are hard times."

Wasyl loosened the reins and clicked his signal for the journey to begin again. The moment had passed, the tension eased, been weathered for now. "We'll get through this, Ivan. Just you wait and see."

* * *

Traditionally, the farmers in the Edna-Star bloc community would take their harvests to Lamont where they were sold to the Home Grain Co. Ltd, owned and operated by American businessman Wallace Carroll. Mr. Carroll operated his elevators on a supply-demand basis and his prices fluctuated each year. Although it had been a bumper crop for the harvest, the commodity prices for bushels of wheat and rye had declined, hitting rock bottom in the Fall of 1914. Grains still made their way East on the railway, cars brimming with wheat, but each pound was worth mere pennies. The entire economy was struggling with the war effort and that unease trickled right down to the farmers who fed the country.

Wasyl and Ivan had split the money from their Autumn harvest, at Wasyl's insistence. There was enough to feed their families and sustain them for the winter, and Wasyl knew that the two men would be able to pick up hours with other farmers in the Spring, especially around the Hairy Hill area. He believed there was strength in numbers and had already discussed with Katja that if Ivan and Mary needed, they would be welcome to move in with the Federchuks for the winter.

The priest had read Wasyl like a book when he discerned his leadership abilities in his face that first day at the church. Wasyl was a communicator, well-respected among the farming community, and an active member of the Alberta Farmers' Cooperative Elevator Company. They were a strong lobby group working together to acquire the best prices for their crops. When William Tregillus, their helmsman, suddenly fell ill late in November, he asked Wasyl to take the role. Meetings would need to take place over the next few months he said. A new strategy was needed to overcome the monopoly that existed with the Home Grain Company. The Cooperative needed fresh, innovative ideas. Was Wasyl up to the challenge, he wondered?

Wasyl had stepped in as interim leader for his friend without any arm-twisting. Farming was his livelihood, and it supported his family and community. He considered himself a fair man and was respected for his business acumen among his peers. The Cooperative held meetings each month, the last Saturday of the month, at the community centre in Edna-Star. In December and January the same six farmers showed, but in the spring, there were over twenty-four men. They needed ideas to end the monopoly.

From his post as medical doctor and self-proclaimed government watch-dog, Dr. Smith observed the farmers' meetings with much interest. He had even attended one, congratulating Wasyl on his effective chairing of the meeting; some of the men becoming unruly, but Wasyl calming them down. Clearly, Wasyl was the educated one of the bunch, Dr. Smith had noted with characteristic superiority. After sitting in on that meeting in January, Dr. Smith had joked about checking the six men's cards to see if they had been stamped for the reporting period. This cavalier comment from the doctor shocked Wasyl and he stopped in his tracks.

"We are all law abiding citizens, Sir." Wasyl had responded. "We want what is best for our country."

Dr. Smith had laughed off his comment, but stayed away from the meetings after that. Still, he watched for the regular meetings and recorded the number of men attending. He thought perhaps the information might be useful sometime.

Henri Bourassa joined the Farmers' Cooperative meeting in late February. Wasyl asked him to attend on account of his different perspective. Henri had never taken his grain to Home Grain Co. because of his proximity and loyalty to another grain company in the Metis settlement of St. Albert, just to the west of his land.

"I always secure the price of the crops in the spring. Get it in writing. Better to negotiate then than when I've got bushels to sell in September."

Wasyl nodded. A new strategy. With the two grain companies available for the farmers, they could bargain for the best price ahead of the harvest. Henri said that he would be happy to act as the group's translator with the Alberta Grain Company.

"A small group of us could go; a coalition. I could speak on behalf of those farmers wanting to sell in St. Albert. It is an option."

"Perhaps, we could secure a better price," Ivan stated hopefully.

Wasyl nodded. It was decided. The three men would go in early March, discern what crops would sell for the highest price and adjust their planting to meet the needs of the elevator company.

Wasyl shook hands with Henri as he left the meeting.

"Thank you, Henri."

"We are a community, Wasyl. We must stand together."

Wasyl prepared for this meeting diligently, scouring the seed catalogues Mr. Benton had loaned him. He wanted to have prices in place for the discussion, to have a base of knowledge should the Alberta Grain Company want crops other than traditional Red Fife. The price for barley was on the rise, he had heard, and there were several varieties in the catalogue. He used his straight-edge to design a grid where he systematically wrote the name of the crop, the seed price, and anticipated yield. Then he divided this by two, on account of the possibility of drought and loss. Then he divided it into two again, thinking of his friend Ivan. Cost versus sale price. These numbers would be vital in his negotiation with Henri and the elevator owner of the Alberta Grain Company.

Katja busied herself with needlework as Wasyl worked at the table beside her. The fire burned steadily, casting shadows on the walls, dancing daintily. Wasyl's brow was furrowed and his eyes narrowly focused on the figures, and Katja knew this meeting was of great importance to their family and those of the entire bloc community. She had washed his best pants and cotton shirt and laid them on the bed post for him. She asked him what else she could do for him to help. He looked up at her, reassuringly.

Wasyl's thoughts burdened him as he finally lay down beside Katja. He turned his face to the warm embers. Ivan had spoken to him in confidence about wanting to start a family, but felt he and Mary could not yet support a child. This negotiation could make that happen for his closest friend. And for Katja and his own children, Wasyl wanted a cow for the farm, to provide fresh milk for his family every day.He wanted to save for modern machinery like Henri's. He must negotiate a fair price that would sustain his fellow farmers of Lamont Country.

Rising early, pulse racing, Wasyl tucked the seed price pages into his woollen jacket's top pocket and secured his suspenders. He stepped outside to sunshine and blue Alberta sky and prepared the horses and wagon. Ivan had already arrived and was playing peek-a-boo with Pavla in the kitchen and warming himself with tea. They had arranged to pick up Henri en route to St. Albert that morning.

* * *

The men in boots were swift. The two officers stopped Wasyl's wagon just outside the St. Albert boundary. Wasyl could see the grain elevator like a mirage in the distance, waiting for him.

"Papers," the captain ordered.

Sitting on the outside, Henri reached into his coat pocket first, handing his French passport over for inspection to the first officer. The second officer began walking to the other side of the wagon. Ivan's eyes were downcast and he shook his head at Wasyl. Wasyl reached into his right-hand pants pocket. The papers were always there, folded just so; tightly as Ivan had shown him so they would not fade with the dust of the fields. His pocket was empty. Couldn't be. He reached into the other and couldn't hear the captain order them out of the wagon. Voices blurred. *Katja*, he thought. He reached into his coat pocket and felt the crinkle, the folds. *Thank God*, he thought.

"I have them here, Sir."

He handed the officer the folded papers, the seed prices and ledger he had prepared the night before with facts and figures. He realized it too late.

"Is this some kind of joke?"

The officer ripped up his work. Wasyl watched, silently.

"Your registration papers, Farmer."

"God forgive us, we don't have them. We just left them today. We had a special meeting here in St. Albert and..."

"You know the law. No papers?"

Ivan knew what was coming next and slipped off the wagon to make a run for it. Silty dust clouded the two of them as he and the captain rolled in a dangerous embrace.

"You better keep your friend here in line." The captain had his baton out now.

Ivan was pushed back toward the wagon and Wasyl got down beside him. He picked up Ivan's hat and gave it to him. Dignity, he silently urged him. Brushing him off, Wasyl spoke calmly.

"We need to do what these men ask of us, Ivan. That is the law. We have done nothing wrong."

Wasyl glanced back, helplessly at Henri, whose eyes had welled up, as he watched his friends being led away to a waiting covered wagon and thrust up into it like cattle.

"Katja," Wasyl mouthed. The cloud of dust from the North West Mounted Police wagon filled Henri's eyes and nostrils.

Katja knew immediately that her worst fears had come true. Henri guided Wasyl's team of horses up the pathway to their homestead. She had found the papers about an hour after he and Ivan had left. They sat, folded with his reporting card, on his bedside table. In the haste and excitement of this important meeting, they had been forgotten, remaining there, haunting her these hours he had been gone.

"I'm so sorry, Katja. Wasyl has..." The rest was a blur to Katja. She cried out and sobbed on Henri's shoulder until her tears seeped through to his skin.

"There, there," he said, trying to comfort her.

He looked beyond her braids to Olek and Pavla, the little one with her thumb tucked comfortably in her cheek, watching their mother from the doorway, head tilted, brow furrowed, wondering.

"Now, you've got those little ones, Missus. You need to tend to them. I will return when I have any new information for you on where they've been taken. There was a group of them taken away in a wagon. They are not alone. They have each other at least."

Katja pushed back her kerchief in an effort to console herself. She had heard they. What did Henri mean they've been taken?

"And Ivan too?"

"Yes, Missus, the two of them in a crowd of many more. Just outside St. Albert. Never even made it to the grain company." He paused, feeling guilty about planning this meeting. If they hadn't done the trip…

"Unfair is what this is. Unjust." He tipped his hat to her as he handed her the reins of her horse and undid his own horse reined at the back.

"I've got to tell Missus Kelemchuk now." Henri sighed deeply, sorrowful.

"No, I should be the one to tell Mary."

"I'd be grateful, Missus. I'll find out what I can for you."

Katja watched the circle of dust swirl in the air as Henri's horse trotted back down the path, like the poof of the magician's wand at the carnival show in Drobomil so many years ago. Just like that, her Wasyl had vanished.

When she turned around, the reins of their horse team in hand, Olek and Pavla stood in the doorway, staring.

"What is happening, Mama?" Olek spoke first. "Why are you crying?"

Katja wiped her eyes as she crouched low and encircled her children, embracing them in her comfort.

"Papa and Uncle Ivan won't be home for a spell," Katja began. "Mr. Bourassa was telling me that and it saddened me."

Olek's brow furrowed deeply.

"Where did they go? When are they coming back?"

"Oh, Olek," Katja said. "I don't know those answers just yet, and neither did Mr. Bourassa. He is going to try to find out and give us more information. Now we have to be brave. Papa would want us to. We have to water the horses then visit Aunt Mary. We have to let her know everything will be okay."

As Katja led the horses to their trough with fresh water, she tried to block out the searing pain clenched in her chest. She felt breathless and gasped for air as if she were underwater. *Everything was not alright*, she thought. Pavla tugged on her tattered apron hem.

"Mama, Mama, pick up."

Katja scooped up Pavla and hugged her tightly. She pushed back her tears and forced herself to be brave. For the children. For Wasyl.

"Come now, Pavla. Everything will be okay." Katja set her down.

Olek stood rooted by the doorway. He was happy his mother had stopped crying now. He didn't understand why that man, Mr. Bourassa, had made her so sad, but he was glad she had stopped and he had left. He had brought Papa's horses and wagon, but not Papa. Somewhere on the journey, his papa must have gotten lost, he thought.

"We need to go find Papa," he stated firmly to mama when she came back to the house.

"Yes, Olek. We will find him. For now, though, we must see to Aunt Mary. Will you be a brave boy and help me?"

Olek nodded. He took Pavla's free hand, respectful of her thumb, comforting her.

"Come, Pavla. Mama needs our help."

Mary heard the wagon before she saw it. The Kelemchuk pathway was overgrown this late in the summer and Ivan and she had been so busy with clearing the land, they had not had the opportunity to push back the scrub. *That was a quick journey to St. Albert,* she thought. She wondered if maybe things had not worked out with the meeting. Ivan had been so full of expectation.

She opened the door, excited to hear the news. Anticipation turned to dark realization and Mary backed up, stumbling, inside her doorway when she saw it was Katja and her children in the wagon. She and Katja had shared the same unspoken fear since that day at the community hall. She shook her head at Katja.

"No," she said aloud. "Tell me it's not true, Katja. Tell me they're coming home."

She cried and Katja embraced her. Olek squeezed Pavla's hand in the wagon, angry that he didn't know what was going on. Now Mama made Auntie cry. "Stop that," he said, pulling Pavla's thumb out of her mouth. "You need to be a big girl now." Pavla stared first, shocked at this abrupt act of her brother, then started to sniffle, holding back tears.

"Mama," she cried out.

Katja released Mary and her body puddled. Katja lifted Pavla out of the wagon and the little one ran to Mary enveloping her shoulders with her small arms. Olek pouted at his mother, his anger smouldering.

"Why do you make Aunt Mary cry?" he demanded.

"Olek, she is sad for the reason I already told you. Papa and Uncle Ivan had to go away," Katja said. "We cry because we don't know when they are coming home."

Olek tried to digest that information in his three-year-old mind. Papa gone.

"Who will take care of us?"

"Me, Olek, of course. Me and Aunt Mary."

Olek seemed satisfied by that and his hardened pout and squint-ed eyes softened. His Auntie had stopped crying now and was hold-ing Pavla in her arms.

"I need you to be a good boy and play with Pavla now," Katja urged.

Olek nodded. Something terrible was happening and he didn't know what to do. He would help Mama. He would protect her and Pavla until Papa was home.

Chapter Eighteen

The two women emerged from Mary's zemlyanka with a plan. Mary didn't want to be alone and neither did Katja. Without question Katja invited her to live at the Federchuk homestead for as long as need-be. The two of them would be safer, stronger, and more stable than each on their own.

Mary packed a few belongings into a cotton sack. She didn't know if it would be a few days or longer that she would be away. She looked around the zemlyanka, Ivan's home. She felt guilty leaving, but couldn't stay, not without him. She could always come back, she thought. Her thoughts were jumbled and her brow ached with tension. Katja was waiting with the children in the wagon. She pulled the drawstring to close the sack. She must go.

The horses whinnied and glanced back at Katja. The sun was just sliding behind the top branches of the aspen, camouflaged by the Autumn leaves as they approached her home. Katja raised her face and closed her eyes, only for an instant, and felt its warmth and felt protected. Wasyl's voice was all around her. "We are safe here."

That night, after Olek and Pavla had been settled, Katja collapsed at the wooden table. Mary sat opposite her, her eyes still red and puffed with circles of sadness. Katja put her head in her hands and felt the rush.

"Oh Mary," was all she said between her sobs.

Mary sat silently. She forced herself to stand on her leaden feet and walked around the table, directly beside Katja and placed her arm around her friend's shoulder. Katja turned her head to Mary and hugged her waist.

Mary felt her belly then, filling out with the life inside of her. Katja noticed this movement and looked up at her friend. "Baby, yes?"

"Yes, Katja," she whispered. "I'm going to have a baby."

Mary was shaking. "I'm about twelve weeks in, Katja. I'm so afraid, and now, without Ivan..."

Katja tried to reassure her. "Even in sadness, there is hope."

Henri Bourassa and two other farmers from the bloc banded together to help Katja and Mary with their field harvest. Henri had purchased a motorized tractor and baler and Katja marvelled at the speed and ease with which it accomplished what would have taken Wasyl and her several weeks to accomplish by hand. Her only income that Autumn came from the sale of the wheat that Henri cut and sold for her. He sold it to the same cooperative in St. Albert that Wasyl was going to meet that day. Henri told Katja he needed to do this, to assuage his guilt, and asked nothing in return. Katja would make the Bourassas a fresh paska bread every Sunday, decorated with breaded leaves and flowers as her thanks.

Bettina took her aside one week after church and whispered, "You don't have to do this, you know. I know your husband would have done the same for any family in the bloc."

But Katja continued. It was for her dignity and Wasyl. Wasyl would not want her to take something without giving something in return.

"Even when we have so little, there is always something we can give back," he would say.

The cow grazing peacefully outside her home was Henri's gift to her children. "They need fresh milk through the winter," he had said. "She's a beautiful Canadian Holstein that will be bred in the spring. Until then, she's yours for the milking." Katja knew that when Wasyl came home again, he would make arrangements for repayment with Henri and Bettina. For now, she was most thankful, and gratefully forked the straw grasses in the small covered pen Henri had built for the cow. Katja looked into the animal's calm brown eyes, a connection, then was distracted by the cow chewing up the grasses almost as fast as Katja forked them in. She was earthen brown and the colour reminded Katja of the majestic elk she had seen by the stream her first week here, but never since.

"She needs to be milked twice a day, now," Henri said. Olek had jumped for joy. "I want to learn how to do it."

Henri had pulled up Olek and sat him down on his knee on the little three legged stool.

"He's never too young to learn, Katja," Henri reassured her. "If you give your permission."

Katja nodded. She watched Olek's quick hands on the teats and held Pavla tight on her hip. From behind, Henri could have been her Wasyl, his hat and overalls a match. Her thoughts turned to him daily. Her worries would drown her if she let them. Dear Wasyl. What was he thinking and doing? Was he hurt, was he warm, was he hungry? She had so many questions she had to bury some deep inside, her worry would help no one. Henri hoped they would hear official word any day now about where the men were taken. But when that would be for certain, he couldn't say.

Milk sloshed in the bucket as Olek carried it with both hands, fists tightly clenched right up to his chin.

"I did it, Mama. I'm a big boy, now."

"Yes, you are, Olek."

Henri nodded to her and tipped his hat back.

"I'll be going now, Missus. Now, both you and Olek can milk her." He patted the Holstein on her neck. "See you ol' girl!" The cow turned her sleepy eye to him.

"Let's get that milk inside. I know Aunt Mary would love some, Olek," Katja urged him. She smiled at Henri and asked him to give Bettina her best.

Chapter Nineteen

In such a small close knit community as Edna-Star, news travelled quickly. At church on Sunday the priest spoke about the internment, then about hope. Official word had been given that seven men from the bloc community had been imprisoned over the past several weeks and were housed in a forced labor camp in Banff National Park, called Castle Mountain. Mr. Benton had given Katja and Mary a copy of The Edmonton Gazette where an article from The Crag and Canyon newspaper, out of Canmore, had been reprinted. It announced the opening of the camp and advised Canmore residents, particularly lady folk, to be on guard, for there were criminals in their midst. *And what is their crime?* Katja thought, as she read the article. *That they came to Canada and wanted a better life for their families?*

The priest spoke of forgiveness and peace at this time of war. While the congregation prayed for the men, fathers, sons, and brothers, Katja also prayed for Mary and her baby. She peeked out during the prayer at Mary's face, serene and calm. Mary's parents had urged her to move home to the village and live with them until Ivan returned, but Mary would have nothing of that. She would link Katja's arm in hers, insisting they would weather this together. Katja was grateful for Mary's company and conversation. Their division of labor for the mundane household chores happened naturally and Katja marvelled at their unspoken understanding of their need for time alone as well.

Katja would hover momentarily when Dr. Smith came to call on Mary in his professional capacity, to see how she was coming along. Katja felt protective of Mary in her vulnerable state, especially knowing the history between the doctor and her friend. The first time he came she was hanging up laundry. His horse, Milly, announced his arrival with a whinny. Although Katja remembered her amusement at his overall demeanour on the day he had first trod this path, time and circumstance had worn her down and now Katja found his putting on airs tiresome.

"Hello, Miss Federchuk. Lovely day isn't it? I've come to check on Mary. Is she inside?"

"Hello, Dr. Smith. Yes, Mary is inside. I can get her..."

Katja didn't have a chance to say more as Pavla and Olek came running up, tangling themselves in her apron.

"What is it, darlings?"

"Pancake's eggs are hatching! Just come and see!"

Katja laughed. "The cycle of life. I will tell Mary you are here."

She went inside and told Mary that Dr. Smith was here to see her. "If you want me to send him away, I will," Katja told her.

"No. It is fine, Katja. It is for the baby. Please don't worry."

Katja opened the door where Dr. Smith was twirling Pavla in the air and Olek was grabbing his pant leg shouting, "My turn, my turn!"

"Mary will see you now, Doctor."

"I will just be outside if you need anything," she winked at Mary and nodded at Dr. Smith and closed the door.

Edward removed his hat, allowing his eyes to adjust to the darkness of the room after the sunlight outside. The room smelled of freshly-baked bread. Mary stood by the kitchen table and motioned for him to come and sit.

"Hello, Edward."

Dr. Smith reached out to take her hand and reached it to his lips.

"Hello, dear Mary. How are you feeling these days?"

"Well, thank you." Mary gently but firmly pulled her hand away and wrapped it in her apron in front of her. "Katja is like my sister and takes great care of me."

Edward glanced around the room, seeing the garden vegetables on the counter. "You are eating well, no doubt?"

"Yes, we have more than enough, thank you. We have the chickens and..."

"That's good," he interrupted. "Any concerns with the baby so far?"

"No, none. I have been feeling fine, thank you."

"And have you heard from your husband, where they've been taken?"

Mary was startled by the brazen question and lowered her eyes. "Not from Ivan, directly, but my father says Ivan and Wasyl have been taken to an internment camp in Southwest Alberta, near Banff National Park. Remember, the priest said it too, at Sunday Service."

"Of course. That's what I have heard as well. Mary, I promise to let you know if I hear any more specific news."

"What kind of news?" Mary wasn't sure of his motive just then, but she believed Edward. For all his airs, she did believe he cared for her still and did genuinely want to help the people of Edna-Star. Otherwise, why did he come back?

"Living conditions, how long they'll be there, those kind of details."

"Thank you, Edward. Any news would be most welcome." Mary walked to the door and opened it. She could hear Katja and the children laughing at the chicken coop. "Thank you for coming, Edward."

"Good day to you, Mary, and my regards to Mrs. Federchuk."

Mary watched Edward mount his horse with the skill of a great English rider, his coat tails flapping as he turned his horse down the bramble path. He knew her eyes were on him, which is just where he wanted them.

Mary looked at Katja approaching with Olek and Pavla.

"Two new chicks."

The women smiled at each other. "Everything alright?" Katja asked.

"Yes, sister."

Chapter Twenty

His letter came not three days later. It was postmarked Castle Camp, P.O. Alberta. Wasyl's writing was on the front. He had written simply, in his block letter style, *KATJA FEDERCHUK, P.O. EDNA-STAR, ALBERTA*. Henri dropped it off on one of his frequent visits to check on his cow. Katja enjoyed his drop-in visits, and knowing that he and Bettina were there for her, Mary, and the children meant the world to her. She was alone, but not lonely. Wasyl had made this community her home. She held Wasyl's writing in her hands. She tucked it into her apron, not ready to read it yet, especially not in front of Henri, then took it out again to feel the writing of her name; his writing. Black ink; solid; forever. It had been six weeks since he was taken. Henri explained that the post office in Castle Camp had opened on September 1st, that was why word from Wasyl had taken so long to arrive. Henri said he got all his information from his brother in the city. "It's in the local papers," he said.

Katja remembered the paper that Dr. Smith had held up for all to see, their Bishop declared a traitor in her country's eyes. She had felt a sudden shame then for being Ukrainian, a fleeting feeling of shame for people believing something that just wasn't true about her people. And now the camps. They were work camps for enemy aliens. That was what the officer had said. They would be holding enemy aliens. She stared at that envelope feeling the injustice of Wasyl's imprisonment growing inside her. Wasyl could calm the fire right out of her. He would talk her down and tell her everything would be okay, if he were here. Katja worked to control her breathing and keep her shouts of injustice deep inside. She must do so for the sake of her children and for Mary.

"Henri, is there anything for Mary?"

Henri shook his head. "You take care now, Missus. I'll be in touch."

Katja opened the door to the house. Mary was in the kitchen rolling out dough for supper's bread.

"I'm just going down to the river, Mary. I'll bring the buckets and fill the animals' troughs." Mary nodded. "Watch the children for me?"

"Of course," Mary answered. She could see Olek chasing Pavla in and out of the laundry line, laughing and carefree. She touched her belly. She had seen the letter exchanged between Henri and Katja and knew Katja wanted to read it in private. And no letter for her. She knew why. Ivan had whispered it to her one night when she had asked him to read her a poem from her father's anthology.

"I can't read words, Mary. Never had the chance to learn."

Mary hadn't dwelt upon that. "Well, I will teach you," she had said. She knew Ivan could read a compass and map like an explorer. He just hadn't had the opportunity to learn to read books and be schooled in the old country. She would teach him, over the winter, she would teach Ivan to read and write. But then he was gone and his words came to her at night in her dreams, not in letters like Wasyl's did for Katja.

Since Dr. Smith's visit she had been feeling weaker and appreciated Katja's offer to take over the more physical chores that needed doing. She felt she needed to stay in the house, close to her bed for the weakness and cramps that overtook her sometimes. The rhythmic action of rolling the dough eased her pain and calmed her breathing like waves going in and out of shore. From the kitchen window she watched Katja with loving eyes until the last of her friend's skirt flounced into the bushes.

Katja relished the warmth of the sun and lay back on the meandering shore. She set the letter on her belly, face down, and prayed for Wasyl's health and happiness. The chickadees twittered above her and she felt a sudden sense of being watched, a presence somewhere in the bushes. She sat up and glanced warily about, scolding herself silently for such foolishness. She must be nervous to read the letter, she thought. She should just do it. She counted to herself, one, two, and three and slid her finger across the envelope, slicing it open.

Wasyl's words flooded her. Her eyes skirted across the page, dodging words like *prison, quarry, typhoid, escape*. She settled herself, took a deep breath, and began to read.

September 10, 1916
Castle Mountain

Dearest Katja,

I trust this letter will find you healthy and safe with Olek and Pavla at your side. And how is Mary? Ivan sends her his love and I am writing on his behalf as well.

We are safe, brought to Castle Mountain, about 600 miles south and west. It is a work camp. The mountains here are enormous and beautiful, in a fierce way. They are our prison, marking the boundary of where we must stay.

There are over one hundred of us here, Poles, Rumanians, and mostly Ukrainians. We talk little and work a lot. We sleep in tents for now and I wonder what will happen as winter comes upon us. By day, we carry and cut rocks at the quarry. For building, the guards tell us;

I don't know for building what.

The guards don't want to be here. They look at us like we are dirty, like we are scum; like we have diseases like typhoid or something worse. There is tension between us and the guards, but Ivan and I listen and work hard. They say if we work hard we may leave sooner.

I want to come home sooner, to you, my family, so I will do as I am told. Some prisoners don't listen and they try to escape. There have been shots. I will listen. I will come home to you Katja.
Love, Wasyl

At this, Katja choked back emotion and held the letter in her lap as she looked at the stream and the pines across the water. That was where she had seen the elk, she remembered. She heard a rustle and scanned the shoreline. She could barely discern the brown-speckled plumage camouflaged as it was within the colours of autumn. The falcon watched her, its golden eyes piercing her heart. Her memories flooded back, Wasyl's lullaby; the dove and the falcon.

Chapter Twenty-One

Mary had not missed a Sunday service since she was a young girl with pneumonia, but she could not rouse her weakened body out of her bed that morning. She whispered to Katja who was up and preparing breakfast for the children.

"Katja, I can't go today."

Katja knelt beside her friend's bedside.

"Then I won't go either. You feel sick? Morning sick? I'll get you a bucket."

"No, no, it's different. It's a throbbing, a cramping. I just think I need to lie down today."

"I'll get you some tea. You stay here. Everyone will understand."

Olek watched Mary from the table shyly. He hoped it wasn't his cow's milk that made his auntie sick. He brought it for her everyday, just as Mama had asked him to.

He moved away Pavla's cup, just in case, and tipped it off the table, shattering the glass.

"Olek!" Katja scolded. "Please be careful."

Pavla whimpered at losing the milk and at her mother's temper. Her thumb brought her comfort as she watched her mama flurry about with a cold cloth for Mary's head and a bedding roll to elevate her swollen legs and ease her cramping.

"Mama?"

"Shhh, Pavla. Mama's busy now," Olek said, his eyes filled with worry.

Olek spoke softy to Pavla, knowing it was his job to take care of her while Mama took care of Mary.

"Mama," he whispered. "I can stay home with Auntie."

"Oh, Olek," Katja's heart was bursting with worry and love. "Olek, I will need you and Pavla to come with me. We need to get Dr. Smith."

"Mary," she comforted, "we'll be right back. Here is some water, Mary. I'll be right back. We're getting Dr. Smith." She paused. "Edward."

Mary's eyes were closed and fluttered ever so lightly. She was very pale and Katja readjusted the wash cloth on her head. So hot already. Mary was with fever. She must go now. Mary needed a doctor now.

Katja had gone into the church. She nodded to the priest, who paused and peered over his eyeglasses, and only had to whisper, "Mary needs you," to Edward, before he crossed himself, stole out of the church, and was up on his horse. He arrived at the Federchuk homestead well before Katja and the children.

Mary was bleeding. Edward's first intention was to stop the bleeding. He talked Mary through his examination and procedure. Edward took no notice of Katja when she entered. She silently brought him more washcloths and fresh water from the well. Katja took the children outside to give Dr. Smith room to work and Mary privacy. When Olek asked about Auntie, Katja said the doctor was helping her and that everything would be alright; but Katja worried the baby was not alright.

When Dr. Smith emerged, he said Mary needed time to rest. "Katja, she'll need ongoing rest for sometime. I think she should go home to her parents in town."

Katja paused, speechless. She felt Mary's arm linked in hers. "We will be together," they had said. Katja silently berated herself for her selfishness. Why hadn't she suggested this to Mary when they first got word of Wasyl and Ivan being taken? Of course, Mary should go home with her parents. Why had Mary stayed with her so long, working so hard, and now the baby. Mary and her baby. What was happening with the baby? She dared not to ask and Edward sensed this.

"She is still with child. I will need my equipment to do a more thorough check, but I can feel the baby and there is movement."

Katja sighed with relief. "But the bleeding?"

"A sign of internal distress," he answered. "She needs rest now, Katja. She should be in town, close to medical care, you understand."

"Yes, of course, we must get her to her parents."

"Her father and I will return with the covered wagon and take her back with us. I would appreciate it if you would pack up her belongings, Katja. She won't likely be coming back for some time, maybe the spring."

The spring? Not coming back? Dr. Smith's words tumbled over in her brain. Katja breathed heavily, her mouth dry, as she nodded. "I will do this."

She looked at Olek, who was tugging at her skirt. "Auntie alright, Mama?"

She bent down and looked into his worried eyes, speckled with fright. "She's going to be fine, Olek. Auntie is going to the village to live with her mama and papa for a while. She will be just fine."

There, she said it. She said it and now it was true. Katja was on her own with Pavla and Olek, the chickens and the cow, and five cold months of Father Winter ahead. On her own.

Chapter Twenty-Two

Survival of the elements was one thing, Katja knew she could do this. Survival of loneliness was another. Her days were occupied with chores from first light to sun-down and her nights were marred with sorrowful dreams that roused her. Those nights Katja would wind up Wasyl's music box and listen to the sweet lullaby, slowing her breathing to its melody. Those nights were more frequent now that Mary had moved back to her parents' home. Their parting had been filled with enough tears to fill the milk bucket and then some. Mary feeling so weak and like she was letting Katja down. Katja feeling so guilty that she had caused this breakdown for Mary. They'd clasped each other's hands and tears fell silently. Mary's father had talked quietly with Dr. Smith beside the wagon until the ladies were ready to part.

"I will visit you on Sunday. We will come to visit on Sunday," Katja whispered. This was not goodbye. She had lifted Olek and Pavla in turn so they could kiss Aunt Mary's cheeks.

"I will keep these kisses with me forever," Mary told them. Katja held Olek on her right hip and Pavla on her left, standing lopsided as the wagon carrying Mary rambled down the path. She paused for a moment. What to do and where to start? First, the bedding. She must wash the bedding and not let the children see the crimson colour, for fear it would frighten them. She handed Olek the egg basket.

"Collection time, dear Olek. And may you please take Pavla with you? Mama is going to do some washing. I'll be at the well."

Wasyl had built the well their second summer on the land. It was near their first hut, the little house, the one they used as the winter store house now. Katja easily lifted the well sweep, drawing water from the shallow well that Wasyl and Ivan had dug. They had discovered the high water table on one of their walks to the stream that first winter and noticed how the ice cracked first in one area and burbled over long before the others in Spring. At home, in Drobomil, they had the water witch to thank for finding the aquifers. Here it was the magic of nature and Wasyl's keen observation that had found the water source to build the well. It was here they dug and the fresh water was carried easily from the well to home and to the animals' troughs.

Katja laid out the sheets on the rough ground and began to pour bucket after bucket on the sheet, crimson tentacles streaming off the side. She had brought her lime soap and scrubbed, removing any last traces and rinsed the bedding again. By the time she hung it on the line Olek and Pavla had returned to the house with eight fresh eggs and were ready for a game of hide-and-seek in the sheet; Mary's pain and suffering washed away but not forgotten.

"And how were those baby chicks?" Katja asked.

* * *

Nights were the loneliest for Katja. She would keep the fire going, tidy, sweep, and prepare the dough to rise through the night for tomorrow's bread, but after all that and tending to the children, there was still time, too much time, for Katja to think. The dark of night came on quicker now and Katja would sit by candlelight, the fire flickering, meditating on the children's dreamy breath of slumber, and she would write.

At the Benton's shop in town Katja scoured the shelves for writing paper. The choice was fancy white, bleached paper with borders of flowers bursting off the page, sold in packs of ten sheets with matching envelopes. Katja stared wistfully at the packages, knowing she would not bring herself to pay the price, not with winter coming upon them and their life strings hanging by a thread. Mrs. Benton sensed this and as Katja contemplated what she and her children would have to do without in exchange for this paper, left Katja for the back room. Mrs. Benton emerged with crumpled packing paper. "Take this for your letters, Katja. It will work well and just needs cutting and ironing." Katja laughed at that, imagining herself ironing the rough, waxy brown paper.

"Thank you, Mrs. Benton. It will be perfect!"

That night she spread out the sheets and selected one, not too big and not too small, for the message she wanted to write. Once the children were asleep, she quietly retrieved Wasyl's fountain pen and inkwell, covered by his handkerchief in the top drawer of his side table, and carried it tenderly to the pine table. The black ink was so final on the page and the paper so precious. Katja worked out her thoughts before putting pen to paper. She wanted to send him hope. She would write with as much joy in her words as she could muster, telling him about the day-to-day goings-on; the milking, the baby chicks, and the harvest. She knew this information would buoy his spirits. Wasyl's first letter lay before her. Mary; she must tell Wasyl and Ivan the news about Mary.

September 25, 1916
P.O. Edna-Star

Dearest Wasyl,

Thank you for your precious letter of September 10th. It is a treasure to Olek, Pavla, and myself. I read it every night and hold it to my heart and pray for your health.

We are all well. Henri and his machines assisted with the harvest this year. You would be fascinated to see such big machines with such tender hands of steel pull and thresh the wheat.

Katja paused. She needed to tell them. Her hands trembled.

I must tell you that Mary has moved back to Edna-Star to be with her family. She has been tired these days and Dr. Smith and her father felt it was best for her to be home. Please pass on to Ivan how much she misses him and that she and the baby are fine.

She stopped and re-read her words. Is it the truth even if she omitted all the facts? Yes, she decided. This was hope and they needed hope. She needed to send them hope. She added to the letter.

Pavla loves dancing to the music box. I take her hands and she twirls like a ballerina. Olek laughs and asks who will play hide-and-seek with him.

We miss you, Wasyl, love you and wish for you to quickly return to where you belong.

Love always and forever,
Your Katja

Katja folded the letter and placed it on the table. Tomorrow, she would mail it when she went to town to see Mary. She would let Olek and Pavla draw on it with the white candle wax in the morning. She stoked the fire one more time, the embers glowing wildly. Its orange light flooded the quilt as she lay on her side, her face to the warmth. That night she slept without waking for the first night since Mary had left.

Chapter Twenty-Three

Milly the horse neighed, its harness jostling up and down, welcoming Katja, Pavla, and Olek to its side, glad for the company. Katja released the reins on her team and tied up the two horses loosely on the wood fence post. "Say hi to Milly," she whispered playfully to her team.

Olek led the way to the Onyschuk house, up the pebbled path to the great wooden door. There was a knocker in the shape of a horseshoe and Katja scooped up both children, one on each hip so they could grasp the knocker together. Three grand knocks!

Mrs. Onyschuk, her grey hair upturned in a chignon, greeted them with smiling eyes. "Come in, Katja, come in, children," she beckoned them into her parlour. "Mary will be so glad to see you all."

"We've brought saskatoon pie," Katja offered. "For your dessert. The children helped me pick them, didn't you?" Katja looked at Olek and Pavla proudly.

"Mama, I'm hungry," Pavla said, tugging on her skirt.

"Well, come on into the kitchen then," Mrs. Onyschuk said. "We'll have tea and biscuits until the doctor is done."

They walked through the carpeted hallway and Katja felt her boots grow lighter on her feet as she stepped on the soft plush floral design beneath her. The Onyschuk kitchen was robin's egg blue, bright and cheerful, with a marigold sunbeam streaming in.

"Sit down, please," Mrs. Onyschuk directed them. "I'll put the kettle on."

"So how is Mary doing?" Katja asked quietly.

Mrs. Onyschuk glanced sideways to the children's expectant faces. "She is well, really well." She smiled at Katja. "Dr. Smith has seen to it."

Katja smiled back. She felt the crinkle of Wasyl's letter in her pocket. She had not yet read the letter in its entirety to Mary. She had come back from the stream that day and reported about the falcon. Though she had left the letter for Mary to read on the table, Mary had been feeling so weak, she had lay down and the letter was left untouched.

"Wasyl says he and Ivan are well," Katja had reported that night as she tended to Mary.

"My Ivan," Mary closed her eyes.

Katja had made the decision then not to worry Mary with any more of the letter. And now she hoped Mary was ready, and Katja could send Mary's letters to Ivan too. She was eager to share all this with her.

Katja sipped her tea, its warmth surging through her. She still wore her mother's gift about her shoulders, the shawl wearing thin, but still treasured. She had not had word from home for some time. She had received a letter earlier in the summer that Anne had sold the farm and was moving in with her sister into Drobomil. That had been the last word. War damaged all things, sparing no one in its wrath. Her mind wandered to her children, who might never meet their Baba in the old country.

The stairs' rhythm gave away Dr. Smith's presence. He entered the kitchen. "Oh, Mrs. Onyschuk, I didn't mean to interrupt. Hello, Mrs. Federchuk; children." He nodded at them. Olek hid his face behind Katja's arm and then peeked out.

"Gotcha!" he said.

Dr. Smith laughed. "May I speak with you alone, for a moment,

Mrs. Onyschuk?"

"Oh yes, most certainly."

They walked to the parlour, Dr. Smith nodding politely to Katja as they left.

She waited impatiently for Mrs. Onyschuk to come back, their hushed voices murmuring through the wallpaper a temptation to her.

Mrs. Onyschuk stood in the doorway wringing her hands. "The doctor says she's stronger now and doesn't have to be bedridden all the time. Great news, it is. Would you like to tell her, Katja?"

"I'll tell her!" offered Olek.

"Let's both tell Aunt Mary," Katja said. "May we go up and see her now?"

"Of course. Tell Mary I'll bring her some tea shortly."

Olek clambered up the winding staircase and Katja instinctively reached down to carry Pavla.

"I do it, Mama," she said. Pavla began the climb, one knee up and two hands up, over and over, as Katja walked protectively behind. Mary's door was ajar and Olek was up on the bed sitting beside Mary as Katja and Pavla entered.

"Olek, be careful," Katja fussed.

"It's okay, Katja. I love him here, and Pavla, dear Pavla." Pavla stood at the side of the bed, arms up, wanting to hug her auntie. Katja boosted her up.

"Now, my turn," she said and reached down to hug Mary.

"Oh, Mary, you are better and stronger, Dr. Smith says."

"Never mind me, Katja. I have so many people doting on me. How are you doing?"

"Well, we are well," she managed. She held back how lonely she was, how filled she was with worry every minute of every day about

Wasyl, the winter ahead, and how she'd ever manage alone. She held back every word of that.

"It's me, Katja. You can tell me the truth. I know you are worried. I can see it in your eyes."

"I am worried, Mary, but I want to know about you now. How are you feeling, Mary?"

"Anxious to leave this bed. Edward has ordered me to stay here and I'm bored and eager to get up and about. I don't think lying here can be very good for the baby."

Olek's ears pricked up at that. "What baby?"

"This baby." Mary put Olek's hand on her swollen belly. "Baby is in here, Olek." Olek's eyebrows bunched up. "You're funny, auntie," he said.

Katja smiled. "Remember, Olek, you have some news for Aunt Mary."

Olek paused. "Oh yes, you can get up now, auntie. Let's play hide and seek!"

Mary laughed and looked at Katja and her mother who was at the doorway with her tea.

"Really? I don't have to stay in bed anymore?"

"Dr. Smith says you can get out a little bit at a time. Now come and have your tea, dear."

"I'll have it in the kitchen, please," Mary said proudly.

"Strong-willed you are, Mary," her mother said.

Mary slowly swivelled her legs to the floor, her calf muscles beneath her nightie like shrivelled prunes after days of being bedridden. Her swollen feet eased into her slippers as she reached out her hands to Katja. Katja's right hand stroked the letter in her pocket as she reached out to Mary.

"Just like the first time we met," Mary smiled, linking arms with

Katja.

Katja scooped up Pavla with her free arm. "Not going down, no you don't," she announced to Pavla. "Be careful, Olek," she added as her little boy slid down the staircase on his bottom.

Pavla and Olek went into the garden with Mary's mother giving Mary and Katja time to be alone.

"I brought Wasyl's letter, Mary. Would you like to read it now?"

Mary's cast her eyes down staring at the brown tea droplet that had fallen on her nightie and pulled her shawl tightly around her shoulders.

"May you read it to me, Katja? I don't think I can do it."

Katja solemnly read the letter, with great emphasis on how well the husbands were doing and how hard they were working so they could come home sooner. "Soon," she repeated to Mary.

Mary wiped her eyes, her nostrils flaring as if breathing fire like a dragon. "I'm so furious and anxious all in one, Katja."

Katja hugged Mary. "I understand, Mary. I feel that way too. I've written to Wasyl and Ivan that you are well and living back home now. We must stay strong for them, Mary."

Katja didn't know where this inner strength was coming from. Perhaps it was the falcon who inspired her with Wasyl's fierce protectiveness. She would tell Wasyl about the falcon in her next letter.

Chapter Twenty-Four

Katja's letter arrived in the internment camp on a train. The same train that brought Wasyl and Ivan here now brought him his wife's words of love from home. Wasyl heard the guards talking about the train coming twice a day now, sometimes bringing more internees, sometimes bringing winter supplies. The captain they called Davis placed the letter in front of him in the mess hall at supper that night. Wasyl could barely contain himself, but slipped it into his overall pocket while he felt the other prisoners' eyes boring into him, willing a letter from their own loved ones for themselves.

Davis had looked at him with kind eyes. Wasyl was a model prisoner and worked hard for all the guards. His overalls were ill-fitting, but he never complained. His rations were never enough, but he made-do. He had not yet received his second blanket for the winter, but he believed it would come. Wasyl thought he saw human understanding and a glimmer of compassion when Davis gave him the letter.

Ivan nudged closer to him on the wooden bench and asked, "What's it say? Will you tell me what she says, Wasyl? How is Mary?"

"Hush now, Ivan. I'll see to it you know what's written in this letter soon enough. Eat your dinner now and the right time will come."

Wasyl watched as Ivan unconsciously lifted his arms reaching for his blanket that had kept him warm from their cross-Atlantic journey. It was his safety blanket and Ivan had kept it with him at his hut all these years. A ratty old thing, balled up, with holes like Swiss cheese. He kept it folded neatly at the end of his bed. "Why are you keeping that old thing?" Wasyl had asked once. Ivan had looked cold then, his face ashen, lost in thought. "To remember what I left, the life I left behind."

Wasyl could still see Ivan cocooning himself in that raggedy old material on the bunks of the S.S. Arcadia. They were prisoners in the storm then, and prisoners of war now.

After supper the men were paraded back to their tents; massive white canvas tents they had to erect themselves on orders of the guard when they had first arrived. It had seemed ironic to put up the tents that would serve as their personal prison. The tents were matching white with sharp peaks where the poles strained to hold up the heavy material, supposedly water and wind-proof. Wasyl had taken great time and effort in setting up his the tent he would share with eleven other men. He bravely asked one of the younger officers for spare poles to make the slope more severe. This would encourage the sheets of rain to flow down and would keep him and his fellow prisoners safe from the wet mud and slush. Still, he went to bed cold and always felt damp.

That afternoon, a team of medical doctors had arrived by wagon to give inoculations for typhoid fever. No choice in the matter, just all prisoners lined up and prodded with batons like cattle to wait for their turn. At least it was an afternoon free from working the quarry. Wasyl stood in line, conjuring images in his mind of Katja, Olek, and Pavla laughing and playing games outside their homestead. It was his way to escape from here, this work camp forced upon them. Other men were so embittered that they bickered with the guards and argued with each other. Wasyl learned from watching them, biting his tongue and turning the other cheek. He had seen men shot for their attempts at escape and beaten for their insolence, put into cells where they would emerge crippled, hardly able to walk.

He watched and learned and waited.

October 16th, 1916
Castle Mountain

Dearest Katja,

I trust this letter finds you well, safe, and healthy. I think of you and the children every day and my hope keeps me going. I look forward to the day we can be together again.

Thank you for news of Mary's safe homecoming to her family. It buoyed Ivan's spirits to know they are safe and healthy in the village.

Ivan and I work hard in this camp. The mountain days and nights are cooler now so Mackinaw coats were assigned to us today. These are made of wool and warm, but get wet and the dampness never seems to leave them. We wear leather mitts to cut the stone in the quarry and another team is clearing brush to make a road they say. Ivan and I hope to be transferred to that team soon.

There is talk of moving the camp into the townsite. The guards say the winter in the mountains will be colder than on the prairies.

Dear Katja, we keep our heads low and our hearts open. Ivan and I have food to eat, a place to sleep, and each other. We have hope.

I send you and the children my love.

Yours,
Wasyl

Wasyl read the letter over, filling the empty lines in-between with thoughts that he would never put down on paper, nor speak to her. Hands and feet so cold and wet at night that prisoners were losing feeling in their toes. Blankets so full of moth-bitten holes, the men would layer them together to keep warm. Hungry as dogs, rationed on fermented cabbage and rolled oats in place of meat. Guards with bayonets and revolvers that they waved around threateningly at the worksite. The "hoosegow" solitary cell for prisoners who dared speak out or ask questions. Questions. Wasyl had so many questions and no answers. He didn't know how long he would be kept here. Each morning, he and Ivan ate together silently in the barracks. A small fire burned in the centre and men huddled on the benches to be close to the warmth. There was talk of moving camp indoors to buildings and it couldn't happen too soon. Wasyl's hope faded some days and he could see Ivan losing his patience with the conditions they were living under. Still, Wasyl knew he had to keep silent. He had to work hard and he had to go home. He would go home.

There was snow that night and in the morning work duties were called off as prisoners were lined up outside of their tents. The temperature had fallen and prisoners stood, hands wringing to encourage blood flow, as they awaited the Captain's word.

"We have to rearrange the tents, around the commandant's," Davis ordered. Guards nudged prisoners, weary from sleep and cold and limbs numb with sadness. They moved in a trance, lifting up pegs and working together, faces ashen and expressionless. What good was this? The tents did not block the wind or keep out the snow. Wasyl felt the wetness of the grainy snow seep into his boots. He scrunched up his toes trying to keep circulation flowing. He must stay warm. Ivan shivered beside him.

"How long will they keep us in these tents, you think?" he whispered.

"Don't know, for sure."

"I'm losing faith, Wasyl."

Wasyl nodded, understanding. He refused to say the words himself. He looked at the line of men: grey overalls ripped with holes exposing sores on skin, unkept hair, coughing and hacking, and he stopped.

"We must never lose faith. That is when we have lost."

The commandant's tent became their new dining hall. The guards set up four fire pits, one in each corner, and the commandant's stove was in the centre. The smoke would swirl about the tent, escaping instantly when the tent door opened with the arrival of the ravenous prisoners, as hungry for rations as for heat. The old dining hall was being used as a barrack for the onslaught of new prisoners arriving on the trains; Wasyl could still see life in their eyes and held onto that. They were from the outside world and it still existed, waiting for him. His Katja, Olek, and Pavla were waiting for him.

Chapter Twenty-Five

Wasyl's letter had arrived the day before, on November 5th, and Katja had brought it home from the post office tucked tightly in her apron pocket until she had a quiet moment to read it in solitude. A light skiff of snow had fallen on the prairie that night and Katja had woken up to fading embers in the stone hearth. She used the straw hand-broom to sweep back in the ashes that had blown out with the wind. Her doubts were creeping in this morning. Could she make it through the winter herself? Katja pushed the worries down, busying herself with the fire, kindling it with dry birch bark. She loved the spark of warmth that burst with the bark, like a firecracker exploding. The firelight lent a warm glow to the room, autumn-coloured hues to tint the early winter snow. Katja looked outside and knew she would have to tend to the animals and ask Henri about winter shelter. Was it enough? Would the animals be able to brave the cold? Would she and the children survive?

She fingered Wasyl's first letter in her apron pocket. It rustled beside the new crisp envelope. It had been over two months since Wasyl and Ivan were taken to the camp. Every day was more difficult than the last. Just these few words between them were all she had to hold onto. The letters were always in her pocket so she could always feel him near.

Katja lit the candle on the table and settled herself. As Olek and Pavla slept soundly, cocooned in the family quilt, she read Wasyl's letter, word for word, over and over. Katja knew Wasyl too well to know that he was only saying what he wanted her to know; this was not all he wanted to say, but all he could share. She tried to read between the lines and knew he didn't want to worry her, just the same as she did not want to worry him. He spoke of having the woollen coat and mitts for warmth but what about at night? He spoke of the quarry and the road building, as if he had a choice in his task, and yet she knew he was a prisoner and would do what the guards asked, with no real choice at all. He wrote he was eating, but he didn't say what it was they were eating and if he and Ivan felt healthy. It was what Wasyl didn't say in the letter that consumed her. Her heart was laden with worry, sinking inside her as each day passed, like a decrepit anchor buried in quicksand and pulling her deeper into darkness.

While the sun shone most days Katja could feel hope, but her sense of isolation overwhelmed her at night. She would pull the quilt up to her chin and smooth it over Pavla beside her and Olek, next in line, his blond curls spilling onto Wasyl's pillow. Olek had her wild free curls and ocean blue eyes and Pavla wore the face of Wasyl in petite form. Her features were fine and miniature Wasyl in every way, right down to her eyelashes. When she smiled and her cheek dimpled just so, Katja's heart skipped a beat as she saw Wasyl in every look. At night Katja would wind the music box she kept on her night-stand, watching the couple dance round and round; the fire crackling its warmth in the background; the smell of bread dough rising; sometimes the sound of the wind howling and sometimes whispering to her from the trees; the chickens mucking about, scratching; every sound of the homestead amplified in the silence.

As she read, Katja's thoughts drifted to Mary and their visit earlier in the week in the Onyschuk garden. Mary's spirits were high that afternoon and her flush of colour was heartwarming to Katja as her good health seemed to have returned. It seemed to Katja that

Dr. Smith was paying close attention to Mary and he was just leaving as she arrived for her visit. Katja worried about the intentions of the doctor but when she tried to ask Mary about it, Mary shrugged it off.

"He's lonely himself, I suppose, and I am his patient and a friend who just happens to be married." She laughed.

"What do you talk about?"

"All sorts of things. He's so well-read, he often tells me about his books, his mother's garden, and life in the city. I often ask about life in the city and the shops there."

Katja watched the light in her friend's eyes as she talked about Edward. She had no doubt that Mary was still smitten with Dr. Smith, and he her, but they were keeping their relationship at bay, for Ivan's sake and the baby.

As if reading her mind, Mary continued. "We're good friends, Katja, that is all. It's so good to have friends and someone to talk to again. And you, I love talking to you too!"

Olek had climbed on Aunt Mary's knee and she stroked his curls gently. Pavla sat upon Katja's lap, snacking on the molasses cake Mrs. Onyschuk had made that morning, until she spied a dragonfly in the garden and clambered down for the chase.

Moving back home had steadied Mary back on the pathway to a healthy pregnancy. She was active and helping out her mother in the kitchen, but not overworked and not doing hard physical labor. It was clear she was staying here for the winter and for the baby's birth. When Katja greeted her on these visits, she was struck by the softness of Mary's hands contrasted with her own calloused, ridge-filled palms. After milking, she would rub the remaining salve Henri had given her for the cow's udder into her palms, massaging her fingers and softening the ridges, but they would return the next day, harder than ever.

"How are you doing, Katja?"

Katja caught her breath for a moment. She looked away, following Pavla's leaps and skips after the dragonfly. How could she tell her best friend about her loneliness, her fear, and her desperation? She longed to share these feelings of despair but to what end? There was no time for that.

"We are well, thank you, Mary. The harvest is in, thanks to Henri, and I am preparing the stores for winter. Olek does most of the milking and now that Pavla is walking, well running actually…" With this, Katja nodded to her little butterfly fluttering about the garden, bare toes tickled by the grass. "With Pavla being more independent, it gives me more time for the chores."

Mary looked down in her lap. Silence fell hard between them. "I'm sorry, Katja."

"Sorry for what, Mary?"

"Sorry I'm not there with you, to help you. I feel I've let you down."

"Oh, Mary. You are helping by being here and keeping yourself and that dear baby safe and healthy."

She hadn't received a new letter yet and knew Mary wondered at news from the camp. Mary slipped her hand under her ribbon sash and pulled out a neatly folded letter.

"Would you send this to the camp with your next letter for Wasyl, Katja? It's for Ivan. I'm hoping Wasyl will read it to him. I was going to teach him this winter, and then…" Her voice trailed off.

"Of course." Katja took the letter and tucked it into her pocket with Wasyl's. She needed to keep him close.

"I haven't heard from them for awhile, but these things take time."

With this, Mary covered her face with her hands.

"I'm trying to be brave, Katja, really I am, but I just don't know how long this will go on. How long will they be there?"

There were no answers. Not yet. Katja had not heard anything official and reminded herself to speak to Dr. Smith on Sunday after service and see if he had any insight.

"We have to be strong, Mary," she comforted.

Olek ran up then and threw his arms around his auntie. "I love you, Auntie Mary, maybe more than the flowers!" And with that, Mary's laugh returned and her eyes lit up.

These waves of emotion careened inside of Katja too and it was the children and the day-to-day work of the homestead that kept them in check. But they crept out at night and swarmed inside her head and the only way out was to drift away on waves, feeling the ebb and flow of emotion until the worries floated away.

Chapter Twenty-Six

Olek took the three-legged stool Henri had brought over and set it down where he had been taught. He and Pavla were helping Mama with the morning chores, Pavla collecting eggs and Olek milking the cow. Mama usually came with him to the stall and worked about at his side, there just in case. This morning Mama was at the well with the wash and Olek decided to surprise her.

"Pavla, let's get all the chores done for Mama, so we have more time for play." The skiff of snow had melted and the sun beamed down from the prairie sky, the promise of another play day.

"We should wait for Mama," Pavla advised, her dark eyes squinted. "She says so."

"I know, but I want to do it now. I know how to do it. C'mon, I'll show you how to milk too."

"Really? You'll teach me?"

"Sure. It's not so hard and we'll do it together, just like when Mr. Bourassa showed me."

Pavla glanced down the hill to where she knew her mama was soaping and scrubbing.

"Okay," she said. "Let's surprise Mama."

Henri had told Olek that where you place the stool for milking is the most important. It has to be close enough to the cow so you can reach, but not so close she will be disturbed by you. The cow was used to Olek's voice now and when he and Mama came in for milking the cow would turn her big head in greeting.

This morning, she snorted and lifted her nose showing her teeth and gums when Olek and Pavla arrived.

"See, she's smiling at us." Olek said and Pavla giggled. Olek felt like a big boy as he set the stool in place. "Now, you sit here Pavla and don't move suddenly. She don't like that."

Pavla trembled with excitement. The cow was still in front of her, seeming about one hundred times bigger than when she was with Mama. Olek stroked the heifer's side.

"There there now, girl. Time for milking."

This calming voice he had learned from Henri. He took Pavla's hands in his and moved them forward to the udders.

"No, I don't want to do it. It feels yucky."

Pavla pulled away, Olek bracing her with his weight. She screamed, tipping the stool forward, and falling directly under the cow's belly. The cow stepped forward, snorting and shuffling at the disturbance. It all happened so fast, before Olek could move Pavla out of the way.

Mama was there in a flash, breathless from her run, and scooped up Pavla. His sister's shrieks clawed at his heart and Olek tried to focus on Mama's commands.

"We need a splint, a piece of wood to set her leg, Olek."

Mama had come running, hands wet with wash water and had found her baby Pavla lying crumpled in the stall, straw strewn around her, her right leg splayed to the side, twisted and wrenched. The cow, her baby, the stool. It was too much.

"Wood and rags, Olek. Now."

She patted the cow's bottom to move her out of the way and knelt down to Pavla. "There, there," she comforted, pulling her upper body to her. "Mama's going to help and then we'll see Dr. Smith." Pavla nodded meekly through her cries of pain.

Katja pulled her close, muffling the sound. She could feel Pavla's heart beating hard against her and needed to act quickly.

Olek returned to the stall carrying a thick twig and some rags.

"Here, Mama. I'm sorry, Mama, we were only trying to help you."

Katja bit her tongue. She wanted to yell *what were you thinking?*, but it would do nothing to change the circumstances they faced.

"I know you were, Olek. Now you need to kneel down here and hold your sister's hand."

With motherly gentleness, Katja placed the wood against Pavla's calf. She ripped the cotton cloth easily into strips and wrapped and tied the splint in three places. She scooped up Pavla.

"We have to get you to the doctor, now, Pavla."

Pavla choked through her tears. "I brave, Mama, I be brave girl."

Katja held her close. "You are brave, dear."

Olek walked beside her, sniffling, filled with shame and guilt. Katja rumpled his curls.

"It's okay, Olek. She's going to be okay, now. We've got to get her to the doctor, is all. I need you to stay with her while I set up the wagon."

Katja's heart beat wildly and blood pulsed through her hands making them clumsy with the harnesses. The horses had not eaten yet, and were not anxious to go. Katja prodded them and tried to be calm, knowing they would pick up on her emotions. Her sense of isolation overwhelmed her. She covered her face with her hands for an instant and she called Wasyl in her heart.

"Oh Wasyl, I really need you here."

Pavla's sniffles spurred her on.

The sound of wagon wheels coming down the road was sweet music to her. Somebody was coming. Someone to help.

It was Henri coming to call and as soon as he saw Katja with the horses, Olek and Pavla set down on the dirt, and the little girl's leg all splinted up, he paused.

"Looks like you could use a hand here. I was just coming 'round to see how you were all getting on."

"Your timing is perfect, Henri," Katja garbled. "We need a doctor. Pavla's leg is hurt badly."

"I can see that, Missus. You stay here with your children and get them inside by the fire. I'll fetch Dr. Smith for you."

"Thank you, Henri. Thank you so much."

The wagon wheels spat up dust as Henri circled in the yard over the ruts and back out to the main pathway.

Katja lifted Pavla gently and carried her inside. Olek held her skirt and pushed open the door for her. The falcon watched silently from the lone pine tree outside as the trio went indoors.

Chapter Twenty-Seven

"Gotcha, gotcha!" Olek tried to play peek-a-boo with Dr. Smith as he tended to Pavla's leg.

Katja scooped him up and hushed him with her hands to her lips.

"Not now, Olek," she whispered. "Hush now." She set Olek down on the edge of the straw bed so he could still survey the scene.

The doctor remained focused, aware of the importance of time in setting and casting the leg in order to promote maximum healing. His own father's pronounced limp came to mind as he wound the bandage tautly around her tiny leg.

Pavla watched him guardedly, her black eyes serene but intent. She looked up at Katja who nodded at her and smiled reassuringly.

"Good girl, Pavla," Katja encouraged. She was grateful that Dr. Smith had given Pavla medicine to ease the pain of the break. It was a relief to see Pavla calm again.

Pavla counted the times the doctor wound the bandage around her calf.

"It was eight," she said.

"What was eight?" Dr. Smith asked.

"Eight circles," she motioned. "Eight," she said again.

"That's very good counting, Pavla. Yes, it was eight times around." He patted her on the head, her black eyes smiling. "How does your leg feel, now?"

"Stiff like I cannot move it," Pavla said.

"That is perfect. Now, Pavla, you are not to move it, nor is your mother. You will have to be carried for the next eight weeks, so the bones can get strong again." He looked at Katja, who seemed to shrink from his words.

"I'm sorry, Katja. It's the only way. She's too young for crutches just yet."

"I can manage," Katja mumbled, fighting tears. "I will manage," she said again, more emphatically, convincing herself. Olek was at her side tugging on her skirt and she automatically put her hand on his head, ruffling his soft curls.

Dr. Smith nodded. "I will come every week to see how she is doing. The cast needs to remain on until the new year."

"Thank you, Doctor. Thank you for helping us. I don't know how to thank you." Katja looked furtively about the room wondering what she had to offer. "Will you stay for tea?"

"Yes, thank you, I will. I should like that very much."

Katja winked at Pavla who winked back. "And some hot milk for you, my little one?"

"Yes please, Mama." Pavla rested on the bed.

"And milk for me too, please. Don't forget me." Olek got up beside Pavla.

"Why don't I tell you both a story?" Dr. Smith interjected.

"A story, a story!" the children shouted.

"Okay with you, Missus?" Dr. Smith looked to Katja. She nodded shyly, eager herself to hear the story that the good doctor would tell.

He confidently pulled up one of the pine chairs close to the bed. "All right then, let's begin. Once upon a time there was a handsome white swan named Rodan. He lived near a stream that flowed through a village much like ours. Everyday, he would peek through the rushes by the stream and watch the lovely female swans frolicking in the water, splashing and preening their feathers in the summer sun. He secretly loved one of the swans, Milena, but she was so shy, she would swim away whenever he came near."

The tea kettle whistled and Katja turned to tend to the tea as the children remained transfixed by the story. Though her back was turned, she continued to listen intently.

"One day, Rodan was feeling very brave and rustled his way to the side of the stream. Today was the day he would tell Milena he loved her. He saw her splashing across the stream and called out her name. Milena didn't hear him calling her because just then a stinging pain struck her in her right leg and she paddled furiously with her good leg to shore. She looked down and saw her white feathers stained red from her bleeding leg. She had been shot."

Katja turned around with the warm milk, surprised with the turn of events in the story.

Dr. Smith looked up at Katja. "Don't worry. It's a happy ending," he assured her.

She brought the tea, warm milk, and sweet bread to the table and Dr. Smith continued.

"The hunter who had shot Milena was full of sorrow. He was aiming for a deer to feed his family, not a swan. Swans were sacred in this place and he immediately ripped the sleeve off of his shirt and wrapped and wrapped Milena's leg, eight full times 'round."

Dr. Smith winked at Pavla.

"Rodan watched all of this with shock and his feet felt like they were glued to the edge of the stream. 'Wait,' he whispered, but Milena and the hunter were gone. The other swans chattered, as Rodan started out, following the trail of his love."

Dr. Smith stopped momentarily, reached over to the table and took a sip of the hot tea. "Lovely, thank you," he acknowledged Katja.

"Go on, more, more," Olek encouraged.

Dr. Smith laughed. "The best is yet to come." He continued, "The trail led to the hunter's home where he had a barn for his animals. Rodan watched as Milena was laid gently in a bed of straw. He saw that the man meant her no harm and when he was gone Rodan crept close to Milena and pledged his love to her. Her eyes were closed as he approached and when he spoke his words of love, they fluttered with life. He repeated his pledge to love her for the rest of their lives, no matter what. That's what swans do, they mate for life."

With this, Dr. Smith paused expectantly. The children were silent; no questions, so he continued.

"When the hunter came out to the barn the next morning to feed Milena, he wondered only for a moment about the second swan in her bed of straw before welcoming Rodan to his family as well.

"Rodan stayed by Milena's side, caring for and encouraging her day by day. When her leg was healed, he encouraged her to jump and fly again, but Milena could not. Milena could walk and run, but she could no longer fly. Rodan grew more and more worried about this as the nights grew ever colder and rain turned to sleet and snow. Swans will fly south to warmer climates in the cold months and Rodan's instincts told him it was time to leave. But how would he leave without Milena?"

Dr. Smith paused again and asked the children, "And what do you suppose Rodan did?"

Olek blurted, "He carried her, he carried her."

Pavla said, "He didn't go, he didn't go."

Dr. Smith looked at Katja, his eyes warm and genuine. She felt her eyes welling up now and blinked away to spread the tears across her eyes. *Wasyl*, she thought.

"Rodan left because he had to," she said.

Dr. Smith nodded. "And one day, Rodan left because he had

to. But swans remain true and loyal to their one true love for their whole lives and in the spring, Rodan returned. Rodan and Milena had a flock of baby swans that spring and when it was time to leave again in the autumn, Rodan and their babies flew south, all the while promising he would return. And he did, every year with love in his heart for Milena, his one true love."

Pavla and Olek clapped then. "Again, again," they shouted.

Dr. Smith laughed. "Pavla is our little swan now, he said. She must be cared for tenderly." With this, he looked at Katja and touched her hand on the table.

"I will help however I can," he said.

"Thank you, Dr. Smith."

"Please, call me Edward."

Chapter Twenty-Eight

P.O. Box Edna-Star
November 7th, 1916

Dearest Wasyl,

Thank you for your letter. It came when I needed to know you were well and you sound safe. We are also safe, Wasyl, though much has happened.

I want to tell you we have a falcon who watches over us. He hides in the tree-tops, but we know he is there, ever-present. I think of your lullaby whenever I catch a glimpse of him.

The harvest is in and Henri taught dear Olek to milk the cow. He is a determined little boy like his father.

Now, there is some sad news. Pavla also tried to milk the cow and now has a cast on her right leg. She fell off the stool and we were so lucky that Dr. Smith cast it that very afternoon. She must wear it for at least twelve weeks and so we are spending much time in the house.

Katja paused and re-read the letter so far. Would this news make Wasyl worry? Should she begin again? No, she decided. She must continue and besides, paper was so valuable.

The snows are starting now, Wasyl, and Henri checks in to see that the animals are well. We feel ready to weather this first winter alone, but miss you so very much.

I want to know more about how you are and how you are being treated. Are you eating well, my dear? Are you warm? How will you stay in tents for the Canadian prairie winter? I wonder about these things.

Mary is healthy and her pregnancy is going well. Being in the village is the best for her now. She has given me a letter to send to you with this one. She asks that you read it to Ivan and I assured her you would.

Please know you are in our thoughts and hearts every day, Wasyl. Pavla and Olek send you hugs and kisses too.
Love and Loyalty Always,
Katja

*   *   *

The flurries of November and early December swirled around the homestead and Katja found herself housebound out of necessity and self-preservation. She missed seeing Mary and missed Sunday service, and with the exception of the occasional visit from Henri to see how she and the children were faring, Dr. Smith was her only visitor.

Edward returned each week, with a story and time to play with Olek and Pavla. Katja found herself looking forward to the sound of Milly's snorts and neighs as the horse trotted down the familiar pathway to the house. The blanket of snow silenced her hooves now, but her sounds of excitement were unmistakable and every Wednesday Katja caught herself listening just a little more intently for Dr. Smith's arrival.

After his visit with the children one afternoon, Dr. Smith sat with her at the pine table in front of the fire and announced his intentions. "I would like to provide Christmas gifts for Pavla and Olek."

"But, I can..."

"Katja," he reached over and put his fingers to her lips. "I know you can, but I want to. I've grown very fond of them the past weeks, and I want them to know they are important to me."

Katja was struck by the feather touch of Edward's finger tips on her lips, their presence lingering on them.

"I'm sorry, I shouldn't have..."

Katja felt speechless and surprised by the doctor's brazen act. She tried to regain her composure. "I just don't want you to feel that you have to provide anything for us. We are doing well."

Edward resisted the urge to kiss her, instead reaching out to take her hands. He had felt a bond between them on that first visit to the farm those few years ago. Her smile and laughter had transported him back to a time in his life before everything became so complicated with his mother, Elizabeth, and Mary. He had left her that day, confused by his feelings. Hadn't he professed his love for Mary Onyschuk who was wonderful in every way? Hadn't he and Mary discussed the possibility of an engagement? So, how was it then, that he could feel starstruck again with Katja, and a married woman at that?

He didn't have time to uncover the answer as he'd left Edna-Star that night, called home to tend to his ailing father. He mused, during those months away, that maybe he was meant to love many women throughout his lifetime. Maybe it was possible for him to love different things in different women. He was still young. There was plenty of time to settle down, wasn't there?

"I know you are doing well. I am proud of you, Katja. You are the reason your children are well."

"Thank you, Dr. Smith." She felt a need to return to the formality between them; to distance herself. Katja felt mesmerized by his touch and looked away, shyness overcoming her. "That is very kind of you to say."

She was thankful to him for the weekly company and how happy he made the children. Olek would clamber up on the doctor's knee as soon as he sat on the bed by Pavla. Her sweet daughter would chatter to him about her breakfast and the song she was learning and how she couldn't wait to dance as soon as the cast came off. Katja longed for this laughter and with Edward's visits her children came alive, their vibrant eyes shining and smiling with life. Why, then, did she feel so uncomfortable with how he looked at her?

Katja pulled back her hands to her sides and fingered the apron pocket with Wasyl's letter.

"And how is Mary? Please do send her my best wishes."

Edward knew that the moment of intimacy had passed. He levelled his rushed breathing and said kindly, "Mary is well. She asks about you and the children. She longs to be here with you and I can understand why." He looked lovingly at Pavla and Olek. "Her pregnancy is progressing nicely and this makes Mary strong."

The doctor paused. He felt compelled to ask, "And how is Mr. Federchuk? Have you heard from him? I heard there was a post office set up in the Castle Camp."

Katja stood up and stepped back, gripping the edge of the table Wasyl had built. Suddenly this all seemed surreal to her. It seemed strange to be speaking about her husband to the doctor. She felt guarded.

"Yes, Wasyl has written to us. He speaks of the prisoners and says that they are warm and fed, but work very hard in a rock quarry."

"Yes, I have heard that too. Sounds like a work camp to me and they should be paying men like your husband a fair wage." Dr. Smith stopped himself. He didn't want to say too much about his own political opinions about these camps, but they seemed to him to be an underhanded way to develop the national park without fair treatment and pay to these men.

Katja was confused by his words. "What do you mean wage?"

"I've said too much, Katja. My apologies. I'm glad you hear from Wasyl. He is the best one to tell you about the conditions. And now, I should take my leave."

Dr. Smith put on his warm jacket over his woollen vest and Katja thought of Wasyl's vest. He had not been wearing it the day he was taken and she left it hanging on the bedpost awaiting his return. She suddenly wished she could take it to him, knowing the warmth it would provide in the mountains.

Edward turned to Pavla and smiled. "Only a couple more weeks, now, until we can unwrap that cast."

He faced Katja. "Of course it will be some time before she can walk and run like before, but it will come. May I?" he asked and he reached for her right hand.

He took the limpness in her arm as accommodation and lifted her hand to his lips.

"Until next week. Keep well, Katja. Children."

He nodded and placed his topper upon his blond hair. He held the door with two hands protecting it against the prevailing force of the wind.

"Thank you," Katja whispered as the door shut.

Chapter Twenty-Nine

December 9th, 1916
P.O. Box Cave and Basin, Banff

Dearest Katja,

I hope this letter finds you and the children well, and Pavla healing that leg of hers. How brave you all are. I hope and pray to be reunited with you all soon.

Our camp has moved for the winter to a townsite. They call the camp Cave and Basin and there is a hot spring here that we can use for bathing. The hot water feels like heaven in these cold temperatures. We now sleep in barracks with a stove in the middle. We take turns tending to it and with the crowded conditions, there is always someone sleeping right next to the fire to keep it going.

You asked about conditions in the camp and I will try to tell you, Katja, but you mustn't worry. Ivan and I are fine. I read him the letter from Mary and he was very moved. He is having a hard time of it, I'm afraid. I work beside him most days, but when we're separated, I just don't know how he is doing. He says he can't take much more of the work and after wrapping his bleeding blisters again tonight, I agree. I've asked one of the guards to take him to the infirmary for rest and treatment of the infection that seems to be eating his hands away.

We both have watched prisoners come and go these last few weeks. There was an explosion just before we left Castle Mountain and a rock crusher hit one of the prisoners on the head, killing him instantly. We all just gawked at that, nobody moving or knowing what to do, including the guards. It could have been any one of us that happened to. I tell you it was terrifying, Katja.

That's when Ivan started talking about leaving; escaping really, except he called it leaving. Another prisoner started a fire in the brush and escaped through the smoke screen. Smart idea. Ivan liked that one.

It's hard to see him thinking about this, Katja. I tell him keep his head down low and work hard and we will get out. See, some fellas are being taken to Collieries Mines just East of here...they're getting out and they'll get a wage in the mines. I tell Ivan to wait and see, and now his hands are a mess...

Wasyl stopped writing suddenly. He had let himself just write and not think and now he knew he couldn't send this letter to Katja. He was out of line and the guard would never allow it out of the camp. He crinkled it up and boosted himself off his lower bunk. He walked to the fire stove and threw the crumpled ball in before one of the guards could stop him; his words becoming glowing orange embers. It would be one more week until he would be granted tokens for the canteen to get another sheet of paper, but he needed time to think about what he could and couldn't say to dear Katja. He needed time.

Wasyl looked up at Ivan in the top bunk, his hands bandaged and wrapped like a mummy, clutching his head, and peeking out beneath the woollen blanket. Wasyl had to find a way to convince Ivan to be strong now. He could see his friend spiralling downward and knew if he couldn't intervene, this would all end badly for Ivan and maybe him too. There was little opportunity to talk to each other privately in the barracks as the guards wandered between the rows of bunks and clapped their batons into the palms of their opposite hands menacingly. Wasyl had seen one of the guards hit a fellow prisoner when walking to the quarry at Castle, accusing him of walking too slowly. He couldn't chance having anything happen to Ivan and had to find a time to talk deeply to him. Wasyl stared at the blackened flakes and chastised himself for wasting the paper, but only for a minute. The letter wouldn't have gotten out of the camp.

He nodded to Pascal Perchaliuk, a fellow prisoner who had just been transferred to Cave and Basin from Lethbridge. Pascal was watching him closely. He had arrived the day before last and Wasyl had taken notice of him right away. Pascal reminded him of Ivan from the S.S. Arcadia, the same earnest face, hopeful eyes in a body still growing; gangly and all limbs. Wasyl took him under his wing. Pascal had been a coal miner before the internment operations had begun and had just been out of work two days when the guards came for him. No time to say goodbye to his family, his mother and father in town. He told Wasyl he was Canadian, that he was born in Canada and that, "this here was a wrongful conviction and he would be enlisting in the army in a few days and fighting on the side of Canada any day now and wouldn't Wasyl just wait and see him do it too."

Wasyl had nodded and smiled at this upstart youngster and concurred in his heart that all of them had been wrongly convicted, without trials and without justice. Pascal's vulnerability and innocence touched Wasyl and he felt the need to protect him, like Ivan. Pascal hopped out of his bunk and joined Wasyl at the fire stove.

"What was that you threw in there?"

"A letter. Too much information though. Have to be careful what we say about this place."

Rubbing his hands together nervously, Pascal told Wasyl, "Yes, well I'm gonna get out of here. Papa is fighting this in court in Calgary and he says I'm gonna be out before the week's end." He waved a letter at Wasyl. "Says it right here, it does. I'm gonna get out."

Wasyl smiled at Pascal. "Can you take us with you, brother?"

Pascal's court case did go through as his citizenship papers were presented to the court in Calgary, and on Friday at roll call, Captain Davis announced that Prisoner 255 was being released. Pascal would be on the next train out. Ivan twitched with envy and he and Wasyl watched as Pascal rolled his bedding and clothes into a pack. Pascal lifted up the straw mattress at the end of his cot.

"Well, they ain't getting these," he whispered to Wasyl. "Take 'em. There's only a few, but you can get more paper. To write another letter to your Missus."

Wasyl clutched the canteen tickets in his palm and thanked Pascal.

"Take care, Pascal. Perhaps our paths will cross again one day."

"I'm gonna tell everyone I can what's going on here, Wasyl. I'm gonna get you all out. Ya hear? You're all gonna get out!"

With his raised voice some of the other prisoner's heads turned, eyes soulless and searching, trying to comprehend Pascal's words in context. One guard they called Marcus took hold of Pascal's arm.

"C'mon Pascal. You have caused enough trouble already. Train's waiting for you."

And Pascal turned and winked at Wasyl. He mouthed, "I will get you out!"

Ivan took in this exchange silently.

"Can he really get us out too, Wasyl?"

"I hope so, Ivan, because the more people that know about the camp, the better. Maybe, people will see how unjust it is to keep us from our families and homes and have our lives taken away." He caught himself. He could see Ivan's eyes welling up again and put his arm around his shoulder.

"I want to be home when Mary has the baby, Wasyl," Ivan muttered. "I want to be there. I have to be."

"Patience, Ivan. We must have patience."

Inside, Wasyl said a little prayer, *please don't let Ivan do anything stupid.*

Slowly he walked to the canteen. A fellow prisoner was manning the booth and didn't say anything when Wasyl handed him the tickets.

"Two pieces of writing paper, please," Wasyl said.

The man nodded, making a notation in his logbook that this was the second time Wasyl was getting writing paper in two days. Either this prisoner was storing his tickets or stealing them. Maybe he was not such a model prisoner after all.

* * *

Wasyl and Ivan volunteered for the new work project, opening up the road to Lake Minnewanka. It meant days in the brush with the snow and slush soaking their leather boots, but it was a welcome break from the soul-crushing and back-breaking work of the quarry. The bush served as a windbreak and when the occasional chinook came and the sun beat down on him, Wasyl could imagine spring and remember working the fields for his first crop.

It was a crisp December day when Captain Davis gathered all the inmates outside the barracks and announced the new project. Road building had been a major project from Banff to Lake Louise, he said, and now the government was expanding to Lake Minnewanka.

"Who would like to join the work party?" he asked the men.

Wasyl had glanced around and then he nudged Ivan.

"Let's do it! When do we ever get a choice here?"

Their hands went up and were counted with twenty-four other

men who were eager for a change. It was over breakfast that morning that Wasyl first learned that the internees were involved in a variety of development projects, from road-building, to the quarry, to building the Ice Palace for the Banff Carnival, to clearing Buffalo paddocks, and constructing a ski jump. He had only known the work of the quarry since his arrival and to think he may now have a choice in his work buoyed his spirits considerably.

Breakfast was usually a quiet affair of funnelling unleavened pancakes or slurping rolled oat porridge, but this morning it was a flurry of chatter as the men shared stories of their work. Wasyl watched the men's faces growing animated as they shared stories of their different work sites. There seemed to be pride in their voices, Wasyl thought, as he observed nodding and laughter among the men. They had been isolated in their lack of knowledge about where each group of men went each day and why some groups hung back or came back later, and nobody dared ask or maybe they just didn't care enough to ask. Discovery of the work projects gave some diversity to their lives and cause for conversation. Wasyl was grateful for this diversion too because it gave him time to talk intimately with Ivan without the guards taking undue notice of them.

"Ivan, we need a plan."

"Yes," Ivan agreed. "I need to get out of here, Wasyl. Mary said she needs me in her letter and I gotta get back to her, I just gotta. I like the smoke screen idea."

"Hold on, Ivan. I mean a plan to be released, just like Pascal. Men are leaving to get jobs in mines. Perhaps a company will come for us. We've got to keep our heads low and work hard, do ya hear? Good things will come to those who wait."

"I don't have that much time to wait, Wasyl," Ivan retorted. "I gotta go soon, before Mary and the baby…"

"Mary is being looked after, Ivan, and what good are you to her if you're kept here longer because of bad behaviour or worse, you come back dead?"

Ivan looked up, eyes wide. Wasyl was sorry he had said it, but it just came out. He shocked himself with talk of death.

"I ain't coming back dead, Wasyl. But, I am getting outta here, with you or without you."

The conversations around them had settled now and the guards were motioning to the door for groups to gather with their black batons.

"My group here," Captain Davis ordered. "Line up here, men. We need four of you to pull the supply wagon for the first leg and then we'll switch off mid-way. Everyone will pull."

Wasyl was reeling from the conversation with Ivan and couldn't put his thoughts in order, but heard Ivan volunteering.

"I'll pull first," Ivan said.

"Good, good." Captain Davis counted out three more men. "You four get to it. We'll start out in front and bushwhack for the wagon. Any trouble back there, you yell."

Captain Davis led the charge and Wasyl and another two men marched quietly behind him. The worksite was in a different direction than the quarry and led the prisoners over the railroad tracks. Wasyl looked longingly at the tracks, knowing they headed eastward to home. When would he ever get home?

That night he was more exhausted physically than ever. It was as if his body had gotten used to the movements associated with lifting and transporting the boulders and using the pickaxe to splice away the sandstone. Tonight he ached in altogether different places from the brush removal which required sustained side-to-side rhythm. *It will pass*, he thought to himself, as he took out his writing paper. *I will get used to it and this too shall pass.*

Chapter Thirty

December 15th, 1916
P.O. Box Cave and Basin

Dearest Katja,

How are you and the children? I think of you every day as the snow flurries here deepen around us, and I hope you are warm and safe in our home. I miss you terribly and pray everyday to be reunited with all of you.

We are coming to our most special season, Katja. Do you remember our first Christmas on the prairie? I can still see the vest hung on our bed post, from our first Christmas together. I am yearning to see you all.

Captain Davis says there will be a service to celebrate, but it will not be Christmas without you and the children. How I long to be with you.

Wasyl felt his eyes welling up and stopped writing. He couldn't afford to ruin this letter as well, what with how the canteen clerk had eyed him so suspiciously, and his own desire to keep in as close contact with Katja as possible. All he had were her letters now. He had to be careful with his words and get this letter to her. It may be his last before Christmas. Less than four weeks away. He would send this letter and his small paper game for the children tomorrow. Surely, it would reach them in time. He had used the second piece of paper to make a folded number game for the children. On the top triangles, he had written 2, 4, 6, 8 and on the inside, he had written the letters L, O, V, and E. Under each letter was a memory of his children ending with the words, "and I love you!" It was a small token of his love for them. He returned to writing with care.

My Katja, my love, I imagine you celebrating Christmas by the fire with your most delicious kutia and kolach bread. I will imagine the table set with the two cloths and you beaming with happiness at the joy of sharing the meal with our children. I will be with you in spirit, just as our ancestors will be.

Please do not worry about me. Ivan and I have joined a new work party and are building a road from Banff. The best thing is that we are in the forest surrounded by brush, sheltered from the winds. We are warm in the barracks and the food has increased these last few weeks to sustain our strength.

Dearest Katja, all I want to say is that I love you and think of you always. Believe in the power of prayer and I will come home to you soon.

Love Always,
Wasyl

* * *

January 10th, 1917
P.O. Box Edna-Star

Dearest Wasyl,

Thank you for your letter and hopeful words. Your words stay with me each day as I do my chores and I read the letters over and over to the children. They always want to hear your words. Your words are the last thing they hear each night.

The children and I braved an early afternoon storm to go to the Christmas service at the church and visit Mary and her family for tea. Then we came home to our small meal together. We placed the dudkh, wheat sheaves carefully dried and saved from harvest, on the table, remembering our ancestors and it was Pavla who said, "and Daddy too. I want Daddy to be here too". And of course you were with us, Wasyl. We ate the kutia and kolach and as we lit the candle Olek said the prayer. He is a wise little man sometimes and has knowledge beyond his years. He is a terrific help with Pavla, who is following doctor's orders and not using her leg. She laughs that she gets to be in the baby sling again and loves to be carried on my back. "Like a baby monkey," she laughs.

After the Sviata Vecheria, the children opened the paper game you sent and played and played; you were right, it became a game of memories as we each shared a special memory. I shared my memory of seeing the elk that first Spring and the trumpeter swan family with three babies, just before I gave birth to Olek.

Olek asked where the swans go in the winter. Pavla had an answer for that from a story Dr. Smith had told us as he was splinting her leg. He told us the story of two swans separated by distance, but never separated in love. Like us, Wasyl.

My faith is stronger than ever now and I truly believe that you will come home soon. Please know we think of you every day and count the days until you will sit with us at the table again.

We look forward to your next letter with great anticipation. I miss you with all my heart.

Love, Katja

Katja signed and sealed the letter to be brought to Mr. Benton's post office when the weather improved. There was much more to say about Mary and the baby, about Pavla and her healing leg, about her own fears about warmth and keeping food on the table and their very survival without him. It had to remain unspoken.

Without faith, she had nothing.

* * *

February 1, 1917
P.O. Cave and Basin

Dearest Katja,

Thank you for your letter sharing news of your Christmas celebration. I could imagine the warmth in our house and the joy and laughter as the children woke up that morning. How I longed to be there.

Despite the fences, Christmas found us. The officers arranged for a special service here in the barracks and then we were marched across a bridge to the community centre where we were served a meal that had three courses. There was borscht and fish for dinner, and stewed fruits for dessert. The meal was made for us by the church community in Banff and we bowed our heads to them in much gratitude. The women reminded me of the nuns we met so long ago in Montreal who fed and housed us our first night here in our new country. I will never give up on the kindness of people, Katja. People are inherently kind, they are good, they only get led astray. Stay true to your faith, dear Katja, as I do.

Our work on the road continues daily, save for the doctor's inoculation visits when we have the afternoon off to line up. The medicine must be working, for I feel stronger and healthier than I have in weeks. Perhaps it is hope inside me that has given me this boost in spirit and body.

Ivan is anxious for word about Mary and asks that you send her his love and send us any word so that he may know about her and the baby. He knows she is very close to her birthing day now and remains hopeful he will be released to be by her side.
In loving faith,
Wasyl

Katja reread the letter twice before looking at the heavens for answers. She couldn't tell him what had happened. How could she? She wanted to beg for his forgiveness, herself a prisoner in guilt. How had she let it go that far? Katja held her head in her hands. She couldn't be absolutely sure there would be a baby yet, anyway.

* * *

February 14, 1917
P.O. Box Edna-Star

Dearest Wasyl,
*   Thank you for your news. I was so glad to hear your spirits are high. I will share your letter with Mary when I next see her. It is difficult to go very far with the children and wagon with the menacing drifts. I work every day to keep them low and at bay, but still they seem to have grown each morning when I awake.*
*   Mary is close to having the baby now and she has prepared the baby's basket with a hand-sewn blanket she keeps by her bedside. She used a square from Ivan's blanket as the centre piece and cut it into a heart shape. Her heart aches for him as I do for you. I have only seen her once since Christmas because of the weather.*
*   The best thing about the incessant flurries and unrelenting winds is that we have been forced to stay inside much of the time allowing lots of time for stories and healing for dear Pavla. Dear Wasyl, our Pavla's leg is stronger than ever. Dr. Smith has seen to it. She uses a wooden walker to assist her, but often she puts pressure on it and takes steps all on her own. I don't know what we would have done without Dr. Smith and his healing. He has been so kind to the children and tells stories to them each week when he visits.*

Katja stopped. How is it she was able to write about Dr. Smith's kindness? She wanted to shout that this man had betrayed them, that she was full of shame and remorse and wished he had never came into their lives, but she could not write these words, not with the divide of distance between her and Wasyl. It was not the right time. She must write with the hope she knew Wasyl needed. He didn't need her anger and despair. Breathing deeply, Katja refocused her energy on the letter.

Olek loves the memory game and keeps it tucked under his pillow. When he thinks I'm not looking, he asks Pavla the questions and then moves the box in and out to reveal the answer hidden under the flap. It was a perfect gift of love, Wasyl. Thank you. We are all well, awaiting Spring and Mary's new baby.

I hope this letter finds you healthy and happy. Blessings to you and Ivan.
Love,
Katja

Katja was satisfied that the letter was full of love and happiness for her Wasyl. She felt her gently protruding belly and looked over at Olek and Pavla. How would she explain?

Chapter Thirty-One

It had happened so quickly, without warning, and Katja could not even recall the exact details. Edward had stopped in only once since then, bringing Pavla her walker and assuring them all that Pavla was healed. She refused to make eye contact with him. When he heard Milly's arrival, Olek had retrieved Papa's rifle from under the bed. He aimed it at the door.

"Whoa now, son," Edward couldn't take his eyes off of the rifle. "No need for that."

"We don't want you here no more, Sir. You best be going."

Dr. Smith hovered before he left, waiting. Katja's shame silenced her. It had happened and Katja blamed herself that she had let it happen.

Edward had spent the afternoon with them in the yard that day in early January, building a giant snowman with Olek as Katja held Pavla in her arms and looked on admiringly. Katja had asked Edward to stay for supper which made the children joyful, because it meant more stories and more attention. Katja was touched by Edward's kindness to her and the children and it never seemed like too much. Pavla and Olek adored him, she saw that; his youthfulness and carefree manner, his easy laughter, and ability to tease them and tickle their funny bones. She loved seeing her children laugh again and never wanted his visits to end for them. After dinner and stories, Katja laid Pavla in the bed beside Olek and pulled up the quilt tightly around them. "Daddy and I love you so very much."

"And Dr. Smith?" Olek had asked.

Katja paused. Edward got up from the table and came to the

bedside, resting his arm lightly on Katja's back.

"I have grown very fond of you, Olek, and Pavla too."

Katja looked at him then and away, her heart fluttering like she had just gotten off the Russian Mountain ride.

"Now, Pavla and Olek, you stay snug and warm. Mama is just going to be a while longer. Sleep tight, my little ones."

When Katja turned back to the kitchen, she could see Edward taking a bottle of wine out of his black bag.

"Sit with me, Katja," Edward urged, as he poured a glass of wine for her. Katja had not had wine since her wedding and fought the urge to tell Dr. Smith to go. This was improper and he should go. She felt herself in a hypnotic trance as if she were watching herself from afar and heard her voice answer, "Yes, thank you. Just a little."

She longed for company and conversation. That much was true. That much she remembered. And so they had talked and enjoyed the warmth of the wine as the wind outside blew furiously. It began to snow, she remembered, and she had asked him about Milly. He had gone out to put Milly in the barn and came back covered with snowflakes. She had helped him off with his coat and turned to lay it over the chair by the fire to dry. He had grabbed her from behind then, roughly, his hands cupping her breasts and kneading them fiercely. She tried to scream, but he braced his hand over her mouth as he turned her around, face to face, and lay her back on the table.

"Shhh. You'll wake the children."

Though Katja clawed at him, her hands felt numb from the wine. She felt his fingers pushing inside her and booted his leg with her knee. He seemed spurred on by this and his penetration inside her burned, caused her to cry out for mercy. She punched his back and kicked hard at him, until he backed away, panting. She didn't know if he had finished or not, but flew at him, standing there, trousers at his ankles.

"How dare you! Get out of here, get out. Don't ever come back!"

She must have blacked out then, because she next remembered pulling down her skirt as she lay on the floor. Immediately, she prayed for forgiveness. The wine made the room spin as she boosted herself off the sodden floor, rubbing her eyes with streaked hands. He was gone, the door to her home left open to snowflakes softly falling sweeping the floor, pure and white, and cleansing. She didn't see the falcon with its piercing eyes high in the fir tree outside. She shut the door and when she turned around, Olek stood there, eyes wide.

"Mama, are you okay? I heard you scream and cry out. I was so scared, Mama."

Her head ached from the wine and her throat was parched.

"Olek, Mama is okay. I'm so sorry I woke you. I just need some water, dear. I'll come to bed in a moment."

"I will stay with you, mama."

Olek didn't tell his mama that he knew Dr. Smith had hurt her, that was why she screamed for him to get out. He held her hand as she drank water and tucked her into bed, before climbing in on his side. He prayed for his daddy to come home, to keep them all safe. He looked over at his mama, her eyes closed, face streaked with tears and dirt from the sodden floor. She looked like she was floating on the water, her body stretched out so still. He would never let anyone hurt her again.

Chapter Thirty-Two

Squalling and crying like a seagull, Mary's baby boy was born March 1st. He had thick brown hair, scrunchy eyes, a fairy-tip nose covered in freckles, and was as perfect to Mary as could be. She called him Pieter as a tribute to Ivan's father and wrapped him in Ivan's blanket and wept with happiness and sorrow at the same time. The salt from her tears dripped down on Pieter and he startled, opening his eyes to his adoring mother. She stroked the pink cheek and hushed him with her words. Dr. Smith stood in the corner whispering to her mother and Mary lay back in her cot with her baby on her chest. Their breaths were in unison, and Mary felt she had never known true love until this moment.

The weather had turned a corner and Katja and the children had harnessed up both horses to the wagon to head to town for some dried goods and to see about seeds. She planned to stop at Henri and Bettina's and at Mary's too, just to see how she was coming along. The horses were edgy, eager to run now that the scent of green was in the air and the warm sunshine caressed their backs. Katja pulled back on the reins, soothing them with her words.

"Can I do it, Mama?" Olek begged her over and over again.

"Not today, I'm afraid. The horses seem wild, Olek."

"I like wild!" Olek said.

Katja laughed. She could not remember the last time she had laughed. "Oh, Olek. I have to keep my eyes on the road or I'd kiss you!"

"Where are we going, Mama?" Pavla asked.

"First to Aunt Mary's. I have brought her a small quilt for the baby, which should be coming any day now!"

"Yeah!" Pavla and Olek shouted. "New baby!"

Katja marvelled at their joyousness and sense of wonder at Mary's new baby.

She pulled up the horses to the Onyschuk fence and tied up the horses.

"All children out!" she said playfully, boosting them down one by one.

Katja and the children strolled up the path to the front door and knocked three times. Mrs. Onyschuk opened the door, flushed from rushing down the stairs. She looked disappointed to see Katja at first, then broke into a smile.

"Hello, hello, dear Katja. I thought you were my husband, William," she said. "Come in, come in, Katja. Mary's had the baby. A boy! A healthy baby boy!"

Katja wept. She caught herself and wiped the tears away before her children could see.

"Is it too soon to see her?" Katja asked.

"Not for you, my dear. Maybe I should keep the children down here this time. It's been a while since I've seen you, Pavla and Olek. Pavla, I heard you had an accident. Why, that leg looks good as new!"

Mrs. Onyschuk led the children away into the kitchen where the scent of cinnamon buns was oozing through the doorway. Katja began climbing the stairwell, her steps silent on the lovely plush carpet. She fingered the soft, yellow quilt she had sewn using remnants of material given to her by Bettina. She didn't hear him coming down, but his sweet cologne alerted her and she looked up to find his eyes, warm and inviting, staring at her.

"Good day, Mrs. Federchuk," he said respectfully. "There's a new baby and mother upstairs just waiting to see you." Katja half smiled, suddenly weary and dizzy.

"You're well?" Dr. Smith asked.

"Yes, thank you." Katja held the railing to steady herself.

"How are the children? Mind if I peek in on them?"

"I'd rather you didn't, Doctor. Thank you," Katja managed, keeping up formality.

Pavla had asked about Dr. Smith several times since his last visit and Katja had finally said that he wouldn't be coming back now that she was all healed. Pavla had sulked until Olek had gotten out the memory game. Katja didn't want any old feelings stirred up.

"As you wish," Edward said. He smiled at her and continued down the stairs, treading so lightly he seemed to float like a ghost. As if nothing had happened.

Katja took a deep breath and continued up to the closed door. It had been nearly two months since she had seen Mary and she was so eager to hug her and confide in her all that had transpired. But now was not the time. It was the time to celebrate this new baby, this life borne to Mary and Ivan, her best friends in Canada. She smoothed her skirt and focused herself. She squeezed the quilt for courage and knocked softly.

"Hello, Mary. It's me, Katja. May I come in?"

"Come in, please, do come in," came the soft voice, unmistakably Mary. It was as if her friend had been heaven-sent.

"Oh, Mary, he's beautiful!" Katja knelt by the side of the bed and stroked Mary's hand, struck by the miraculous sight of mother and child.

"No no, you must come up here." Mary sat up and propped up the pillows behind her back. "Hugs! It's been much too long, Katja!"

Katja threw her arms around Mary, respecting the baby bundle on her chest, and kissed the baby's soft, brown tufts. "Welcome to the world, baby," she said.

"This is Pieter. And Pieter, this is Aunt Katja."

Katja swallowed hard to keep down her tears of joy for her friend. "You did it, Mary. You did it all on your own."

Mary looked deeply into Katja's eyes. "Please write to Ivan today. Let him know, Katja."

"Of course, I will. I will head to the post office straight away." She suddenly remembered the quilt. "I have this for your baby."

Mary covered baby Pieter with its softness. "It's absolutely beautiful, the colour of the sun. We will treasure this quilt, Katja." She lifted up the baby and Katja tucked the blanket under Pieter who nestled into its warmth like a starling in its nest.

"How are the children?" Mary asked.

"They're wonderful, thank you. Pavla's leg is healed after her accident with the cow. Did you hear about that?"

Mary laughed. "Yes, Edward told me on his visits. I'm so glad she is fine. And Olek? Edward said he had grown quite fond of him."

"Yes, Olek is fine, growing wilder every day." Katja didn't want to talk about Edward and hoped Mary would let it slide.

"I'd love them to see Baby Pieter next visit, okay?"

"Of course. Get some rest now and I'll rescue your mother from the cinnamon bun monsters in her kitchen."

Mary laughed. "She loves it, I'm sure."

"I'm so happy for you, Mary. Really, truly I am."

"Thank you, Katja. I love seeing you. Promise me you will tell Ivan how much we love him?"

"I will. For sure, I will." Katja glanced back at Mary snuggling down with baby Pieter and revelled in that intimate moment of mother and baby when everything is aglow.

Chapter Thirty-Three

Ivan couldn't stop pacing the night Wasyl read him Katja's letter, with news of baby Pieter. "I need to go, Wasyl," he kept muttering. He had beads of perspiration on his forehead and Wasyl thought maybe his friend was with fever. Ivan had woken up with nightmares the past week, since Pascal's suicide.

Pascal had been sent back to the Cave and Basin camp almost as soon as he reached the Calgary station. He explained to the station guards that he had been released, and was going to enlist with the Canadian forces now, but his parents and the court papers were not at the station to meet him and he had no proof, no registration. He had thrown all his release documents into the fire stove in the barracks in his last stab at the system.

"No enemy alien is allowed to enlist," he was told harshly at the train station. To the patrol guards, he looked like an escapee from Castle. His ankles and wrists were shackled and he was put right back on the train.

That night he had not spoken a word. His eyes looked hollow and his face ashen to Wasyl, and Pascal denied all efforts at drawing him out. Shortly after the dinner meal, Pascal had gone to the latrine and cut himself with a razor that was used to sharpen the axes on the work project. It was an officer who found him hours later and shouts went up in the night, lights flashing, alarms sounding and Wasyl knew it was Pascal. The system had failed him. They had all failed the boy.

Pascal's parents had come out the next day, court papers in hand, having won his release, determined to take home their son. Their son's death had happened in the hours of miscommunication that followed. When they learned of the news, his mother had collapsed, fainting to the ground before the prisoners' eyes. Wasyl wanted to run to them, to tell them what a strong young man they had, but his words escaped, forever buried by his own guilt over not doing more for Pascal. Pascal's frail body was wrapped in bed cloth and placed in a wooden casket and once again set on the train. This time, set free.

Wasyl didn't want to fail Ivan too. "Ivan, come sit down. You're going to wear out your boots if you keep that up."

Ivan sat down beside him. "I'm gonna do it, Wasyl. I'm gonna leave here. You gotta help me. You gotta make a diversion for me."

"You need to rid yourself of this foolishness right now, Ivan. It's fools who try to escape and they're brought back here and for what? Longer time and harder work, that's what."

Ivan stopped and looked at Wasyl. He wiped his forehead. "Read the letter again, won't you, Wasyl? The part where Katja tells me about Mary and the baby and the blanket?"

It had worked, thought Wasyl. He would read that letter all night long if Ivan would settle and get some rest. Tomorrow was brush burning on the project at Minnewanka and Wasyl knew they needed a good rest to prepare them for the day in the incessant smoke.

It was the smoke screen that shielded Ivan from the guards that next morning. He was thrashing the brush one minute, and the next Wasyl caught only a glimpse of his orange scarf fluttering in the trees as he ran away from the camp.

"Man away!" an officer called out. "Rifles up!"

The shots rang out in an instant and then the guards ran through the billowing smoke and there was the sound of crackling from the fire and their trampling boots on the charred branches. The prisoners stopped working and stood still, smoke encircling them as they watched the scene unfold. Rifles in hand, Davis ordered the guards to spread out in a spider's tangled web formation. "Find him!"

"Here!" a voice called out from deep in the bush. Guards flocked to the site. "Blood trail, here!"

He had been hit. Wasyl thought. Ivan was shot, but he could still run. "Go Ivan, go on home!" He prayed with all his might that Ivan would do it, that he would get home.

Captain Davis spoke calmly, confident Prisoner 121 would be found. "Everyone back to work. Finish the job. We need more water from the creek to make our water line bigger. Let's get going, boys."

Captain Davis was at Wasyl's side. "Not you. I want to talk to you. Did you know anything about this? Guards say you two are thick as thieves."

"Ivan is like a brother to me, it's true. But no, I did not know he was going to do this," Wasyl lied. "I never believed he would do this," he revised.

It was the middle of the night when Ivan was led back into the barracks, hobbling on one foot using a cane to support his weight on the right side.

"Almost done it," he whispered as he pulled the bedding from his cot. "I almost got away, Wasyl. I was this close," and he held up his fingers a smidgeon apart to show Wasyl. "I couldn't go any further this time on account of my hip. That's where the bullet grazed me." He lifted his shirt to show Wasyl his wound.

"Sleep now, Ivan," was all Wasyl could manage to say. He prayed.

Chapter Thirty-Four

It was near three months when Katja knew with certainty she was with child. Henri and Bettina and a whole crew from town had banded together and spring-seeded the land for her. Bettina stayed behind in Katja's house those days, washing every surface down and hanging out the bedding to air in the April breeze. It had been some time since Katja had cooked for more than herself and the children and she worried if she had enough food as she pulled the braided bread out of the steaming fire pan.

"Men'll be here soon for lunch," Bettina said as she churned the butter rhythmically. "Feels good to be close to Spring, n'est-ce pas?"

Katja looked at Bettina's rough hands moving so freely with the churn and wrung her own, feeling the blisters under each finger with her tips.

"Bettina, may I tell you something?"

Bettina stopped churning, hearing the trepidation in Katja's voice.

"Sure, dear. Anything."

"I'm with child."

There was stone silence as Bettina digested this information. She didn't look up, just asked. "How far along are you?"

"Three months last week."

"Does Wasyl know?"

"Oh no, I can't tell him, I won't tell him. It would kill him."

"And the father?"

Katja hesitated. Uttering his name would make it real. There was no turning back. His name felt rotten in her mouth. "Dr. Smith."

"Well, I never…fils de pute, son of a bitch," she muttered under her breath. "That man has been after every young thing from here to Lamont, and now you, a married woman. Has he no shame?"

Katja hadn't expected Bettina to be so angry.

"I feel so ashamed."

"No mind now. I don't need to know the details to know he is the one to blame," Bettina counselled. "Best thing we can do is care for you and that baby, if you want to keep it."

"Of course I want to keep it." Katja was shocked at the thought of anything else. She had heard of procedures in the city, but…no she was keeping the baby, God willing.

"I'd like to tell Henri. He'll want to know about Dr. Smith. Best thing for our community is to have that man gone, I'd say."

Katja's cheeks flushed with shame. Telling Henri meant telling the village. Bettina reached out and hugged her.

"Now dear, ne pleures pas, no tears. There is not going to be a way to hide this baby, so we might as well face facts head-on. Together."

Katja nodded. She felt a weight lifted from her shoulders, a secret shared with someone older and wiser who would take charge and know what to do with that information. Katja had seen Mary and Pieter two more times since baby's birth, but there was never a good time to share her own circumstances. Mary's joy and the hope that Pieter brought her was palpable and Katja could not bring herself to share news that would most certainly cause her anger and worry. Sometime, but not yet.

Bettina nodded. "C'est le temps de manger! The men are here now. Let's get them lunch!"

Henri came to her before he and Bettina left, the last of the seeding complete. "God willing, we'll have some rain showers to set the seeds, Katja. You need to get those scarecrows out in the fields as soon as you can to do their job. Those scavengers will be out in full force as soon as they smell the Red Fife."

"Thank you, Henri, for everything. You've been such a great support for our family and Wasyl. He is so grateful to you."

"You take care now and don't you worry about a thing. Just keep writing to Wasyl and keep that man's spirits up. Rumours are they're letting some men out to work in the mine and your Wasyl may just find his way out before long."

Katja felt her heart leap in her chest, an extra beat that it may be so.

"Thank you, Bettina."

Bettina nodded and Henri gave a wink and a whistle to his team and Katja turned to Olek and Pavla, beside her. The children clung to her skirt.

"There are leftover buns and butter. Who's hungry?"

"Me!" they shouted in unison. Katja watched the wagon disappear, a load lifted from her.

"After lunch, we need to make a scarecrow family to protect the field. We have all the supplies in the shed out back. Olek, I'll need you to make a couple of trips to gather the materials and then we'll make the scariest scarecrows ever." Olek nodded, slurping his milk and laughing at Pavla who was preoccupied with making scary faces.

* * *

Katja's news spread like wildfire in the village and on Sunday when Katja and the children walked into the church for Easter Service, the hushed silence and furtive glances their way reinforced this. Mary was there and waved her white glove, motioning for Katja to come and sit by her in the second pew. Katja admired Mary's mauve jacket and skirt adorned with lace collar and smoothed Pavla's curls in front of her. Baby Pieter was sound asleep in Katja's quilt, and tucked snugly in the crook of Mary's arm just like he was a part of her body. "Why didn't you tell me?" Mary whispered.

"I couldn't, Mary. I just couldn't. I wanted to, really I did."

"I can help you. Mama and Papa can help you. You and the children can come live with us."

"I'm fine, Mary. We're fine, really." Katja held Pavla's hand tighter and smiled at Olek.

"What about coming to live with us in town just until the baby is born?"

Katja blinked hard. Living in the village. Living in Mary's house. Leaving her house? The house that Wasyl built piece by piece? She could never leave it.

"Let's talk after the service." Katja rose as the priest entered the sanctuary and nodded to Olek to do the same.

Katja tried to focus on the priest's Easter message of forgiveness and hope that love brings. Spring is the time for renewal, he said. Katja could feel the eyes of the congregation boring into her and doubted her decision to come today. She must keep the children safe from her own shame.

Mary looked over at her dear friend and took Katja's hand.

"I love you, Katja."

They walked out of the sanctuary into the waiting sunlight. The priest greeted her taking her free hand in his. His words, "Peace be with you," resonated inside her.

Still holding Mary's hand, Katja saw Dr. Smith in the chapel garden. His head was down and Katja thought if she veered right, he wouldn't see her and she would miss him. "Go play now, children," she urged and Olek held out his tiny hand for Pavla. Mary stopped and faced Katja. "Edward wants to address you, if you'll let him."

Katja looked at her friend, questioningly. She glanced back at Edward, pacing back and forth in front of Milly who was tied up on the white fence opposite the sanctuary.

"I think you should hear what he has to say," Mary said. Pieter's eyes fluttered in the bright sunlight and his mewls began.

"He's hungry, Katja. I'll feed him just over on that bench. I'll watch the children. You go." She called to Olek and Pavla, the wailing chorus trailing as she led them all to a bench underneath a shady tree, in the opposite direction. Katja looked around her to see who else may be watching, but the congregation had dispersed and only Edward remained, steadfastly pacing and glancing at her now and then. She retied her yellow bonnet, adjusting it confidently like her suit of armour. Her legs felt leaden with weight of guilt and shame as she made her way toward Edward. She stopped about a yard away, an invisible barrier preventing her from going any closer.

"Hello, Dr. Smith. Mary said you wanted to speak to me."

Edward looked up, his eyes reddened with sadness.

"Katja. I have betrayed you and my whole community. I am leaving to go back to the city. I loved you from the start, I really did. I never meant to hurt you."

Katja swallowed hard. She would not be taken in by his charms again.

"I want to take care of you and..." he paused. "And the baby."

He handed her an envelope. "It's not much right now, but I will send more from the city."

Katja did not reach out. Edward took a step toward her and she automatically stepped back for self-preservation.

"Now, look here. I'm trying to do the right thing, Katja. Please take it. For the baby. Save it for the baby."

He reached out and thrust the paper bundle in her hand and closed it up tight. "I hope one day you will forgive me." He turned to undo Milly's reins, then turned back. Katja felt frozen in time, like a stone statue; unmoving.

His last words to her were, "And I hope Wasyl will come home safely."

Katja refused to let him see her cry or lash out, even though her anger was like a tinderbox deep inside of her. She wanted him to feel her shame. She said nothing.

Edward tipped his hat to her valiantly, head held high.

Katja turned away, failing to see his last glance at her. She looked at the brown manilla envelope in her hand. Money for the baby. She tucked it inside her waistband of her skirt and faced the sun. Forgiveness, hope, that's what the priest had said. Focus on forgiveness for what has passed between them and hope for what will come. Olek came running toward her, his blond curls flying. "Was that Dr. Smith? Are you okay, Mama?"

"He was saying goodbye, Olek. He's going home to the city where he belongs."

Katja nodded at Mary. "All done?" she asked.

Mary looked down at Pieter. "He's a great baby, Katja. I can't wait until Ivan sees him."

Katja nodded again. "And Wasyl. I can't wait for him to be home as well."

"Come for tea?"

A calm settled over Katja. He was gone. "Of course, we'd love to, wouldn't we, children?"

Pavla tugged at Katja's skirt to be lifted up. She scooped up her little one and twirled her around, lifting her arms high to the sky, filled with happiness and hope. Pavla's squeals of excitement filled her ears.

When the priest found the manilla envelope blown up by the church door the next morning, he thanked the heavens for this gift for the parish sent by God.

Chapter Thirty-Five

Edward left Edna-Star shamed on the outside, but on the inside he felt he was doing the right thing. He could not explain what had come over him that night with Katja, just that he had longed for her for some time. It was like a wave of madness that he could not erase; he could never rewind. He would stand by his word and support the baby. He couldn't yet face that it was his baby and couldn't honestly answer his mother's confrontation when he arrived on her doorstep in Edmonton.

"Home again, are you, Edward? Alone? For how long this time?"

It was his secret, this child. Shame was a growing thing if you let it be, but Edward knew how to suffocate it inside of him, to cover it and blanket it with the money he would send. Yes, he was doing the right thing by the baby, he was sure of it.

Winter session at the university was just ending that April and Edward was determined to get a research post for the spring and summer sessions. After all, his father's reputation was still strong and carried clout, and he was a shoe-in for an internship, he knew. Edward was welcomed back by his mother who knew his philandering ways too well, but adored him nonetheless. To the university he was a gifted researcher who would bring in cash donations to the Department of Medicine. He was destined to follow in his father's footsteps.

Once he had secured the internship, Edward was determined to go on a holiday. He was, in fact, quite zealous about his quest for rejuvenation. He decided to visit Banff in the Rocky Mountain National Park. The railroad ran straight into town and he had heard of the revitalizing health benefits of the natural hot springs. He wanted to fill his lungs with the fresh mountain air.

Then, he thought, he would be ready to return home to Edmonton, refreshed and ready to take on his new posting. His mother had encouraged him to go, not knowing the full details of his hastened departure from Edna-Star. She even toyed with the idea of going with him, then decided against it on account of appearances.

Standing on the C.P.R. train platform in Calgary, Edward felt pity for the men lined up like cattle, prodded onto the open platform; dusty grey overalls and eyes soulless. The reality of these peasant prisoners hit him as he realized they were headed for the Castle Camp. Last he had heard about the Internment camps, months ago it seemed now, this was where Wasyl, Ivan, and other men from the Edna-Star bloc were being held.

Edward swallowed hard as he smoothed the crisp cream linen of his suit jacket and adjusted his silk tie. He didn't want to appear too conspicuous. His fellow coach passengers were buzzing about on the platform, seemingly preoccupied by their own conversations and gathering of belongings prior to boarding.

The prisoners waiting outside of the end car were like ghosts that only he could see and smell and hear. Their shuffling in shackles, the occasional glance up at him with the deadened eyes, their spirits already broken.

Edward coughed and looked away, up to the sky above, and wondered about the weather. It was too much to look these men in the eyes. He boarded without another glance their way. They rode in the last car, the cattle car, and if he played his cards right, he would not have to see them again at the end of his journey.

The train passed through the city and opened up to valleys of wildflowers, Indian Paintbrush dotting the grasses, still green from the snowy melt. Edward felt relaxed and leaned back in his seat, breathing slowly, in synch with the train's locomotive beat. He opened his briefcase and perused the brochure. It was a perfect escape to be sure.

The Banff Springs Hotel rose majestically in the valley of the Rocky Mountains, its copper-plated spires reaching to the heavens. Edward had put thoughts of the prisoners behind him as soon as he had settled on the train and he disembarked at the station, brimming with optimism and an air of elegance. He was on holiday and would make the most of his time here. He walked Main Street with purpose, striding confidently, tipping his hat to the multitude of visitors here for spring holidays. Women in fluttery skirts and ruffled blouses; coiffed men like himself, tanned in their crisp white linens. It all felt perfect.

The mountain peaks remained streaked with white, despite the warmth in the air, like dripping ice cream cones in the sun. Wisps of cloud hovered creating dancing shadows on the cobbled street. Edward determined the hotel to be within a few miles walking distance and crossed the bridge overtop the Bow River. It felt wonderful to be in nature, to be moving again after the journey on the train.

He paused on the bridge, catching sight of an off-road trail along the side of the river. He descended and followed its meandering path leading to an apex of thundering water over boulders in the distance. *The winter melt*, he thought. The river path led him through a woodland and he watched the hotel's spires disappear, then reappear on the horizon. He sat on a flat rock on the shore, stretched out his legs, and let out a sigh that had been bottled up inside of him for months.

Edward closed his eyes and took in the sound of the starlings and chickadees above him, rising above the churning of the tumbling falls. The crashing water filled his senses and a rushing feeling of relief intermingled with sorrow overcame him. He removed his hat and wiped his misty eyes with his handkerchief. He held his forehead and covered his whole face, the white cotton laundered in lavender; a cleansing shroud. His heart had broken at Katja's news, at leaving her, at knowing what had happened between them, and knowing he could never change that; never fix it. His father had always been able to fix things for him, but this last incident was completely on him. He let himself feel the emotion of all that had transpired, the rush of loss flooding out.

When he rose, the sun streamed down between the tree trunks, holding him in its spotlight. He felt a sense of renewal, a chance to begin again. His suitcase felt lighter as he strode with renewed confidence to the hotel. It was the first and last time Edward let down his guard; the fir trees his only witnesses.

The Banff Springs Hotel epitomized luxury amidst the wild backdrop of Rundle Mountain and the towering pines. Edward nodded to the bellman who held open the gold-plated door with his white gloves. Edward knew he was going to like it here.

He climbed the interior marble staircase to a landing and looked out over the Bow Falls from an adjoining window. The spring sun shone through alighting his attention on a portrait. Bathed in warm reds and golden autumn hues, the portrait of lumberjacks felling giant redwoods gave Edward pause for thought as he felt both affinity for the work itself but recognized this scene was not from the West. Reading the descriptor plate, Edward learned that this portrait was of William Davidson, renowned "first lumberjack" of Canada who settled in the Miramichi area of New Brunswick. The gold plaque said that Banff was named for Davidson's home village in Banffshire, Scotland. Edward felt a pang of wistfulness for Europe. He had not returned since he was a young boy and had gone to meet his father's family. Edward had revelled in all the attention bestowed upon him there and warmth crept up in him as he noted the European connection. Perhaps Europe would be his next destination.

He had asked the front desk for a room with a view of soaring Rundle and was pleased to find his second floor room had a lovely view of a green space; soon to be a golf green, the desk clerk had relayed. He scanned the area, noting the workmen below trudging with rocks and scythes to cut down brush. It appeared to Edward that they were like the prairie settlers from Edna-Star, clearing land to make way for development, like Mr. Davidson himself. It was men who drove development; men and their ambition.

He set his brown leather suitcase on the bed and opened it, removing his few toiletries. He set them on the edge of the washbasin in the tiny bathroom adjacent to the great room which contained a wild-rose-coloured velvet armchair. The chair beckoned him with its plush stuffed pillows and perfect view of the grounds. As he sunk into the chair, a wave of peacefulness washed over him. He closed his eyes.

Tonight, he would dine in the hotel and tomorrow visit the Sulphur Hot Springs he had read so much about for their therapeutic qualities. He opened his eyes and, drawn by their muffled voices, looked down again upon the workmen. He noted their grey worn overalls, visibly tattered even from this height. He pushed back the lacy curtain and used his binoculars to get a closer look.

The men's faces were lined with grime, some wincing with pain as they lifted boulders onto a platform. Other faces showed determination as the men sliced at the twigs and brush with their bare hands, expanding the clearing. Edward found himself transfixed watching these men, struck by the paradox of their harsh circumstances and the creation of something that would last a lifetime. He removed the binoculars and scanned the group as a whole. He wondered if they were hired hands and yet, they reminded him of the prisoners at the train station; surely they wouldn't be working here at this posh establishment. He let that thought slide away.

Most of the men's faces were downtrodden, but there was one that caught Edward's eye. The man kept looking up, up at the sky, at the trees and mountains as if revelling in their splendour, glancing up at the hotel too. Edward's eyes hovered on the man and then he felt it, an inexplicable connection as the workman locked his eyes on Edward's face at the second floor window. Unexpectedly, the man waved at him. Edward stepped back behind the curtain, his hand steadying it as it fluttered. He suddenly felt conspicuous, like a spy who had just been caught. He shut the inner red velvet curtain, allowing only the dewy sunlight to seep through. He returned his binoculars to his bag and, without further thoughts on the men below, retreated to the bathroom to run a hot bath and ready himself for dinner in the hotel dining room.

He had heard the Duke and Duchess of Connaught were also staying in the hotel and was eager to make their acquaintance.

Chapter Thirty-Six

P.O. Box Castle Mountain
April 21, 1917

Dearest Katja,

We have returned to Castle Mountain. We spent the first week here erecting the tents and mending the outer ten-foot high barbed-wire fence. The inner fence was intact, but certain parts of the outer fence were flattened as if they had been charged by a big animal. Guards say it was probably the deer misjudging their jumps or else it was bears. The spaces are so big, I think it must be the grizzlies we have heard so much about. I wonder why it is they wanted to come into this prison in the first place.

We have seen elk around the perimeter of the camp. They hover as if to ask us who we are that have come to take over their grazing land. They remind me of the elk we saw together so long ago. Where did he go I wonder? We never did see him again, did we? Perhaps he was our welcome spirit.

Ivan has regained his strength from the hard winter and we are working well as partners. He is focused on getting released and seeing Mary again and meeting his new baby Pieter. When he started to grumble about fixing the fence that was to keep us in, I nodded and said we have to do what we have to do in life. We are dealt the cards we get and we must do our best with that. What else can we do?

Katja re-read and rolled this line over in her head. She was sure Wasyl would be furious at her, at Edward, and at himself. He would

probably blame himself for what had happened, for not being there
to protect her. She nodded at his words. What could she do now,
except move forward?

*We are working on clearing the land from the Banff Springs Ho-
tel now, expanding the golf course for the guests. The hotel is like a
queen's castle, Katja. It stands four storeys high and is majestic with
the mountains as her backdrop. I like this work because it is sheltered
and Ivan and I can talk as we work. Sometimes I look up at the windows of the hotel and see a face staring down at me. Once I waved and
saw a flutter back. My guess is it was a child, perhaps the same age as
our Olek, who was watching us from up there.*

*We had two guests come to the work site today, the Duke and
Duchess of Connaught. I asked Captain Davis who they were and he
told us that the Duke, Prince Arthur, is the first Governor General of
Canada to have royal blood. He said the Prime Minister sent them
here to see how we were being treated here.*

*They watched us work on the golf grounds, chatted with the guards
and Captian Davis, laughing and nodding. I felt like a caged animal
in a zoo on view, but to tell you the truth, I'm glad they saw us working so hard for our country. I looked the Prince in the eye, Katja, I did.
I wanted him to see me for me and to know I am on his side, that I
am a Canadian. Maybe it will change something in our circumstances
and they will see we are not enemies after all.*

*I am so thankful to Henri and the men for seeding and you said
there's been rain, which is good. My plan is to be home for the harvest,
God willing.*

*And so, I sign off with that hope, dear Katja. I am coming home to
you soon. I can feel it.*

Love Always and Forever,
Wasyl

The harvest! Not so long until then. Katja read the letter to the children that night. She sat them down at the pine table and told them that this was a time for hope and prayer for their daddy's safe return. She had chastised herself when she found out she had lost the envelope with the money weeks ago now, and had even gone back to the church grounds to search, but soon came to believe it was meant to be. She was meant to wipe that slate clean and start again. Wasyl's message of hope was all Katja needed to keep her strong. She would do what she needed to do and everything would turn out all right in the end. It had to.

* * *

The Bloc Meeting was held on the first Saturday in May. Katja had bundled up the children against the nip still hanging in the air. There was talk of a school starting up and Katja wanted her voice to be heard. She wanted her children to be educated and to have the same chance she did to learn sums and to read and write. Education meant freedom and she wanted every advantage for Olek, Pavla, Pieter, and her new baby. Her apron blossomed slightly at these four months into her pregnancy. The pleats served as a disguise and made Katja less self-conscious among her neighbours. The town seemed to have calmed down a great deal since Dr. Smith had left and the new physician, Mr. Lazaruk, had begun to settle in well. He had told the villagers right from the start that he would be keeping office hours in town, and would only be visiting the homesteads for emergencies. This was on account of his getting on in years, he said, and everyone respected him for his honesty.

Katja was going to visit him after the school meeting. When she told Olek about this, he had asked her if she was sick. She had answered nothing was wrong, but she knew she would have to tell Olek and Pavla soon. They would come with her, she insisted, and then she would tell them their mama was having another little baby, just like Auntie Mary had Pieter.

Words buzzed like flies in the community centre as villagers, most of them with children in tow, made their way inside. The only other meeting Katja remembered being this full was almost two years ago now, the fateful meeting where the War Measures Act was explained. She shut out that memory and focused her attention on the gathering now.

"Up, up, Mama," Pavla whined.

Katja scooped her up and whispered to Olek to stay close. She needn't have worried for he was occupied, having found a new friend in the crowd; a little boy with a mossy green hat who was making faces at him that he returned with gusto. The gavel sounded and Henri spoke at the front of the stage.

"We have called this meeting to discuss the proposal of starting a village school." "Hear hear," voices in the crowd sounded.

"There are approximately seventeen children of school age in our settlement and the law dictates that a school can be incorporated with eight. It is Edna-Star's time."

There was applause. "Who will speak in favour of this school?"

Katja looked around at the villagers. Their silence engulfed and encouraged her.

"I will," she said, barely audible.

"Who was that?" Henri cast his eyes to the back of the room. "Katja Federchuk, you have the floor."

All eyes turned to Katja as she spoke.

She cleared her throat and clutched Pavla tightly. "We need a school for our children. In the old country, we learned sums and to read and write, and it is because of this we were welcomed to this new land."

Beside her, a bearded man guffawed. "That ain't so, Missus. Me, I can't read or write nothing and when I got off the boat, those men, they was happy to see me. That's it. I'm a hard worker. That's what got me here."

Another man Katja couldn't place added, "I hear ya gotta pay taxes for a school. I ain't paying no taxes, that's for sure. I ain't got no kids."

Katja collected her thoughts and stood her ground. "As new Canadians, the way to prosper is through education and our children in Edna-Star deserve to learn to read and write. They can learn in Ukrainian."

Bettina spoke up then. "I agree. We need a school now, so that our children will not be left behind. We came here for a better life and we want this for our children."

"Who will pay for the school?"

Shouts went up. "Yes, who will pay?"

Henri stepped in. "Hold on there folks. First of all, we are having this meeting to decide if our community wants a school. Then we will vote. If the vote passes, we will appoint a committee of three taxpaying citizens who will be called our Board of Trustees. These trustees will apply to the government for permission to designate a school for our area."

"You haven't answered the question, Sir. That is, who pays?" the bearded man interjected.

"I was just getting to that, Sir. Thank you. Any family who has children at the school will be levied a user tax. If a family has no school-aged children, then there is no tax."

There were murmurs in the crowd as neighbours conferred. Katja looked down at Olek and wondered how she would pay if she was on her own in the Fall. She thought of Edward's money again, the money he said to use for the baby. She could have used that, if only she had not lost the envelope at the church. She crossed herself suddenly, thinking that may be a sin to think like that, to take the money for one child and give it to another. Henri's gavel brought her back to the meeting.

"If there are no further comments, I say we put it to a vote. All those in favour of Edna-Star appointing a Board of Trustees to apply for a school for our village, say 'aye.'" Bettina counted the raised hands. There was a clear majority. Katja smiled.

"Okay, now we need three people to take this on, to be our liaison with the Department." Katja looked around the room. No hands, no voices. She looked hard at Mr. and Mrs. Benton who had three school-aged children of their own, willing them to step forward. Katja had seen their little ones in the shop, surely they would want their children to learn sums to carry on with the family business.

Henri spoke again. "Look, if no one volunteers, then maybe our community is not ready."

"I will do it," Katja spoke up. "I will make the application for our school."

"Are you sure, Katja? It will take some time. There is a great deal of paperwork involved." Henri spoke softly to her, as if they were the only two in the hall.

"Yes, I am sure." Her eyes drifted from Henri and scanned the room. "Who will stand with me and speak for the children?" Pavla kissed her on the cheek, while Olek tugged at her skirt.

Bettina smiled admiringly at her friend, and said, "I will."

"And so will I." All eyes looked to the back of the hall, to the voice. It was the new doctor, Mr. Lazaruk. He had not yet made the acquaintance of Mrs. Federchuk, but he was mighty impressed by her determination today.

"Thank you, Sir. That is very kind of you to volunteer. There, we have our three Board of Trustees."

Katja blushed at the applause and Pavla clapped too, leaving her mama feeling winded.

"Maybe we will have a school for you to go to in the Fall, Olek," Katja looked down at her son's inquisitive eyes.

"Nice to make your acquaintance, Mrs. Federchuk," Dr. Lazaruk said, hand extended in greeting.

"Nice to meet you too. Thank you for volunteering. My boy, Olek, he's ready to learn. I am so happy about the school."

"Of course. It will happen, all in good time. Now we have an appointment to keep, don't we?"

Chapter Thirty-Seven

May 31, 1917
P.O. Box Edna-Star

Dearest Wasyl,

How are you? I hope the warm weather has come to the mountains and that you and Ivan are well. So much has happened here since I last wrote, I must collect my thoughts before I begin.

There will be a new school in Edna-Star! We have applied to the government for an official designation, Wasyl. It may happen as early as the Fall, if approved, and if we can find a teacher, that is. That will mean our Olek may go to school! I am so happy for this. I hope you will be proud of me, Wasyl, as there are three of us who are called Board of Trustees: Bettina, myself, and the new town doctor, Dr. Lazaruk. We have filled out the lengthy application and met with the government official who stamped our papers and said, "Your application is now in process." He reminded me of the government officials who first greeted us when we left the Arcadia, remember Wasyl?

Here Katja hesitated. Here is where she needed to tell Wasyl why Dr. Smith was gone and Dr. Lazaruk here. She desperately wanted to tell Wasyl. She hated keeping this truth from him, but knew it was best spoken in person, and for that, she had to wait. She had to bide her time until he was released and home again so that she could explain. She returned to the letter.

Baby Pieter continues to grow and develop each week we visit. Mary has taken to sketching him as he sleeps so she can show Ivan his miraculous transformation. Olek and Pavla cuddle with him in the Onyschuk's big armchair in their sitting room when we visit, and he shakes his rattle like he's performing a concert just for them. They will be fast friends.

Wasyl, I am thinking of asking Mary to be the teacher of our new school. What do you think? She is youthful, energetic, intelligent, and educated. Do you think this is a good fit for her? Please speak to Ivan if he thinks this is even a possibility. We are not ready for a teacher quite yet, as we have only just applied, and don't even have a schoolhouse but you know how my mind races. I don't want to overstep my bounds here, but feel strongly that we need a teacher who knows our children and our community's values. Mary fits that.

I like to imagine you near that hotel you spoke about. Our new Dr. Lazaruk told me that it resembles a Scottish castle. He has visited the park on occasion, he said. He assured me that you would be well taken care of and there is much talk that the camp will be disbanded by summer. Have you heard this too? What word is there? I like to think that when that Duke and Duchess saw you working so hard, it lit a fire in their hearts to change this law when they returned East.

Olek and Pavla are doing very well. Olek continues to milk everyday and Pavla "checks the chickens" as she says, and has taken to naming them now. The chubby round and flat one is her favourite and she calls her Pancake. They are very helpful to me everyday.

We are happy to see the sun return again 'most every day and to see the kalyna berries in bloom. The prairie summer is not far away now.

I write in great anticipation of your next letter and news of your return.

With love and hope,
Katja

Katja folded her letter neatly. She could hardly wait to share all the news with Wasyl and felt a pang of envy for Bettina whose Henri was always by her side. Bettina had laughed and laughed when Katja had told her about Pavla's Pancake and said she could picture exactly which hen it was too. Bettina had been a source of strength that day since Katja had confided in her and she applauded Katja for her suggestion of Mary becoming Edna-Star's first teacher. It was highly unconventional to have a married woman, and one with children, be the school teacher, but now they just had to convince the doctor and Ivan.

At the post office, Mr. Benton handed her an envelope, eyebrows raised. Katja was surprised to see it was postmarked 'Edmonton' and the return address said, 'Smith'.

"Thank you, Mr. Benton," Katja said. Clutching the envelope tightly, she shooed her children toward the carriage.

"Aren't we going to visit Aunt Mary and Pieter, Mama?" Pavla asked.

"Not today, darling. We'll visit after church tomorrow. We best be getting home now."

She tucked the envelope into her skirt waistband only until she got to the wagon. Then, once in the driving seat, she put it under her right thigh for certain safekeeping. She had forgotten about Dr. Smith's promise of sending money, and as the horses pulled her on this familiar pathway Katja resolved to keep this money for educating all her children.

Chapter Thirty-Eight

Indian Days; Captain Davis had announced that there would be a parade and celebration of Indian Days at the camp. None of the prisoners knew what this entailed, but there had been parades before; usually when Dr. Brett came in his motor car with several other motor cars in line, eyes staring under frilly bonnets and beaver-felt hats, windows rolled up tightly. The prisoners understood that they were a tourist attraction of sorts as they were paraded before the cars, eyes gawking on one side and eyes downturned on the other side of the show. Canadian Pacific Railway was luring visitors to the park and Dr. Brett was bringing some of them on tour with him as part of his visit for inoculations. Wasyl raised his hand in the crowd.

"I beg your pardon, Captain Davis, but what is Indian Days?"

If it had been any of the other one hundred and sixty-nine prisoners, Davis would have dismissed the question immediately, rebuffed the speaker, and denounced him for insolence. But it was Wasyl Federchuk, Prisoner No. 129, who was a quiet leader among the men, a most determined worker, and Davis knew Wasyl was speaking for many of the men when he had asked that question.

"Indian Days represent the best of the Wild West! We will have activities such as target shooting and archery and we will wear these…" He turned to enter the tent behind him and brought out a deer-skin fringed jacket.

"You will all be given these coats in celebration of the occasion." He nodded at the guards who gathered armfuls of the coats as Davis ordered the prisoners to form two lines: small size and large size.

Wasyl scratched his head. He looked at Ivan who shrugged his shoulders. They separated into their respective lines to receive their costume adornment. It was certainly not deer-skin jacket weather in mid-June! This must be some kind of a photography opportunity for the government, he thought.

Wasyl didn't mind though because it was a day off from the back-breaking work at the hotel. With the heat of the June sun, he was taunted daily by the gurgling sounds of the Bow River behind him. Water was rationed at the worksite because all supplies had to be trekked there by the men themselves. Why the guards wouldn't let the men fill their canteens from the river directly, Wasyl could not understand.

"Doctor's orders," was all they said in explanation.

The prisoners were digging up the hotel's grounds now, installing sprinkler systems that would soon be covered with seed. The whole process of this golf course project reminded Wasyl of breaking his own land, digging the furrows for his seeds then covering them as he would soon do with the turf seed.

Captain Davis told the men to take care of their jackets and that they should report to the opening ceremonies at 10:00 am sharp the following morning. What he didn't say, what he couldn't say, was that this was the last-ditch effort of the government to show they were treating the prisoners well. The camp was coming under fire, even from their homeland Great Britain, and talk from powers above was that the camp would be closed unless conditions improved.

Indian Days would change all that, Captain Davis had assured his superior. Photos were to be sent to the Governor General himself, including ones of the prisoners with their dinner of venison and vegetables. That should surely garner some badly-needed support from the federal government. Davis had been head of this camp for three years now and although he despised it some days, it was his job and he didn't know what the future would hold if the camp closed. He might be sent to another internment camp in Vernon, or to Kapuskasing in Ontario, away from his family. He refused to think about the prospect of leaving them.

"This will be something to write home about, hey, Ivan," Wasyl laughed heartily at this prospect. Ivan smiled at this trusted friend, always optimistic.

"I want to write to Mary," he said suddenly.

"Okay, then you shall. What do you want to say? I'm happy to write it for you, Ivan."

"No, I want to write it. I want to learn, Wasyl."

"Okay." Wasyl paused. Ivan had been very excited when he heard about Katja's work to build a school for his son, an education he had never had the opportunity to receive in the Old Country.

"Will you teach me, Wasyl?"

Wasyl laughed, "I'm no teacher, Ivan, but I will try."

They went to the dining hall where Wasyl could spread out the sheets of paper he had been saving each week for his letters home. While other prisoners traded their tickets for luxuries such as cigarettes, Wasyl could only bring himself to choose the most prized commodity of paper, for it meant connection to home. He thrust one at Ivan that was stained from moisture on the top.

"I keep this one for emergencies. You can use it for practice. So, first I am going to write a letter of the alphabet and then tell you the sound. You can write it below to practice, okay?"

Ivan nodded. The pencil felt awkward in his hand, uncomfortable, like a stick of kindling, and he had to restrain himself from throwing it into the fire. As the lesson continued, Ivan grew more frustrated.

At last he asked Wasyl, "May I tell you what I want to write and then you point to the letters to use for the message?"

Wasyl could see that Ivan did not want to practice for days before sending this message. He wanted to send it today.

"Of course, Ivan, absolutely. So, what would you like to tell Mary?"

"I love you, Mary, and I am coming home to you and our baby soon. That's what I want to tell her. I feel it Wasyl. We are going home soon. I just know it."

Wasyl smiled. He wanted to reassure his friend. He also believed that justice would be served. He had felt it when the Duke and Duchess had watched them work so fiercely on the hotel project; their release was imminent.

Chapter Thirty-Nine

When Mary and Pieter went to the Benton's shop on Thursday, Mrs. Benton told her that her husband had expressly asked her to pass on a message of great importance.

"For me?" Mary had asked. "What is it?"

"There is a letter for you at the post office. Mr. Benton wants to give it to you himself. He said if you weren't up to collecting it, he'd deliver it to your door, he's that excited."

"Well, it must be an important letter for that to happen. Yes, I mean we are up to it, aren't we, darling?" Mary nuzzled Pieter who gurgled his agreement. "Thank you, Mrs. Benton, and good day to you."

Mary's mind wandered as she left the shop and headed next door to the adjoining post office. She never received letters and wondered who it was from. If it was from Dr. Smith professing his love like his last note to her before he left, she would just tear it up this time and hurl it into the fire. Imagine his nerve, professing he still loved her after what happened with Katja, and she with a babe in her own arms at that.

It was not from Dr. Smith however. Mary didn't recognize the printing on the front, but noted the postmark read Castle Camp, Banff. She washed away the cloud of dread that enveloped her and decided to wait until she was home to read it.

Sitting in her favourite chair in the sitting room with Pieter snuggled on her lap, she used the letter opener to neatly slice the top of the envelope. This letter felt special to her, like it had its own pulse somehow; sacred. She suppressed her fear. Good news or bad news, she had to know what the letter said.

Her eyes slid quickly from the post office address at the top in one handwriting to the closing, 'Love, Ivan' in what she only could imagine was her husband's own trembling hand. It was from Ivan. He had written to her, painstakingly carving out each letter for her; his message of hope.

Dear Mary,

I love you and Pieter and am coming home soon.

Love,

Ivan

Mary knew that Wasyl must have spent time teaching Ivan and was so thankful. She wished she could tell Katja.

"Mama," she called. "I have received a letter from dear Ivan. He says he is coming home!"

Pieter looked at his mother with shining eyes, gurgling and laughing at her own folly.

Mary asked her mama to watch Pieter that very afternoon and took the family wagon out to the Federchuk homestead. She had not visited since she had given birth, almost one year ago now. Mary was struck by the dullness and hardship of it all, as she directed the team of horses down the bramble-grown pathway to the house that Ivan and Wasyl had built. Nestled in the woods was the tiny whitewashed house with robin's egg blue trim, a stark contrast of colour to the other faded browns and grey of the outbuildings. Pavla was the first to see her and the horses, the bells on her horse's reins reminding her of fairies dancing like in the story Mama had told her last night.

"Auntie Mary!" she called out. "Auntie Mary!"

"Careful now, child," Mary commanded as she pulled up the reins on the team. She steadied herself and hopped down off the wagon seat, crouching down to scoop up Pavla in her arms.

"Aren't you forgetting somebody?" Pavla asked, sucking her thumb. She had never seen her Auntie without Baby Pieter since he'd been born.

Mary laughed and tousled Pavla's hair. "Pieter is with his Baba in the village. Now, where's your mama got to?" she asked, eyes searching the yard.

"Mama's down at the river fishing for dinner. Let's go. I'll get Olek. He's milking."

"Your mama's fishing? Olek's milking? Well, I'll be."

Mary looked down at her peach skirt and wished she had changed into something less formal for the visit. Seeing the homestead brought back memories of the hardships of life here and she admonished herself silently for not remembering, for seeming to have put on airs for the visit. Laundry on the line, children doing chores, and gardening gloves and tools in the pail by the front door. It all seemed familiar to her, but blurred. She feared she had grown soft being at home again, spoiled by her own mama, and resolved to take on more responsibilities when she was home again.

"All right, Missy Pavla. Let's get Olek and go find your mama."

The three of them sang a ditty as they skipped down the pathway to the river where they found Katja with her fishing rod and long line flying back and forth. She smiled fondly at the children.

"Shhhh, I think I'm going to catch one," she whispered.

Katja hadn't yet seen Mary. She watched her line and the fly at the end float down the creek slowly, slowly until snap! she caught a walleye on the end. A little one, but it was sustenance all the same. She looped the line pulling the bobbing fish closer to her. She had been so absorbed in the catch that she had not noticed when Mary took the children's hands in hers and mouthed "Shhh" as they tiptoed on the grasses behind her.

When she turned to her children to show them her prize, her jaw and the fish dropped as she saw Mary there too!

"Mary Kelemchuk! What are you doing out here?" Katja searched behind Mary. "And where did that wee baby of yours get to?"

Mary laughed and hugged her friend. "Pieter's at home with Mama. I had news. I just had to come to see you. I do hope you don't mind."

"Never! I'm thrilled you're here."

"Oh, oh, there goes fishy," Pavla giggled as the flopping fish was making its way closer to freedom back to the creek.

Olek stepped in and grabbed a flat rock from the shoreline and bopped the walleye on the head, killing it instantly. "I took care of it, Mama," he said assuredly and gathered up the rod and line and fish in his arms. "I'll clean it by the well." He started back up the path.

"Well, I'll be, isn't he just the little man, and only five years old?"

"He has grown up a lot, Mary, and he'll tell you he's closer to almost six years old now."

"Let's go have some tea at the house."

"You go on ahead, I'll be right behind you."

Katja rinsed off her hands in the trickling creek and looked up at the falcon watching her intently from the fir tree above. "Thank you," she whispered.

*　*　*

There were rumours in the village after that, started by Mary herself. Seven of the men from Edna-Star, fathers, sons, brothers, cousins, and uncles, were coming home. Their release from Castle Mountain Camp was imminent.

Henri had announced it at the June Bloc Meeting. He had also heard the Camp was closing from the papers in the city and that all the men were being released; some to the railway, some to the mining companies and some, like Wasyl and Ivan, would be eligible for Conditional Release since they were landowners. They had families to come home to.

Mary's news that day in May had sent Katja spinning into a spiral of excitement and relief coupled with fear and dreaded anticipation of telling Wasyl the whole story; explaining herself. She had long since stopped worrying about what part she may have played in the event. She had forgiven herself and moved on. What mattered to her now was her family, including the new baby. She had felt healthy and strong throughout this pregnancy and as she entered her last trimester, with the heat of the summer months upon her, she felt that must keep up her energy, for everyone's sake. Dr. Smith's third envelope with money for the baby was tucked, unopened, on top of the other one into the base of the music box. Her plan was to save this money until she needed it and refused to open the envelopes one second before that.

She and the children were surviving on fish, bread, potatoes, and other root vegetables from last year's harvest. The berries were beginning and Katja was buoyed by the prospect of Wasyl's return, yet something tore at her and gave her cause for worry. She had not heard those words about release from Wasyl himself. She knew that he would write to her only when he knew for sure. He was a dreamer it was true, but he would not want to foist a false sense of hope upon her until he, himself, knew it to be absolutely true. And so she waited, sometimes making three trips to the village a week, after the Edmonton train, just to see if there was a letter for her.

Finally in late June, a letter from Wasyl did come. Mr. Benton made a special delivery to her at home with the letter. He didn't usually do such things, he explained to his wife later at supper, but he could just feel this letter was the one Katja Federchuk had been waiting for.

And it was. Wasyl's words spoke of frustration over not writing for so long as he had to wait until he could get more paper. Did Mary like Ivan's letter, he wanted to know? Then Wasyl told her to hold onto her answer, because she could tell it to him in person. He was being released. Released. Released. Katja found herself reading the word over and over until it sunk in that it was true. It was such a calming word, like a soft breath, long and drawn out. It was only when she held the letter to her heart that Katja noticed Mr. Benton was still there.

"Well, what's it say? When are our boys coming home, Mrs. Federchuk?"

Katja laughed. Wasyl wrote this two weeks ago now. He said they would be released at the end of June. He didn't know the exact day. "He'll be home shortly, I expect, Mr.Benton."

In fact, Wasyl and Ivan were already on the train from Castle to Calgary when Katja read the letter. While his words swam in her mind, Wasyl read his Release Certificate over and over again. He held it firmly in his strong, weathered hands.

This is to certify that I, Wasyl Federchuk, a subject of Ukraine was interned as a prisoner of war in Canada at Castle Mountain, Banff, Alberta.

Identified as follows:
Age: 28 years
Height: 5' 9"
Weight: 145 lbs.

Features: Dark Hair, Hazel Eyes
This is to certify that I have been discharged from internment subject to the following conditions:
That I will not leave Canada during the period of hostilities without permission granted by an authority of the Canadian government;
That I will observe and uphold the laws of Canada;
That I will refrain from any acts of a hostile nature intended to give information to or assist the enemies of the British Empire such as espionage;
That I will report to the Royal North West Mounted Police upon arrival in Calgary, Alta, and thereafter in Edmonton, Alta as often as I am directed to do so by officials.

Dated at Castle Mountain, Alberta, this 28th day of June, 1917.
Signed,
Wasyl Federchuk
#129 (Wasyl had written this in.)
Witness: Captain Davis

He looked sideways at Ivan whose eyes were closed, his forehead leaning on the train window, breathing heavily as if truly sleeping restfully for the first time in ten months. Wasyl didn't have to wonder where Ivan kept his certificate. He had seen him fold it into a tiny square and put it into his pocket, the same way he did with the map of Montreal when they had first stepped foot on Canadian soil. Wasyl kept his on his lap.

Calgary would be the first stop. He reached into the pocket of the buckskin fringed jacket and felt the $33.45 he had been given for transportation costs to Edna-Star. He and Ivan would join the other men from the area and register in Calgary. They were to stay the night and board the Canadian Pacific Railway Line to Edmonton Strathcona the following day.

It was a twelve hour train ride to Edmonton and would cost $10.00, minus room and board tonight. He figured that would still leave him a substantial amount. He put aside the bitterness he felt rising over the unfairness of it all, since a good wage for workers in the mines was $2.00 per day and the $33.45 he had received would not even cover one month at the camp. Still, soon he would be home. That was all that mattered now. Wasyl closed his eyes and breathed in sync with the revolution of the locomotive. He replayed his goodbye to Captain Davis who had shook his hand and looked him in the eye when he gave him his release papers.

"You're a good man, Wasyl Federchuk; a good, honest man."

Somehow, between the two unlikeliest of men, a bond had formed of respect and trust.

"Another place, another time, I think we would have been friends," the captain confessed.

Wasyl had always trusted that Captain Davis would do what was right for the prisoners, including today's release. Tears welled up inside of him and he kept his eyes closed in hopes of keeping his emotions in check. Tomorrow he would see Katja. Tomorrow he would hold his children. Tomorrow.

Only Ivan saw his friend's tear fall. Ivan had not told Wasyl what their friendship had meant to him, but he knew he would not have survived the camp had it not been for Wasyl. Wasyl was the strong one, always had been, in their relationship. His spirit and optimism had guided Ivan and grounded him, especially when Ivan just wanted to escape. How many times had he wanted to escape, and then his failed attempt. Well, he had a pronounced limp to show for it, and his handy cane, a gentleman's walking stick Wasyl had called it. It made Ivan look regal, Wasyl said.

He and Wasyl had not said a word to each other since they boarded. There was absolute silence on the train. Forty-four men had been released today, boarded on the train, meagre belongings in tow; all of them silent, lost in thought or worry or dreams.

Ivan closed his droopy eyes again and let out a huge sigh that had been welling up inside of him. Wasyl had figured out the logistics of the trip; Ivan felt unhelpful without his compass in hand, and had told him they would be home tomorrow. Wasyl had written to Katja and she would tell Mary. His Mary and Baby Pieter.

Back at the camp, Captain Davis went into his barracks and sat on his cot. The gray woollen blanket felt scratchy under his breeches, all his senses alert to the absolute silence of the camp. He had sent two of his officers with the remaining forty-four men, and the other officers were bringing back equipment from the work sites, to be picked up by authorities in the next two weeks. He had been Captain here for three years now, since the camp first opened in 1915. He picked up his logbook and made his final entry.

June 28th, 1917. Clear summer day. Last remaining prisoners, numbering 44, were conditionally released today, 11:00 am. Each granted certificate and $33.45 transportation and subsistence allowance. Boarded train at 11:00 AM with Officers Bradyn and McDonald for Calgary. Two weeks to camp closure.

He tucked his pencil carefully in the spine of the soft logbook and set it inside the metal box on his bedside table. He listened intently and then, sure he was alone, Captain Davis held his head in his hands and wept. He wondered what this all had been for.

Chapter Forty

Katja stood solemnly with Mary, Mr. and Mrs. Onyschuk, and the children at the train station in Edna-Star. It was still light on this June evening even at 7:00 pm. The evening train was scheduled to arrive in a few minutes. Katja clasped her hands under her belly, released them, smoothed her curls back under her bonnet, and interlocked her moist hands again.

"You look beautiful, Katja; radiant," Mary told her. Katja felt her nerves pinching inside her. She felt short of oxygen and tried to measure her breaths carefully for fear of hyperventilating. Pieter was sucking Mary's hair in his mouth and cooing. Olek and Pavla were playing Ring-Around-the-Rosie and falling down on the grass by the station in gales of laughter. Katja started to say something about being careful, not to get soiled before they saw their father, and stopped herself. That wouldn't matter to Wasyl; these little things really didn't matter, only that soon he would be back.

It had been decided that Ivan would stay with Mary at the Onyschuk's tonight and though invited, Katja had declined the kind offer, knowing how much Wasyl would want to see his homestead; even if it meant driving the wagon at dusk, he would do it. She had spent all day yesterday cleaning, sweeping, and adding whitewash where she could until the house glistened. She wanted it to be warm and welcoming. She had shaken the quilt and hung it outdoors to freshen it, put the music box on the table, and baked a fresh babka bread. The house looked and smelled completely inviting.

They could hear the train coming before they could see it. The whole earth beneath Katja's feet seemed to shake under the train's thundering approach. Her little ones jumped up and stood on either side of her, Olek feeling a little shy on one side and Pavla very bold on the other. Katja's mouth felt dry, absent of the very flow of life. She held her breath. The train stopped. First off was the R.N.W.M.P. Police Officer who had travelled with them all the way from Castle Mountain, on Captain Davis' orders. He disembarked and stood at attention as the seven men from Edna-Star stepped onto their prairie soil once again.

Slowly and nobly, Wasyl climbed down the stairs of the train, his eyes locked on Katja. He removed his hat then and strode quickly to Katja, took her in his arms and swung her around. He could feel her swollen belly push up against him and held her close. He held her face in his hands and stared into her blue eyes. No questions now. Not now. His dark eyes melted her and she wept with happiness and kissed him. "Papa, Papa!" It was Pavla calling out. Wasyl looked down at his little girl, the spitting image of himself at her age, dark hair, dark eyes, and an unmistakable air of elfin mischief. He twirled her about and tossed her to the skies. "How's my gift from heaven?"

"Happy, Papa, happy!" she sang gaily.

Olek stood silently, waiting his turn. He wanted his papa to notice what a big boy he had become, what a strong young man he was growing into. Wasyl set down Pavla and crouched down.

"Hello, Olek," he said. He reached out his hand to his boy who shook it with quiet confidence. "Hug?" Olek rushed into his father's embrace.

Wasyl held Olek while he scooped up Pavla. His heart soared, holding his children again. Katja glanced at Ivan's homecoming which was quiet and intimate with Mary and her parents with lots of handshaking and baby holding.

"I will say hello to Ivan," Katja said.

She approached the family and Ivan reached out to shake her hand. He saw her state and looked at Mary for explanation and knew that would come.

"Hello, Katja."

"Hello, Ivan. Welcome home."

"Katja, I wouldn't be home if it weren't for your husband."

Katja looked back at Wasyl playing with the children. "Thank you. I know he feels the same about you, Ivan."

Katja felt very sombre and nodded her goodbyes to Mary and the Onyschuks. She looked back at Wasyl and her children; her family. It was time.

Chapter Forty-One

Pavla chatted to Papa all the way to the wagon as if he had just come back from vacation. To her, time was fluid and he could have been gone one week or one month. It didn't matter anymore because he was here now. Walking to the wagon, Olek became shy again, silent, and Katja took his hand gently.

"Papa will have lots of time to be with you from now on, Olek," she said.

Olek held Mama's hand tightly and climbed beside her and his father. Katja took her place in the wagon and watched as he stroked his horse and Ivan's horse, getting reacquainted, whispering greetings to them. The horses nudged Wasyl as if cuddling an old friend, his scent familiar and comforting to them. He climbed up on the wooden seat and fingered the black leather reins, circling the pads of his fingers on the leather, retracing and remembering. The wooden seat felt strangely hard and he shuffled to get comfortable. He clicked to the horses; homeward bound.

Wasyl's face glowed in the dusky light as he drove the wagon off the main road into the homestead pathway. He felt enveloped by the earth, as though the trees opened up this pathway just for him only to close afterward, keeping his family safe.

The sharp twigs at the side, the new leaves, and their bright early-season-green just bursting inside their pods welcomed him. He pulled up on the reins as he came closer to the homestead. The robin's egg blue trim stood out brightly against the lime whitewash of the house. It looked perfect, right out of a fairy tale, he thought. His home. He looked at Katja and his dear children. *Our home.*

Katja gathered the children and told Wasyl she would get them ready for bed and put the kettle on for him. She watched him as he nodded, lost in thought and remembrance. He wanted to touch everything all at once, take it all in, the cow, Pancake the chicken, the river. Though the homestead remained unchanged, he looked at it with new eyes, wizened by time and experience, and he relished its colour and comfort. He walked past the henhouse up to the well. He scooped out some fresh cool spring water and splashed it on his face, mingling with his tears. What they had endured together, he and Ivan, he thought. And now, both men were home with their families where they belonged.

Wasyl heard the swish in the branches above him before he saw the peregrine falcon land on the very tip, perched still as a statue upon the bobbing branch. He smiled up at the falcon, at its strength; its source of power. One more splash and he would be ready to hear what she needed to say.

Katja's story spilled out like milk trickling from the puzzle jug with its latticed rim. She kept her eyes lowered, peeking out now and then to see if Wasyl's eyes were angry. They only stared at her filled with love; enduring, passionate love, ever understanding and ever true. When she had finished, he took her face in his and kissed her with such passion, she fell limp into his arms. "My Katja," he said. "What you have endured. I will love this baby as I love our children. We are family. We are together. That is all that matters now."

Katja's broken heart felt stronger, as if mended by each of Wasyl's healing words of compassion for her and the baby. She felt her shame washed away as Wasyl wiped her tears and held her face in his. He embraced her so tightly she felt that her very heart was melding into his. "I will always love you, my Katja."

Pavla stirred in their bed then, and Katja whispered, "Thank you for coming back to me, to us. I love you, Wasyl."

Olek squeezed his eyes shut, squinting out, pretending to be asleep and listened. He heard his papa moan and his mama's breathing and he remembered this from before. He rolled over then, ashamed and fearful. What if his daddy went away again? He couldn't bear to think of this. His tears fell on the cotton pillowcase soaking it. Mama came to his side then and held him.

"Oh, Olek, did you have a bad dream?"

"No, Mama, I'm okay. Are you and Papa okay?"

"Yes, dear, everything is alright now. We are together again. Sleep now."

Olek snuggled into his mama and Katja lay down between her children as she had done each night in Wasyl's absence.

"Good night, Wasyl," she whispered.

"Good night, my love," he answered. Wasyl took the spare quilt off the end of the bed post and lay on the dugout floor in front of the fire. He folded his worn grey woollen trousers, carefully laying them to the side, and cuddled in the quilt, wrapping himself in its feather softness. The shadows of the flames leapt up and down like a fire-walker on red hot coals and Wasyl marvelled at their animated dance. Warmth caressed his skin and the smell of Katja on him was intoxicating. He felt completely satisfied, the burden lifted off his shoulders, and its weight laid down before him to be left behind. He tucked his arm under his head, propped on his side, the fire at his back, gazing at his family on the bed across the room. He was home, finally home. He had his family back, his home back, and he was safe. He was free. He felt an overwhelming gratitude to the country he knew would do right by him.

PART IV. AIR

"What is now proved was once only imagined."

William Blake

Chapter Forty-Two

Mrs. Lazaruk opened the door of her tiny stucco bungalow on Whyte Avenue. There on her porch stood a gangly girl, maybe eighteen years old, with blond ringlets spilling out under her scarf, wearing a white blouson and a crimson pleated skirt.

"Hello there," she said, trying not to sound awkward toward her prospective boarder.

Kalyna thrust out her hand with an air of confidence.

"Pleased to meet you, Mrs. Lazaruk. My name is Kalyna Feder-chuk. I'm here for the room."

This young woman looked like a famous actress with those bobbing curls, thought Mrs. Lazaruk.

"Do come in," she said, making a sweeping gesture with her hand.

Kalyna picked up her brown valise and entered, eyes scanning the sitting room, sizing-up the place with its greying lace curtains and fraying brown furniture. It will have to do, she thought.

Mrs. Lazaruk sized-up Kalyna. She had just barely advertised for a boarder when her father had called her up and said to take down the sign from the variety store, he had someone perfect for her. He said her name was Kalyna, a young girl from Edna-Star where he practiced, and she was a shining academic poised to take on the world at the University of Alberta. Now, this girl stood before her, judging her she could tell and she didn't like it one bit. She wondered if she had kept that sign just in case this didn't work out.

"I'll show you to your room now," she said, matter-of-factly.

They went down a stuffy hallway opening up to a dark bedroom facing the backyard. The shuttered windows dimmed the sunlight streaming in, giving the room a sombre glow, but Kalyna could see the space was large enough for a bureau, small study desk, and a single bed. Katja's voice flooded Kalyna's head. *"Be grateful. Mrs. Lazaruk is so kind to rent you this room, and it is so close to the university."*

"Thank you, Mrs. Lazaruk." She turned to her host with a beaming smile. "It's just perfect, really."

Mrs. Lazaruk could see through this girl's practiced facade like a newly-scrubbed window pane.

"Glad you like it," she played along. "Comes with two meals a day; breakfast at 7:00 and supper at 6:00 sharp. Here's your key."

Kalyna nodded and took the key, fingering it like a sacred treasure. They didn't have a key back home. This was the key to her future, she mused.

"Fresh towels every Saturday and the bathroom is right across the hall," Mrs. Lazaruk continued, but Kalyna was already tuning her out, focusing on the key, her room, and her freedom. A young independent woman in the big city of Edmonton, off to University—the first in her family to do so—that's who she was. Independent, confident, and successful. Mrs. Lazaruk coughed and Kalyna suddenly remembered her host.

"Thank you, Mrs. Lazaruk...for everything. Thank you."

Mrs. Lazaruk took her hint and said, "If you need me I'll be in the sitting room."

Kalyna closed the bedroom door behind her, set her valise on the desk, and bounced onto the bed mattress. It felt soft and fluffy. This was home for the next eight months. She opened the wooden shutters, releasing beams of sunshine into the room. Mrs. Lazaruk's yard was an English-style garden filled with roses and delphiniums.

Her crabapple tree swept the sky with its branches, valiantly trying to soar under the weight of its autumn fruit. She should volunteer to pick them for Mrs. Lazaruk. Her mother would want her to be helpful. Be helpful and grateful, that's what her mama had said.

Katja had seen her off at the village train station, where the train took her directly to Strathcona Station right on Whyte Avenue. Uncle Ivan had drawn her a map which she carried in her skirt pocket, folded neatly into quarters just as he had shown her. She had carried her valise with an air of confidence as she marched down the busy avenue, shops bustling and young men's eyes trailing her. She knew she was a beauty but wanted to be known for more than that. She wanted to study law and be the first Ukrainian female lawyer to be admitted to the Alberta Bar.

Kalyna came to the city with a single goal: to use her education to further the rights of women in government, like Louise McKinney. Mama had told her about Miss McKinney who was elected to the Alberta Legislature the year Kalyna had been born. Mama had watched this election with tremendous interest as this would have never have happened in the old country. Mama had told Kalyna that being born in that same year was no mistake. Her daughter too would change the world; make it a better place for women. Kalyna was a gifted student academically who loved reading and writing and would read the newspaper at night to her parents. She viewed law school as a stepping stone to launch her career in the field of justice.

Kalyna stared at the austere beige bedspread, the brown shutters, and the nondescript, yellowing wallpaper on every wall, except the ceiling which was dirty white. This room needed some colour, Mama's colour. Mama had packed one of her quilts for Kalyna. She called them her growing quilts, as each child had their own that

Mama started when they were born. They were made of scraps of clothing salvaged over the years of growing up, then stitched with love into squares, and hand-sewn together to make a growing quilt. Mama had added the last square, a red maple leaf, the night before Kalyna had left the homestead. She had used one of Papa's old red plaid work-shirts and painstakingly cut out the red blocks, nipped and tucked to form the autumn-coloured leaf which puffed out, proudly completing the pattern.

Kalyna unfolded the quilt, releasing smells of the farm; the straw, the chickens, and her mama. She lay it over the bedspread, smoothing out the squares lovingly. Yes, that definitely made the room brighter. "It's a little piece of home to remind you where you come from," Mama had said. Kalyna had been reluctant, not wanting the quilt to soil or wrinkle her new sweater sets and skirts for University, but Mama had insisted and folded it so neatly that it fit in her valise too perfectly to say anything.

Kalyna had had no choice in the matter and now, as she admired her mother's handiwork, she was happy she had brought it after all. She stroked the squares familiar to her: her baby blue frock transformed into a light star blocked in the centre, her yellow wool blanket cut to trim some of the squares, and now the leaf. She touched this last square that her mother so diligently sewed on the very night before she left. It was all that was needed to complete the quilt, Mama explained to her. It fit perfectly. Kalyna liked the way it puffed out and it even crinkled like the autumn leaves. How clever her mother was with her work.

Though she greatly admired her mama, Kalyna had not taken after her in her domestic talents, not like her big sister Pavla. Pavla loved baking bread and cooking with Mama, and they would sew by the fire most evenings while Papa and Olek played games. Kalyna had read. She read everything she could get her hands on; her love of learning and discovery was instinctive. She was born to read and study and learn; this was her gift and her parents had nurtured it lovingly. It meant leaving Edna-Star and the life she had known but she was more than happy to leave. She had felt an odd sense of relief to be escaping from there. She had always felt like an outsider of sorts. She couldn't explain why, but this place, the city and university, it called out to her.

A piece of paper fell onto the floor. Mama had provided her with another name to look up, a professor at the University in the Faculty of Medicine, Dr. Smith. But, Kalyna smiled to herself, that would wait for another day. Today was dedicated to settling in. Classes would begin tomorrow and she wanted to be as prepared as she could be.

Before she fell asleep that night, Kalyna read. She opened the crackling spine of a volume of poetry and quickly turned to the dog-eared page she so loved. Auntie Mary and Uncle Ivan had given her this book as a parting gift and she had read it cover-to-cover on the train ride here.

She had folded over the page of her favourite, a poem by Yeats, which began, "When you are old...". She recited it quietly now, in her room, so as not to wake the sleeping Mrs. Lazaruk in the room next door.

As she read the words, "One man loved the pilgrim soul in you, and loved the sorrows of your changing face," her mama and papa came to mind; Katja and Wasyl, so deep in palpable love their whole lives, through all their joys and sorrows.

Kalyna's most vivid memories of her father were of him dancing with her mother to the tiny music box set in the middle of the pine table. And singing. He would sing to Mama and hold her close and the children would blush and look away. Her papa could make Mama laugh like no other.

Kalyna had grown up closer to her mother, as Papa was often in the fields working outside, and Kalyna had her nose in her books. She longed to go to the creek with him though, where he would rattle off the names of all the flora and fauna like a botanist. Though papa was not educated in the formal sense, he had learned from the land itself.

Beyond those few precious times with her father, Kalyna had always felt like he kept his distance from her. His playful ways of tousling hair and making funny faces were reserved for her siblings and his mischievous eyes seemed to gloss over, to become more solemn and thoughtful—almost wistful, whenever he looked at her. Kalyna had told herself this was because of her gift. Papa had seen her delight in learning early and she knew her parents must have saved for her future education right from her birth. Otherwise how would they ever have been able to pay for her tuition? Pavla and Olek had not shown any disposition toward further learning, that was true, so the savings had gone to her. She was grateful, certainly, but a part of her felt she had earned this right with her dedication; she felt entitled and deserving to go to university, and now, she would put her gift to use towards securing women's rights.

She read Yeats' last line again, "And hid his face in a crowd of stars." That was where Papa was now. Mama had always told her to look up at the night sky and there he would be. Holding the book tightly in her hand, she rose, the hardwood floor cold and rough against her bare feet. Kalyna stood on her toes to look outside one last time. Before she closed the rickety shutters, she silently thanked her father for bringing her here. She pushed back the tears. "I'm here, Papa. I'll make you proud of me."

She placed the magical poetry on her bedside table where Yeats' words could murmur, glow, and embrace her in their grace.

Chapter Forty-Three

Kalyna was the only female in her class of twenty first-year law students. This garnered her a great deal of attention from the young gentlemen in the class, which she shunned, at least on the outside. She dressed as modestly as she could to blend in, to Mrs. Lazaruk's nodding approval each morning, but could not deny the unmistakable looks whenever she entered the halls. Her classes took her beyond the Law Building, and she loved the many lecture halls; the professors with their robes and the regal way they recited their notes.

Her favourite professor was Dr. Rankin, who always seemed to be late for class and would pat and search the pockets of his robes before he shuffled through his papers. Once, after welcoming the students, he had begun his lecture by pulling out his notes to read then realized it was his grocery list. He had laughed heartily at himself and the class had joined him. He was kind, polite, and generous with his knowledge of Common Law, and Kalyna was hooked. He would smile and nod at Kalyna each class and when he called upon her, he would nod his encouragement to her as she answered, like a doting grandfather.

Within a week on campus Kalyna had joined The Gateway, the student newspaper, and had taken up the Law Society Beat, writing updates on the social events of the Faculty. What she really wanted to do was interview each professor and find out how their minds ticked and how they came to be in their respective posts, but she would wait to broach this idea with the editor of the paper, Randall Thebe, a second-year Medical student. Along with Randall, she joined a team of another five young men, and Rose, a woman from the Faculty of Arts who was studying English literature. In Rose, Kalyna found a fellow lover of Yeats.

Rose and Kalyna became fast friends and spent lunch hours together on campus, preferring to sprawl on the lawns in front of the student centre rather than sit in the cafeteria. Rose had grown up in the city; her father was a lawyer with one of the big city firms, Hillier, Myland and Watson, and had always encouraged his daughter to go into Law. Rose explained to Kalyna that her passion was science and she wanted to be a doctor, a surgeon. She had decided to pursue her Arts degree first, then apply to Medicine and was dabbling in some Political Science courses this term, to appease her father.

Rose shared that she had a crush on a professor she secretly called Smitty. He was so suave and debonair, she explained. And, yes, he was much older, but she was attracted to his confidence. "He is an Englishman," she declared. Kalyna shared that her favourite professor was Dr. Rankin, that she was positive he possessed a certain knowledge that only she could understand. They laughed at themselves, their schoolgirl folly, and giggled when Randall would walk by and wave shyly, day after day, hoping for an invitation to sit with them.

It took Kalyna until the end of her second week on campus before she remembered her mama's friend to look up, and made the connection that Dr. Smith and Rose's Smitty were one and the same. Rose was positively giddy the day Kalyna revealed that her mama once knew Dr. Smith. He had been the doctor in Edna-Star when she and her father first arrived, she told Rose. "I have his phone number," Kalyna said.

"Let's call!"

"But you see him every day in class, Rose. This is silly. Why don't you introduce me to him and I will send him greetings from my mother."

Rose thought this was an excellent idea and would make her stand apart from her classmates in Dr. Smith's eyes.

"When would you like to meet him?"

"What about tomorrow at noon, after your lecture? I can meet you just outside the main lecture hall."

That night, Kalyna wrote her third letter to Mama.

September 21, 1935

Dear Mama,

How are you, Pavla, and Olek? I trust this finds you well and that Olek is working hard at the harvest. I hope you are not working too hard, because even though you insist I not worry, I do, Mama. Especially after what happened to Papa, I do.

I am working hard at my classes, making you proud. I just wrote my first paper for Dr. Rankin, my favourite professor. I am anxious to see how I do as this is the first real test of my ability.

Mrs. Lazaruk is so kind and her meals are delicious, although I miss your cooking, Mama. That is what I miss from home the most. I have tried to be helpful and picked her crabapples on the weekend and now the house is filled with the aroma of sweet jelly, worth all the prickles and scratches I bear.

My friend Rose and I had a good laugh when we discovered that her favourite professor is your old friend, Dr. Smith. We are meeting him tomorrow and I will introduce myself. I am anxious to meet him and to tell him how Edna-Star has changed.

I send all my love and kisses to you, Pavla, and Olek.

Your Loving Daughter,
Kalyna

Kalyna folded the letter and sealed the envelope. Tomorrow she would visit the post office on her way to campus. What would this Dr. Smith be like, she wondered as she pulled the quilt up to her chin and cocooned herself in it? She could still smell earth in it, Mama's baking, and the straw from the hen house; home.

* * *

Kalyna rushed across campus to Rose's lecture hall in the Medical Building directly at noon, as they had planned. Rose stood outside nervously explaining.

"He's just collecting his papers and should be coming out momentarily."

"I'm ready," said Kalyna. "How about you?"

"Ready," confirmed Rose.

Just then, the door swung open revealing a striking gentleman, gallant and well-coiffed, in a lengthy blue robe. Kalyna was struck by the colour of the robe as her professors all wore black. She looked into his face as Rose stepped forward.

"Uh, excuse me, Professor Smith, my name is Rose. I'm in your Bacteriology class."

"Yes, I know. I see you every day, Rose. Who do we have here?"

Dr. Smith turned his attention to the beautiful young woman with bobbing blond ringlets. He felt a tinge, a tweak in his memory.

"I am Kalyna Federchuk, Sir. My mother is Katja Federchuk and she gave me your name as a contact here in the city."

Kalyna's words awakened an ache inside of him that he believed was buried. He felt a chill tingle down his spine. He stared at Kalyna disbelieving for a moment, his voice escaping him. Katja he thought. Eighteen years ago. Edna-Star.

Kalyna was his child. He should have made the connection immediately and chastised himself, only now noticing how much Kalyna resembled her mother. Kalyna stared innocently at him with his own grey-blue eyes that seemed to change with the hues in the sky. Her daughter, their daughter. He coughed and collected himself, suddenly aware of the awkward silence between them, and reached for her outstretched hand.

"It is my pleasure to meet the daughter of Mr. and Mrs. Federchuk. How are your parents?"

Kalyna stopped, her confidence waning. She had not even told Rose about her parents, about her father…

"My mother is wonderful, thank you, but my father, Wasyl…" she paused, her mouth suddenly dry, voice wavering, "has passed away."

Dr. Smith stepped back, struck by the news. He had left Katja and Wasyl alone all these years, though he longed to see them and shake Wasyl's hand and tell him what courage he had to go through that hell of a camp. He could never contact him, though he had played out the reunion in his mind many times. Betrayal was his cross to bear. That was enough.

His only thread of contact had been the monthly envelopes of money and now here was his child, at university, standing before him; his flesh and blood.

"I'm very sorry to hear that," he said, regaining his composure. "Your father was a brave man, a hero to many in the community."

"That's what Mama always said, too. Papa was revered by everyone in town."

Dr. Smith could see that Katja had never told Kalyna the truth and he would uphold their secret, as he had promised himself to do.

"What are you studying, Kalyna?"

"Law, Sir, I am studying Law. I want to work for women's rights and better their position in government."

Dr. Smith smiled contentedly. She was fiercely independent like her mother.

"Very good, Kalyna. You and Rose are a great team, a future doctor and lawyer as best friends."

The young women smiled at each other. "We think so."

"Well, nice to meet you, Kalyna. Thank you for introducing yourself. Give my best regards to your mother for me. I'm afraid I must take my leave as I have a pressing engagement. Perhaps we will run into each other on campus again."

"Oh yes, Professor, thank you. I will write to Mama that I met you. Thank you for your time."

Kalyna watched Dr. Smith stride confidently down the hall, his gown swaying at his heels like the waves on an open sea.

"I can see why you fell in love with him," she smiled at Rose. They giggled.

Dr. Smith walked directly to his office building and locked the door behind him. The drawer stuck only a little as he reached in to feel the cold glass bottle. He poured himself a glass of scotch and sat at his grand desk looking out at the grounds of the campus. He had to calm his jumbled thoughts. If Katja was alone now, maybe he could make amends, apologize, and they could tell Kalyna together. Is this what Katja had intended by giving Kalyna his name? His speculations ran wild. He breathed deeply and concentrated on the scotch running down his throat, lighting a fire in his belly.

Chapter Forty-Four

September 22, 1935

Dear Mama,

How are you, Pavla, and Olek? I know I wrote you yesterday, but I wanted to tell you the news that today I met your Dr. Smith. He is a Professor of Bacteriology. He asked about you and Papa and was saddened when I told him about Papa. He had to hurry off to a meeting, but sends you his regards.

He was impressed I am studying Law and this gave me more motivation. I will devote myself to my studies, Mama. I am determined to write more articles for The Gateway, focusing on female students on campus and the role they play in leadership. There is not one female professor here yet. I want to speak out about that.

I am happy at Mrs. Lazaruk's and continue to help where I can. She has invited me on a weekend trip to Borden Park which has an outdoor amusement park and swimming pool. I said I would go even though I cannot swim. I remember you told me about the rides with Papa in the old country. What an adventure!

I promise that I will be careful. I hope this warm weather has been good for bringing in the harvest. I will write again soon.

Love Your Daughter,
Kalyna

She folded up the letter and put it in one of the envelopes she had stacked on her desk. Mama had ensured that she had stamped envelopes with her when she came; a letter each week was what she expected, Katja had told Kalyna with a smile. Well, this was number two in two days for Mama. Kalyna knew she would be pleased.

Tomorrow was the planned outing to Borden Park. Mrs. Lazaruk had surprised her at supper by suggesting the two of them take the streetcar to the East End and go for a swim and then visit the adjacent roller-coaster amusement park. Kalyna had hesitated as it seemed so out of character for Mrs. Lazaruk to suggest such a daring plan. Her face had lit up with excitement at the prospect though and this compelled Kalyna to say yes, she would like that very much, even though she had never learned to swim. Mrs. Lazaruk had clasped her hands like a child and Kalyna thought she was the happiest she had seen since her arrival two weeks ago. As she dressed for bed Kalyna recalled her mama's stories of the roller-coaster ride with Papa in the old country, where she had fallen in love with Papa. Kalyna loved that story.

* * *

The stifling heat enveloped them as they reached the poolside. Kalyna's toes immediately crinkled up to avoid the burning asphalt beneath them. Mrs. Lazaruk had rented two bathing suits for them and had already entered the pool water, splashing about. She gestured to Kalyna.

"There are stairs on the side, dear. Come on in. It's not too deep and you can stand on the bottom."

Kalyna felt wobbly at the knees as she held the railing and felt gingerly with her tiptoes for each step into the pool. The water felt cool on her skin and soon she was chest-deep. Her arms became wings skirting the surface of the crystal clear water.

Mrs. Lazaruk had moved closer to her, dodging the flailing extremities of children jumping in and frolicking all around.

"I will teach you to float, if you like," she told Kalyna, who nodded, gratefully. "You just pretend you are like a star in the sky and the water is your pillowy bed in the clouds, like this."

And Mrs. Lazaruk pushed herself off the bottom, spreading her limbs into a graceful star pattern, her face tilted to the sky, eyes closed, peaceful and still. "You try," she urged. "I'll be right here beside you."

On the third try, Kalyna managed to kick her legs up to the surface, relaxed her back and shoulders, leaned back and floated. What a sensation! This feeling of floating, of complete freedom. She tried again, to the applause of Mrs. Lazaruk. Kalyna thought she could just spend the whole day floating, but soon the children splashing around them prompted Mrs. Lazaruk to suggest they get out and head to the roller-coaster park before the heat of the day was upon them.

The roller-coaster loomed large before them as they entered the amusement park. The sign in front of the ride announced it was 432 feet high above them. Kalyna's eyes followed the rickety track, half expecting the wooden slats to tumble away as the car clacked noisily upon them. Second thoughts were creeping in.

"I'm not too sure..." she stammered.

"It does look high, doesn't it?" agreed Mrs. Lazaruk.

A gentle hand touched the small of Kalyna's back, brushing the wet curls that lay there. Dr. Smith stood beside them, in his beige three-piece linen suit, and with a walking stick to boot.

"Ladies," he greeted them cordially with a slight bow.

"Hello, Professor Smith." Kalyna was surprised to see him there and knew introductions were in order. "Mrs. Lazaruk, this is one of my friend's professors at the university. Dr. Smith, this is my friend, Mrs. Lazaruk." Even as she said it, Kalyna surprised herself. Yes, she had grown fond of Mrs. Lazaruk and she had become a friend to her.

Dr. Smith removed his hat and kissed Mrs. Lazaruk's hand making her blush and beam at the same time.

"Hello," she managed.

"Dr. Smith is also a friend of my mama's," Kalyna explained. "He was the doctor in Edna-Star before your father came." A flash of recognition came over Mrs. Lazaruk, then it was gone. Only Dr. Smith saw and wondered if she knew about the past.

He changed the subject. "Were you ladies thinking of going on this ride?"

"Yes," Mrs. Lazaruk said. "Do you think it is safe, Doctor?"

Dr. Smith laughed, "Safe enough, yes, but not for me I'm afraid. The old ticker..." and he patted his chest.

"Let's go," Kalyna braved before she changed her mind. Mrs. Lazaruk agreed and the ladies gave their swim bags to Dr. Smith who agreed to wait for them at the bottom, just in case of any emergencies, he said. He laughed at that and Kalyna felt queasy as she tightened the lap belt around her and pushed the bar in front to ensure it was locked tight. Her heart beat wildly as she looked at Mrs. Lazaruk smiling calmly beside her.

"It will be alright, dear, you'll see. Just hold on tight." And she patted Kalyna's hand as the car jerked forward on the track.

The thrilling ride was over in what seemed a blink of time, leaving Kalyna with only butterflies, a dry mouth, and her beaming smile. Kalyna knew then that she was her father's child, loving the speed and excitement of this coaster, like flying up and down mountains. Mrs. Lazaruk was also beaming as they approached Dr. Smith.

"You survived the ride!" he laughed.

Mrs. Lazaruk smiled broadly and suggested they all get a lemonade. Kalyna watched as Dr. Smith and Mrs. Lazaruk chatted, conversation flowing easily between them about their high schools, friends, family, and jobs. Kalyna realized that the extent of what she knew about Mrs. Lazaruk was that she could make crabapple jelly, was an excellent cook, liked to crochet, loved swimming, and, now, roller-coasters. She really didn't know anything else about her past. What was her story? Here she was interested in women and women's roles and she had overlooked the very female in front of her.

Dr. Smith had now hooked his arm through hers and was leading a giddy Mrs. Lazaruk to the lemonade stand. How things change so quickly, Kalyna thought. Perhaps, the roller-coaster really was the ride of love. Perhaps it had worked its magic on Mrs. Lazaruk too!

That night, Mrs. Lazaruk hummed as she braised the roast beef in the oven. She mashed the potatoes with a steady beat as Kalyna set the table.

"I had a wonderful time today, Kalyna. Thank you for coming with me."

Kalyna had been reluctant to take the ride home offered by Dr. Smith in his motor car, but Mrs. Lazaruk had been so grateful and it was their first time to ride in a motorized car. It exhilarated Kalyna almost as much as the roller coaster. Another thing to write home about.

"No. Thank you, Mrs. Lazaruk. I had a great time too. My favourite part was floating."

"My favourite part was meeting your Dr. Smith," shared Mrs. Lazaruk. "It has been a long time since I have felt that way."

Kalyna's silence at that statement made her worry that she had said too much. She felt closer to the girl now and felt herself opening up more day by day. "Let's eat," she managed.

Over supper Mrs. Lazaruk relayed her story to Kalyna, the promising career in medicine like her father, the love affair, prospect of marriage, the baby, and the miscarriage. She laid herself bare to this girl from the prairie. She told Kalyna how she had dropped out of university and taken a job at the local library and there she stayed to this day, an old maid with few prospects...until now.

Kalyna looked at Mrs. Lazaruk deeply, and, for the first time it seemed, she saw her beauty and knew that it was her sorrow that made her appear older than her years. Kalyna guessed Mrs. Lazaruk was probably no more than thirty-five years old, and felt guilty she had dismissed her when they had first met. She was almost her mother's age, but today displayed the joy and wonder of a child, and now she was clearly smitten with Dr. Smith.

Love can change many things. Its power itself is life-changing. This she knew from her parents. That night, she prayed for happiness for Dr. Smith and Mrs. Lazaruk.

Chapter Forty-Five

Katja sat at the table, the three letters before her, two of them from Kalyna. Kalyna's letters were filled with such joy at being at university. Katja held them tightly and knew this was the road her youngest daughter was destined for. She wanted to write back to encourage Kalyna and to tell her how proud she was of her. The third letter could wait.

September 29, 1935

Dear Kalyna,

Thank you for your letters, which have arrived one after another. How exciting to hear from you and know that you are approaching each day at university with such confidence and dedication. All of us in Edna-Star are so proud of you and I know your father would be too. We knew you would go to university from a very young age and this was our dream for you, Kalyna.

Katja drew a big breath.

I am glad you have had a chance to meet Dr. Smith. He played a role in our early years as your father and I settled here in Edna-Star and built the home our family grew up in. It is important to know the past while moving forward to the future, dear Kalyna. Dr. Smith is part of that past and now, your present.

I look forward to hearing about your adventures in Borden Park with swimming and the roller-coaster, my goodness! Your words took me back in my memory to the Russian Mountain Ride I took with your father all those years ago in the old country. Do you remember me telling that story, Kalyna? It was when I fell in love with your father. I love holding onto my memories of him and of us, as a family.

Yes, the harvest is going well. Olek is working hard with Ivan and Henri and they go to our neighbour's farms to help each other out. We will sell the grain directly to the Wheat Board this year and the price is very good. Olek is pleased. It is hard for him to go to the same fields where your father's accident was. I am so proud of him for doing so, bravely, each day.

Pavla has been working with Mary in town as her teaching assistant this fall as more children are attending school now. Mary tells me that Pavla has a gift with children and supervises them at recess play time and is now teaching them music. I think she must have your father's gift of singing!

All is well, here, Kalyna. No need for worry. We think of you every day and wish only the best for you in your studies.

Love,
Mama

P.S. Are you using the quilt?

Katja re-read her letter. Was she being too bold with her hint, she wondered? She set Kalyna's letters aside and eyed her pruning scissors resting by the kitchen basin. She could always cut off that last line, if she decided to. The candle still provided good light to her as she read the third letter to arrive that day. It came in an envelope, stark and crisp, just like Kalyna's money had, but those had stopped now that Kalyna had turned eighteen years old. She had not heard a word from Edward all these years and now, her daughter had seen him and they had spoken.

She stared at his handwriting, the loops and valleys so delicately written by fountain pen. Even his script carried his air of elegance, she thought. She had not wanted to be unfaithful to the memory of Wasyl, but felt that Kalyna was ready to know where she came from. That is why she had given her daughter his name. Kalyna yearned for justice for women, for all people, and Katja felt that justice can only come with understanding. That's why she had done it, why she had sewn Wasyl's release certificate from Castle Mountain Internment Camp into the leaf piece, the last piece of Kalyna's growing quilt. She wanted Kalyna to know the truth and in the truth, to find her own peace. She read.

September 24, 1935

Dear Katja,

How long it has been since I last saw you in the church yard? Eighteen years have passed now and I still think of you every day. And now I have met our daughter. Her beauty and confidence reminded me of you immediately. Her shining eyes are determined and I am proud to see her at University. I can see she is a force to contend with, and I want to commend you and Wasyl on raising such an intelligent and independent young woman.

I was so sorry to hear of Wasyl's passing, Katja. Over the years, I have imagined myself meeting him on the street and please know I should have liked to shake his hand and tell him how courageous I think he was. I mean that, Katja. He was a hero.

I admit that I was surprised that you had given Kalyna my name to look up. I wasn't sure if you wanted her to know the truth about her family or not. I could see that she didn't know who I was and so I vow to you to keep our secret for as long as you wish it to be so.

I have befriended Mrs. Lazaruk, the woman Kalyna boards with, so I shall be able to keep tabs on Kalyna and send updates to you, if you wish. Only if you wish.

I believe time heals all wounds, Katja, and I long for your forgiveness. I am grateful for being able to meet Kalyna and only desire the best for her and you.

Fondly,
Edward

Katja held the letter tightly to keep her hands from shaking.

Chapter Forty-Six

It was the Saturday before Thanksgiving when Kalyna found it. She routinely laid out Mama's quilt with the maple leaf at the top, just kissing the edge of her pillow, at night gently stroking her chin. The crinkling was more than the fabric, Kalyna had decided, so she asked Mrs. Lazaruk for her stitch remover and, one-by-one, hand-clipped the threads which bound the quilt piece together. The tiny folded paper inside reminded her of the map Uncle Ivan had given her, folded like an origami box, only squished flat. She saw right away that it was an important document. It had a seal with the Government of Canada stamp, signature lines, and typed lettering. She hesitated in reading it, only for an instant, and her eyes jumped across the page, held hostage by words like '*Internment, Castle, 1917, release.*'

She slowed her breathing and sat down on the bed. This had belonged to her father. His name was typed in black and white and his signature was at the bottom. It was some sort of a release form, a promise not to engage in espionage. Her thoughts darted in her head. She felt she was seeing something she shouldn't. Wasn't this spying? Was her father a spy? What was this? She read on in disbelief, trying to digest the information before her. The details shocked her. Her father had been interned during The Great War as an enemy alien in the country he called home.

All his life, her father had reiterated what a gift it was to be born Canadian and professed his love for this country which gave him freedom, and here was evidence, right here in her hands, that his freedom had been taken away at a time when Canada had been at war. Had her father really believed what he said? Why did he keep this from her? Why had she never known about this? Did her siblings know? She sat on the edge of the bed, clutching the quilt in one hand and the release letter in the other. Mama still didn't have a phone or she would have called. She felt like she was bursting and had to tell someone. Mrs. Lazaruk.

Kalyna knocked on Mrs. Lazaruk's door. "Mrs. Lazaruk?" Kalyna tried to measure the urgency in her voice. "Do you have a minute? I need to talk to you."

"Come in."

Kalyna had never been in this room in the house before and the colours, the magenta, melon oranges, and marigold yellows sprang upon her like a bursting flower garden. Mrs. Lazaruk hid her colour in here, she thought.

"What is it, Kalyna? You've been crying."

Kalyna reached up to her face which was, indeed, damp. She had the sensation of time passing, frozen in the moment of reading the letter.

"I found this..." she stammered. "In the quilt Mama made for me."

Mrs. Lazaruk reached out for the letter. She knew it was important for the seal shone through the translucent paper. Her hand trembled as she read Kalyna's letter. Her own father had told her once of such atrocities, but said it must remain in the past, best not to speak of it. This was one of his reasons for practicing all these years in Edna-Star, he said. He believed that the Ukrainian settlers were the backbone of the prairie settlement and he wanted to be a pillar of support for them, as they had been for his generation.

"Wasyl Federchuk was my father," Kalyna managed by way of explanation. "Can you tell me about this Castle Camp? Can you tell me what you know about the internment? What does it mean?"

"Sit down, Kalyna," Mrs. Lazaruk urged. "One thing at a time."

She looked deeply at Kalyna who seemed to shrink before her eyes. The young woman's shoulders were hunched over as if encapsulating her heart, protecting it from the news to come.

"The best one to answer all this is your mother. She must have wanted you to know this information if she sewed this into your quilt."

"And I will ask her, Mrs. Lazaruk, but she doesn't have a phone, and my trip to see her isn't for weeks. Please, tell me anything you know."

Mrs. Lazaruk sighed. "Ukrainians don't speak of this time because the older generation still lives in fear of the barbed wire fence," she began. "All I know is what my own father told me years ago. I'll tell you that, child." Mrs. Lazaruk swallowed hard. Her mouth felt dry and burning with the words, the story, she was retelling.

"During The Great War, the government of Canada enacted the War Measures Act enabling them to imprison those they felt to be enemies of the state. Ukrainian-Canadians were one of the groups that they regarded as supporters of Austria-Hungary. Therefore, this group and many others were seen as enemies of Canada and Britain. Hundreds of men, and even entire families, were imprisoned in work camps across Canada for the sake of the country. 'For peace and protection', they said." She paused. Mrs. Lazaruk looked directly at Kalyna, her eyes studied and intense.

"That's it, Kalyna. That's all I know." Mrs. Lazaruk had noted the date on the release form and looked at Kalyna. Was this girl seventeen? Eighteen? Born in 1917? Then, it struck her that Kalyna didn't know yet. Another secret, another shock was yet to come for this dear girl.

Kalyna was silent, deep in thought. "Thank you, Mrs. Lazaruk," she said stoically. She retrieved the form and went back to her room. Closing the door as quietly as she could, she directed her anger to the quilt, throwing it on the floor as her anger exploded. It was so unfair. Why had she never been told? She could have done something, said something to her father to let him know he was a hero. That was what Mama always called him, and so did Dr. Smith. They all knew! Everyone but her. It was like the village secret kept locked up tightly in a wall of silence they had built around her. She stooped to pick up the quilt and hugged it to her chest. The maple leaf fluttered, hanging by loose threads as if taunting her.

Why had Mama waited until now? She must have had a plan, Kalyna was sure of it. Mama must have wanted to wait until she thought Kalyna was ready for the news, but why? Why now?

Powerless as she felt, Kalyna needed to talk to Mama so she ripped off a piece of lined paper to begin her letter. It hit her. Mama knew that now Kalyna had the power to do something. She wasn't born in the year of Louise McKinney for nothing, she could hear her mother saying. This was her destiny, she felt power in her fingers as she wrote to Mama. Now she had the power of knowledge and words.

October 5, 1935

Dear Mama,

I found it. I found Papa's document in the quilt. I know you must have wondered when it would happen. I read it over and asked Mrs. Lazaruk to explain. I wished I could call you, mama. Why didn't you tell me? Why didn't I know before Papa died? Why now?

I have so many questions and I know you may say it's best to wait until I am home for the Christmas break from classes, but it seems ages away. I want to do something about it, Mama. It seems so unfair. The father I knew was the most loyal Canadian citizen, who spoke so highly of his government and the freedom his country bestowed upon him and his family. Was this all a lie? Was he really a spy? Why did you keep this from me?

After she wrote that last line, Kalyna regretted it, only for an instant. No, she wanted to know the truth. 1917 may have been the year for Louise McKinney and women's rights, but it was also a stain on Alberta's history of human rights, one that had never been spoken of in her home or village. 1917, the year she was born and the year Papa was imprisoned and released. 1917. She sat down on the bed, dizzied by the realization, the thoughts swirling in her head. How could it be? She crumpled up the letter and threw it at the peeling wallpaper.

Mrs. Lazaruk could hear her sobbing across the hall and got up once to comfort her, but sat down again on her bed. Kalyna must know now, she thought. The last secret was out. She felt a pang of guilt in knowing what Kalyna had not, what her father had shared with her about Kalyna and her family.

Sleep evaded her that night and in the morning Kalyna decided she had to go home to Edna-Star and speak to her mother in person. She just couldn't wait. This news about her father, the camp, and her birth had sent her for a tailspin and she would be unable to concentrate on any of her classes until she had spoken to Mama.

In the morning, with tear-stained cheeks, she told Mrs. Lazaruk her decision. Mrs. Lazaruk had heard the tossing and turning during the night and consoled Kalyna the best she could, listening and nodding. When she heard Kalyna's determined intention to take the train to Edna-Star, she suggested they ask Dr. Smith if he would like to drive her and go back with her. She would go as well to pay a visit to her father. She would telephone Dr. Smith right now and ask about the time, if Kalyna wished it to be so. Kalyna didn't really want to go alone and told Mrs. Lazaruk she would appreciate her coming and her support, and Dr. Smith's too if he was able to take off the time. By twelve noon, it was all settled and Dr. Smith's Chevrolet Coupe was outside, motor purring. He got out to lift her valise inside.

"I'm happy to take you home, Kalyna. Mrs. Lazaruk said it's of great importance."

"Yes, thank you. I'm very grateful, Dr. Smith. I hope it's not too much of an imposition."

Edward Smith wanted to embrace his daughter and tell her the truth, and that nothing would ever be an imposition for him as long as it was for her, but it was not the time, not yet. He had a promise to keep.

* * *

Mrs. Lazaruk remained in Edna-Star with her father while Edward's motor car laboured on the dirt roads to Kalyna's homestead. Olek heard the sputtering before he saw it. He picked up his rifle, as was his habit, to greet the coming visitors. Dust swirled for a moment and then Kalyna appeared as if an apparition to him. He ran to her and swung her around.

"What a surprise, Kalyna! It's not enough that you've gone up and went to the big city school now is it, now you've got yourself a motor car?"

Kalyna smiled, betraying the hole in her heart.

"Not exactly, Olek. My friend, Dr. Smith, drove me so I could see Mama. Where is she?"

But Olek fixated on Kalyna's mention of Dr. Smith. The Dr. Smith of Edna-Star, the one who had hurt his mama all those years ago? Could it be?

He aimed his rifle at the car door, opening to reveal a man he once knew and had played hide-and-seek with.

"Whoa now there, Olek. No need for that, my son." Edward had a flashback to the last time he had seen Olek.

"I'm not your son, and why are you here?" Olek's anger boiled up inside him.

Dr. Smith looked at Kalyna.

"Don't be rude, Olek. Dr. Smith drove me here from Edmonton. Where's Mama? We should get Dr. Smith a drink of water."

Olek muttered under his breath but put the end of his rifle down.

"Good to see you again, Olek," Dr. Smith reached out his hand.

"Dr. Smith," Olek muttered, hands at his side. "Mama's inside, Kalyna."

Kalyna went inside, returning moments later with a cold glass of water. She handed it to Dr. Smith and nodded at Olek to keep him busy outside, while she and Mama talked.

Olek gestured to the stumps around the fire pit and sat down with Dr. Smith.

"So how've things been, since your father..."

"Since he died, well, they've been difficult, to tell you the truth, but the thing about this place, Dr. Smith, is that everyone stands up for each other and have each other's backs. We take care of each other."

"That is good to hear, Olek." Dr. Smith cleared his throat. He could feel Olek's anger seething again, the boy's eyes asking him why he had hurt his mama all those years ago when they had trusted him so much. Edward looked away to the house that had stood the test of time, encapsulated in the past, unchanged in almost twenty years. He looked back at Olek.

"I'm a professor now, Olek. I left all those years ago to go back to the university to honour my father and to follow in his footsteps."

"Is that all you're going to say?" Olek glared. "I know about Kalyna, Dr. Smith. I was five years old. I remember things. I saw things. I know Papa was gone then…"

Dr. Smith's throat was parched. He sipped the water calmly.

"Olek, I can explain. I came here to see your mother and apologize again. I can't change what happened. It was a terrible mistake and I've tried to make amends." Olek's silence urged him to continue. "The past is a funny thing, Olek. When we are young, our past seems like yesterday and when you are my age, it transcends a lifetime. It's always there, lurking, but you keep moving forward, dodging the memories, burying them a little bit. Sometimes the past creeps up on you and bars your way and you cannot keep going forward until you address the issues in front of you. That's where we are now. I'm here to address what happened. Kalyna came into my life for a reason. I believe this."

Katja emerged then from the whitewash door and gestured Dr. Smith in.

"Hello, Edward. Please come in."

Olek watched the door close but the wood could not stop his sister's thunderous sobs from reaching him.

Dr. Smith left the house that day with his heart aching. He had said what he needed to say and that was that. Katja had looked right through him, with sympathetic eyes, for a lifetime he had lived unfulfilled and unloved. Kalyna had hidden her face in her folded arms, like a baby bird hiding in its nest. She had not looked up even when he left. Olek managed a nod to him and he directed his motor car toward Edna-Star. Edward swallowed hard and licked his lips, parched with dust. He could taste disdain for his past. He would never be able to make amends.

Kalyna stayed the week on the homestead, healing herself by keeping busy tending the chickens, sewing and cooking, and reading. She visited Aunt Mary and Uncle Ivan and went to school with Pavla, admiring her big sister's easy way with children in the village. Life in Edna-Star had carried on without her just fine. Though not ready to go back to Edmonton, Kalyna desperately missed campus life, Rose, Randall and her classes. She was eager to return and reignite the spark of learning she felt was driving her in Law.

Mama had explained everything with honour and grace and said that forgiveness was the highest of all qualities that Kalyna must learn. "Without forgiveness, there is nothing," Mama had said. "If your father could forgive the government for imprisonment, surely you can forgive what has happened. You are alive, you are healthy, and you are destined to change things."

Mama's words resonated inside Kalyna as she boarded the train back to Strathcona Station on Sunday. "Change things."

Chapter Forty-Seven

Mrs. Lazaruk shunned Dr. Smith after that, a love too good to be true, she said, and set to work redecorating her sitting room. Kalyna never asked for an explanation and could only assume Dr. Smith had told her his side of the story as they drove back to Edmonton that day. The sadness in Mrs. Lazaruk greeted her every morning and Kalyna tucked away her personal feeling of guilt for any role she had in this.

She had seen him only once after that on campus, and had hid behind a column until he passed. She had told Rose everything, crying on her shoulder as her friend gasped and hugged her tightly. Rose never mentioned her Smitty again.

With this chapter closed, Kalyna threw herself into her research of the internment camp and her father. She was determined to understand the legal undercurrents of the camps; how and why the government had interned so many of its own citizens.

Her letter-writing campaign began in earnest, directed at the Member of Parliament for Edmonton East, Samuel White. She asked for his assistance to bring this issue of atonement to the forefront of the government's agenda. She said it was a matter of national importance, a quest for dignity, and an opportunity for forgiveness. Her letters, polite but pointed and mailed with zeal, were returned with silence. When no response came to her three letters, Kalyna mustered confidence to try another tactic.

Emboldened by her determination to right the wrong done to her father, she found herself on the doorstep of Mr. White's constituency office in downtown Edmonton. The sun was trying to shine

through the looming clouds, which promised precipitation of some
sort, probably an early flurry. It was Friday after classes and Kalyna
had urged Rose to take the trolly with her to Mr. White's office. She
stared at the black door and the copper nameplate. There was no
turning back. Surely he would speak to her directly now. He just
had to. She would not leave without a face-to-face meeting. Kalyna
raised the brass knocker, moulded onto a winged lion, and knocked
on the grand door three times. Footsteps shuffled toward the door.

"Yes?" A head peered out around the door.

"Good day, we are here to meet with Mr. White on a matter of
great importance. Is he in?"

"Well, no, he is not, dear. He is in Ottawa." Kalyna's face fell. She
breathed rapidly. Failure again.

"Come in, come in out of the cold. I am his secretary, Miss Pringle. Perhaps I can help."

They followed Miss Pringle down the corridor to the first office
on the right. Mail was piled up on the mahogany desk in a criss
cross pattern. Miss Pringle followed Kalyna's eyes.

"Is one of these yours, perhaps?"

"Yes, ma'am." Kalyna replied. "More than one. I've been writing
to Mr. White about a matter of great importance to me and my family and wish to know when he might return to Edmonton."

"He should be back over the holiday, Miss…"

"Miss Federchuk. Apologies, I am Kalyna Federchuk and this is
my colleague, Rose Ross." Her smiling eyes met Rose.

"Well, I can certainly leave Mr. White your names and tell him
you were here and I'm sure he will address your concerns as soon
as he returns."

"Thank you, thank you very much," Kalyna said. She took a
piece of paper from Miss Pringle and wrote her name and phone

number at Mrs. Lazaruk's. Underneath, she wrote, *This is a matter of national importance.*

"Please tell him we called."

"That I will," Miss Pringle nodded.

There were still four weeks before the winter break on campus and Kalyna was determined not to be deterred. She needed to plan her approach carefully, but how?

"Rose, what do you suggest? What is my next step? I feel a bit at a loss."

"Well, since I am your colleague," she laughed and squeezed Kalyna's hand, "I do have an idea. Why not start local, with people you know and trust at the university?"

Kalyna embraced Rose. That is what her father had always said. "Surround yourself with like-minded people and change will come."

Kalyna took her case to her Dean of Law, John Wells. Professor Wells knew Kalyna from class, having taught her in the first semester. He admired her fierce independence and fighting spirit for justice. Professor Rankin had also spoken highly about her abilities. She clearly loved the law itself which was an unwritten prerequisite of the faculty.

The university campus was like Edna-Star in the way word travelled quickly between families, and in this case faculties. He had received the newly-appointed Dean of Medicine, Professor Edward Smith, for a meeting only last week, who had urged him to assist the student, Kalyna Federchuk, with her upcoming request.

"What request is that?" he had asked Dr. Smith.

"A matter of law and justice, Sir," the professor had answered. "I think it's best to hear it from Miss Federchuk. I'm certain she will be contacting you soon."

Special requests from fellow deans were rare so Dean Wells was more than prepared to hear what the young woman had to say.

Kalyna smoothed the pleats on her skirt nervously as she stared at Dr. Wells' office door. In her book bag, she carried her father's release form and two of the letters from Mama that she had exchanged with Wasyl from the camp, relaying information about the work projects he and his fellow prisoners were engaged in, the attempted escapes, and harsh conditions.

"Evidence," Mama had told her. "You'll need some evidence, to back up your request."

Dr. Wells' eyes never lifted from her face. He listened intently, glancing down at the papers only when she referred to specific lines in her oratory. Her sincerity and passion captivated him. Her intention was clear and concise. She, Kalyna Federchuk, wanted the Government of Canada to acknowledge that they had imprisoned their own citizens, wrongly, and apologize to the country publicly.

Her voice trailed off as he took out his pipe and set it down, its smoke curling like a snake dancing to the flute player's sweet tune. Kalyna watched it meditatively, a load lifted from her shoulders.

"Are you finished your legal argument, Miss Federchuk?"

"Yes, Sir. I am, thank you."

"Well, I must say I am mightily impressed with your knowledge of events and your evidence. You will be a fine lawyer one day. This *injustice,* as you say, has had considerable impact upon you, members of your family, and your village. I can see your passion, and indeed your fire, and this is what the law needs, it needs passion. However, Miss Federchuk, this time you speak of was a time of war and in war our country needs to do what it needs to do to protect itself and its people. Do you not agree? Does war not change the rules of the game? The War Measures Act does seem to fit into that category, does it not?"

Kalyna restrained herself from shouting. She breathed deeply, measuring her thoughts and pausing before she answered.

"My opinion is that when a free country imprisons its own citizens for fear they will turn against them, it is unjust. You may not agree, Sir, but I will continue my fight for justice with or without your help."

With a guarded confidence, John Wells answered her plea.

"Miss Federchuk, it is not for me to agree or disagree, but for you to prove the injustice. That is the study of Law."

Kalyna stood then and began to gather her papers.

"Thank you for your time, Dean Wells. I genuinely appreciate it."

"It was my pleasure, Miss Federchuk. I have only one thing to add for your consideration. This quest you are on is for a war past, and the political situation is growing unstable once again. Perhaps it is best for you to let this information settle for a spell and resurrect it when the country is not embroiled in its current turbulent economic state. It is jobs and security that are presently at the forefront of everyone's mind, not reliving history; not now. The time will come for your argument to be heard. That I am sure of."

"Thank you, Sir. I will consider that." Kalyna felt like she was choking, pushing down her rebuttal, but held her trembling hand out to him respectfully.

"Good luck to you then, Miss Federchuk, and good day."

Kalyna waited until she got around the corner, down the hallway, and could stand behind the big white pillar before she allowed her tears to fall. Two dead-ends and nothing to show for her determination. It's as if everyone did want to bury the past and just forget about it. If not now, when? And what Dr. Wells had said about jobs, about the economy; perhaps, she should let this go for now. Perhaps there were bigger fights to fight just now. But when would be the right time? And how would she know?

Chapter Forty-Eight

Olek thought the summer drought of 1938 would be the worst in his lifetime, but he was wrong. The winter months held virtually no snow, resulting in a drought so severe that the following Spring, 1939, even the grasshoppers had migrated for lack of subsistence. Ivan and Mary left their land to the forces of Mother Nature and moved back to The Onyschuk family home in Edna-Star. Pieter had moved to St. Albert, billeted with another farm family, and was studying to be a pilot. Olek lived in Ivan and Mary's original home on the land and tended both theirs and his mother's fields, what little there was to tend.

Money was so tight, they had heated their homes with the dried wheat in their stoves because they couldn't afford coal that spring. The Federchuk family still had two horses and their wagon remained in good condition, and Mama would never sell her dairy cow, though Olek had presented many arguments in favour. But Mama would not be swayed, urging Olek to take his fishing rod in hand to the creek instead, break the thin film of ice, and will a perch or walleye to bite the bobbing dried kalyna cranberry. Pavla still worked in the village school, when there were students, and gave her meagre wage to Mama for food. The dust and dryness of the land seemed to suck out the very life from the farmers in the bloc community, and Kalyna's letters were a great source of joy for Katja. Kalyna was nearing the end of her fourth year in Law School and would soon be articling with one of the biggest firms in Edmonton, Hillier, Myland and Watson. Olek admired his sister for her determination and often wished he, too, could escape to the city.

He watched Mama reading one of Kalyna's letters over again by the fire and knew he would never be able to leave her. The lines on her face spoke to him and told the story of the land he loved so much; his father's dream. He had fallen in love with Henri and Bettina's youngest daughter, Chantelle, and wanted to tell Mama, but that would have to wait. Even love has to wait, he told himself.

Kalyna's private letter to Olek came as a surprise. They had never been that close, Kalyna always with her nose in the book and Olek in the fields, but she had written just the same. Just to him.

April 9, 1939

Dear Olek,

Mama writes of the harshness of the winter months. She speaks endlessly of your kindness and hard work, Olek. I feel compelled to say thank you to you. Thank you for giving your strength and endurance to Mama. Without you she could not survive, and you are a gift to her everyday.

Olek felt himself blushing as a lump rose in his throat.

I wanted to ask for your help, Olek. Help in remembering. Remembering when Papa was in the camp. Remembering the years when Papa came home and how life was for him. Did he talk to you and Mama about his time? I want to know more and I can no longer ask Papa. I dearly wish I had known to ask him so I could carry his story with me. It is one of the hundred or more questions I wish I had asked him.

Olek felt the letter trembling in his hands. He did remember even when he had tried hard to forget. He could remember Mama's tears when he asked about the baby. Later, they had talked about betrayal, about forgiveness. Then there was Papa's silence; whether it was resignation to what had happened or profound sadness, Olek didn't know then, and it passed.

When Kalyna was born, the river of Mama's tears dried up. It was as though the miracle of the new baby brought Mama and Papa renewed hope and the family felt whole again. His papa was the bravest man he knew. If the same thing had happened to him, Olek wasn't sure he could stand it. His papa. He took his handkerchief out of his pocket and wiped his eyes. Why his sister was so insistent on dredging up the past, he didn't know or understand. Papa always said, "Better to let things stay in the past than to carry the burdens forward to a new day." A new day. Why couldn't Kalyna be content with the new day?

Olek, I know you must wonder why I am pursuing this so rigorously. It is for Papa and Mama and for all the internees of Canada. This has been hushed and forgotten and I want the story of the survivors and their families to be told and understood by all Canadians, great and small. Please help me.
Your loving sister,
Kalyna

Olek set the letter back into the envelope and stroked the seal. He carefully folded it in his breast pocket next to his heart. He thought about Kalyna, the most well-read person he knew. Maybe she was right. To pursue justice for her father would protect future generations not just for today, but for the future.

Perhaps it was time to tell Mama about his love for Chantelle after all. It was a new day.

* * *

In the city, John Wells' words resonated with Kalyna each and every day. She had received a written response from Mr. White, her Member of Parliament, echoing Mr. Wells' sentiments. It was a valid argument, he said, a genuine concern. It was true, but it was not for the time when Canada had so much on her plate.

"Take time and build your case," he had urged her. She had heeded his advice and written to Olek to try to recover firsthand memories of the time. Olek would be able to help, she was sure of it.

Kalyna watched the impact of the floundering economy affect the city she had come to love. The Bennett Buggies pulled by horses clip-clopped down Whyte Avenue replacing the motor cars of more prosperous times. The buggies were testimony to the fact that the price of gasoline was out of reach for so many citizens, not just in Edmonton, but, if Kalyna were to fully understand the articles in the newspaper, the economic collapse was world-wide. Headlines reported that another world war was imminent.

Staying devoted to her writing and studies at this turbulent time, Kalyna graduated that year at the top of her class. Dean Wells presented her with the gold-gilded degree and shook her hand firmly.

"Well done, Kalyna. And more to do."

Mama, Pavla, Olek, Auntie Mary and Uncle Ivan, and Mrs. Lazaruk attended her convocation. Kalyna looked up to find them in the bleachers and thought she saw them wave but couldn't be sure, the spotlight was blinding her. She could see the Deans of the University before her though, and her eyes were drawn to the bright blue robe adorning Dr. Smith. His eyes connected with hers, radiating pride and genuine joy.

Kalyna smiled at him, sincerely. A moment of forgiveness. He nodded. He understood her message. She felt at peace then, with him and with everything. He had respected her desire to be left alone these years. She had reached her academic goals and felt a surge of pride.

Her family celebrated that night at Mrs. Lazaruk's home with roast beef, mashed potatoes, and carrots; a fine meal for a golden celebration. Rose and Randall came for dessert. They were engaged to be married that summer, Randall having secured a job as a journalist at The Edmonton Gazette and Rose with a position in the same library as Mrs. Lazaruk.

Olek slipped her a letter that night after dinner when they were out on Mrs. Lazaruk's patio, the scent of the new roses just beginning to blossom surrounding them.

"This letter came for Papa after he died. I kept it from Mama because I didn't want to upset her. It looked very official and was postmarked Ottawa."

"Who's it from?"

"I don't know why exactly, but I never opened it. It was addressed to Papa; it felt wrong to open it." Olek admitted to himself that it was strange that he had never opened it, but had kept it hidden all these years. "I think I meant to read it, but there was always something to tend to. I kept it from Mama to protect her." Olek held the envelope out to Kalyna. "Maybe now it's time."

Kalyna knew this was the missing link to her case without knowing what was inside. There was an energy in the letter itself and it burned in her hand as she held it. She looked at the postmark, squinting in the failing light of dusk shrouding the yard. It was post marked from Ottawa, July,1932.

"Thank you, Olek. Thank you for passing it on."

Kalyna slid her fingernail along the top of the envelope, slicing open the white paper. She unfolded the letter slowly and carefully, as if it was a treasure map. Her eyes scanned the letter to the closing, unable to resist knowing who it was from, cascading past the delicate cursive loops to the signature. Captain Davis. There was a Captain Davis mentioned in Papa's letters to Mama. That same Captain Davis had signed Papa's release papers. She could hear her heart beating as she read.

June 28th, 1932

Dear Mr. Federchuk,

Today marks the fifteenth anniversary of your release and the closing of the camp at Castle Mountain. I remember that day like it was yesterday, the white tents dismantled, billowing in the wind like flags of surrender, the moth-eaten blankets bundled only to be burned before the last train car pulled away.

I have lived for the past fifteen years wondering about you and the other prisoners. Not a day goes by when I don't question what it was all for, what good the camps did, for anyone, and for our country.

Did you get your life back, Mr. Federchuk? Was your family intact upon your return? I wonder and pray for you and your family every day.
Respectfully,
Captain Davis

Kalyna reread the letter many times that night. Captain Davis was probably close to her father's age when he was in the camp, she guessed. And so he would be in his fifties now. Was he still alive? Suddenly Kalyna was hit with a fervour that she must find Captain Davis. He and Papa must have shared some sort of connection, superseding their roles as captain and prisoner. Her papa could win anyone over, she remembered. The letter empowered and emboldened her. One more link. She put it under her pillow that night, making a wish for its power of influence to wash over her.

May 15, 1939

Dear Captain Davis,

My name is Kalyna Federchuk and I am the youngest daughter of Wasyl Federchuk. I am grateful to you for your heartfelt words. My father passed away eight years ago, and your letter remained unopened until now. I would be very grateful if I may ask you some questions about Castle Camp and my father's life there. I will await your response.
Sincerely,
Kalyna Federchuk

Kalyna reread her letter just before she posted it. She was eager to meet Captain Davis, but a face-to-face meeting would have to wait.

As her professors, Honourable Member of Parliament Mr. White, and the newspapers had predicted, the onslaught of the war consumed the country and, indeed, the world. Many young men in Kalyna's own graduating class proudly joined the forces, believing that freedom was well worth fighting for and expecting to be home by Christmas. It was the same in Edna-Star. Young men ached to protect the freedom that their parents had sought so valiantly years before when they crossed the Atlantic. Aunt Mary and Uncle Ivan's only son, Pieter, had been one of the first to serve in Belgium, and Kalyna feared he had been killed even before the news reached her.

Tears flowed in Edna-Star for their golden child, a brave young man, fighting for his country; a hero like Wasyl. Kalyna had grown up with Pieter, born the same year, best cousins. They shared a sense of adventure, Pieter with flying airplanes and Kalyna escaping into her books. The news of his death seeped inside her, landing in the bottom of her stomach like a rock, solid and unmoving. This war had changed everything; her country, her city, and her family. Its impact and intensity was far-reaching and Kalyna buried her face in her hands. When she emerged she felt a renewed sense of service to the country she loved.

October 7, 1939

Dear Miss Federchuk,

Thank you for your letter. I was very sorry to learn of your father's death. Wasyl Federchuk was a good man, a quiet leader in the camp, and respected by all of the guards and prisoners alike. The time of the camps is buried, but not forgotten, and I would be honoured to share my memories of your father with you.
Respectfully,
Captain Davis

*   *   *

October 20, 1939

Dear Captain Davis,

Thank you for your response. I have so many questions. It is difficult to know where to begin. I am a newly-practicing lawyer and desire to know not only my father's story, but the story of the camp itself. My mother has told me there were many other internment camps across Canada as well. Will you help me to uncover this information and assist in my quest for atonement with the Federal Government?

Kalyna paused. Her letter was very pointed, perhaps too over-bearing, but if not now, when? The words echoed. After all, Captain Davis had reached out to her father. Wasn't atonement what he too may have been seeking? She signed, sealed, stamped, and posted it before she changed her mind.

The war was all-consuming and when no letter came from Captain Davis, Kalyna concluded that he too had been swept up in the war's fervour, by virtue of his position and standing with the forces.

Chapter Forty-Nine

Kalyna quickly became renowned in Edmonton legal circles as the articling student-of-choice for cases of injustice. She dedicated her keen sense of justice for underdogs to cases of employment rights for men and women, fiercely arguing for equal pay for equal work. Kalyna Federchuk was forthright in her summaries, passionate about people, and built up her cases like a fortress. She worked tirelessly at the provincial level, lobbying the members of the legislature with great resolve. Her firm held her in high esteem and she was asked to remain on as partner.

Always fiercely independent, Kalyna struck out on her own, hanging out her own shingle and as her practice in Edmonton flourished Kalyna hired two junior lawyers to assist her in her research work. She was asked to speak at many events in Edmonton and on campus. Dean Wells never forgot about her and would invite her as an itinerant speaker on Human Rights. She shared with him her work on the Aboriginal Nations' resolution and he would nod.

"How's your other case coming?" he would ask.

"Waiting, biding my time," she would answer. She longed for a response from Captain Davis and still found herself looking hopefully at every letter the firm received to see if it was from him.

Throughout these war years, Kalyna's heart was never far from Edna-Star. She was diligent in keeping in touch with her mother although her letters often seemed to offer little substance. Mama told her it was not so much what Kalyna wrote that mattered, it was just important to stay in touch and held steadfast that no, she wasn't getting a phone anytime soon.

Olek had married Chantelle, Henri and Bettina's daughter, and they were raising a family of three, still farming and eking out their living from the land. "I can never leave," Olek had told Kalyna the night of his wedding. "This land is Papa and it is my home."

Pavla continued to work at the schoolhouse and still lived with Mama, helping out on the homestead. Aunt Mary and Uncle Ivan had taken over the grocery shop from Mrs. Benton who wanted to move to the city now that her husband had passed away. Dr. Lazaruk had retired and presently stayed in the very room where Kalyna's ideas about change had blossomed all those years ago. Kalyna still visited Mrs. Lazaruk for Sunday dinner and the doctor would regale them both with tales about Edna-Star in the good old days.

She received the phone call in her Edmonton office in the Spring of 1956. Mama was sick with pneumonia, her breathing severely laboured and the doctor had told the family to fear the worst.

Olek said, "You need to come home, Kalyna. Mama needs you and we need you here." Kalyna put down the phone, gathered her papers into a folder and handed them to Stephanie and Barb, her new junior lawyers.

When the call comes, children go home. There is a magnetism that pulls the heart back and a yearning for that last moment to hold and look into the eyes of the person that loved you the most. Kalyna's only hope as she boarded the train was that she would not be too late.

Mama lay on her bed, cocooned in the same quilt from all those years ago, tucked lightly and lovingly over her frail petite frame. She looked like a child to Kalyna, as Olek and Pavla ushered her into the house with hushed voices. The house seemed smaller now, compressing both Mama and her. The open room with the fireplace on one side, the familiar pine table, and Mama's straw bed were all in view. Kalyna saw the small undulations as Mama's chest rose and fell, slowly and haltingly.

Sometimes there was no breath. It was as though Mama had forgotten to breathe in that cycle and then she would begin again, laboured and rattling. Kalyna knelt by her bedside while Olek got her a pine chair to sit upon.

"Mama, I'm here. It's me, Kalyna."

Mama's eyes fluttered then, her fingers on her left hand wiggled and Kalyna took hold of her hand. Mama's skin was porcelain white, translucent, as though the colour had already drained itself from the paper-thin flesh. Kalyna stroked Mama's fingers, soothingly, softly, and sang her the lullaby she used to sing to with the music box. "Too Ra Lu, Ra Loo Ra..."

Mama's blue eyes opened and she smiled. She tried to sit up, which set off a coughing spasm. Pavla appeared on her other side with a glass of water.

"Here, Mama, drink this. It will help."

Kalyna watched this helplessly. She suddenly had so much to say to her mama, and there seemed little time. She held Mama's hand and asked if she could sit with her.

"I want to tell you about one of my greatest days, Mama. It was long ago, before I graduated, but I remember it like it was yesterday."

Kalyna could not explain why she had chosen that moment and that story about swimming and the sensation of floating to tell Mama. She only knew as she sat with her and told her about staring at the blue sky above her, her eyes alert, her hearing muffled by water, she felt as if she had entered another world, a peaceful world where she had never felt so calm. Mama closed her eyes, but Kalyna knew she was listening and imagining.

"You just lie back, Mama, and pretend you are a star in the sky, floating amongst the clouds."

Olek made funeral arrangements for Mama the next day, and Pavla and Kalyna packed up her belongings to give to the Red Cross Agency. The sisters said little to each other, each engulfed in their own sorrow. It was at the train station that Pavla broke the silence.

"You know, she talked about you all the time, Kalyna," Pavla said. "She was so very proud of you and your work."

"She was equally proud of you, dear sister. Each of her letters spoke of your teaching and commitment to the community."

Kalyna felt the same sense of isolation then that she had when she was a child. She loved her community, Edna-Star, but she didn't belong here. She had always felt this separation and it was present even now. She longed to return to the city.

Chapter Fifty

Kalyna swallowed hard and pushed her feet solidly into the floor. Since Pieter had died, she had a fear of flying, of letting herself be in someone else's control. The steward nodded, ushering her forward. The gate attendant waited impatiently. Each step felt like a brick landing in mud, her legs like spindly noodles barely holding her up. Perhaps, she didn't need to fly.

"I need you."

Kalyna turned around to face the voice, the presence behind her, but there was no one, only impassive faces and a small child staring up at her.

Kalyna pressed on, forcing each step into the tunnel leading to the entrance to the plane on the tarmac. No turning back now. She controlled her thoughts; she told herself, *Think of something else, dammit.* Kalyna had not forgotten about Captain Davis but had not heard from him since that pointed letter over sixteen years ago. She felt for the envelope in her pocket, comforted by its presence. This was her primary quest when she was in Ottawa.

Time is mysterious and its passing even more curious. Pausing on the porch of the red brick bungalow, Kalyna double-checked the house number, comparing it to the flowing cursive numbers and letters on the envelope in her hand. This was it, Captain Davis' home. Would he even still be living here after all this time? Would he welcome her in? Would he want to talk to her?

She knocked quietly; timidly. No answer. She knocked again, louder this time, and with confidence. Shuffling and a woman's muffled voice came from behind the door. Kalyna's eyes were drawn to the door knob turning slowly.

"Hello. Who's there?" a voice asked through the safety chain.

"Uh, hello." Kalyna answered. "My name is Kalyna Federchuk, from Edmonton. I was writing to Mr. Davis about a matter of great importance. He knew my father many years ago."

The chain clanged, the door shut, and there was more shuffling and a muffled male's voice.

The safety latch and chain were removed and Kalyna stood face to face with a towering, elderly man she could only assume was Captain Davis.

Kalyna suddenly felt alone and fearful. A wave of heat flushed her body as she reached out to the officer to shake his hand.

The woman beside him spoke. Kalyna had been so struck by the commanding presence of Captain Davis that she had not noticed the petite woman at his side.

"She is wanting to shake your hand, Harold," she said. "Right in front of you now."

Captain Davis reached out and found Kalyna's outstretched hand.

"Kalyna Federchuk. I am pleased to make your acquaintance."

"Do come in," the woman urged.

Kalyna watched as the woman guided Captain Davis to a brown easy chair.

"I am Mrs. Davis," she acknowledged. "My husband has spoken about your father for many years."

Kalyna looked around for a place to sit, the room spartan and immaculately kept.

"I keep it like this for Harold. He needs it to be simple, on account of his eyes, you see. He's blind."

She disappeared momentarily into the kitchen and returned

with a soft padded chair.

"Have a seat now and I'll make some tea." She patted Captain Davis's hand gently as she left the room.

Kalyna sat silently, wondering where to start.

Captain Davis broke the silence. "I may be blind," he said, "but I can see your father in you. I felt it in your handshake; the same strength, the same courage."

Kalyna felt a lump in her throat. She felt overcome with emotion. "Thank you, Sir. Thank you for seeing me. When you didn't write back all those years ago…." Her voice trailed off.

"War changes everything, Miss Federchuk; the first war and then this second. Somehow all that matters is survival. Hard for you to understand, I know. Then, I had my accident and I lost my sight."

Kalyna nodded, then chastised herself. "Yes," she agreed. She could hear the tea kettle whistling in the kitchen and Mrs. Davis humming. She willed his lovely wife to come back and join them.

"So tell me what it is you want to know, Miss Federchuk."

"I want to know everything. I want to know the beginning. How the camps came to be, the sentiment behind them, the reasons…"

"You must know some of the background from your mother. Your father wrote many letters to her, saving every coupon to trade in for the writing paper at the canteen. When I would ask him when he would buy himself something, he smiled so broadly and would say, 'But I am buying something for me. These letters mean everything to me.'"

Mrs. Davis floated back to the room silently, placing Captain Davis's tea in his special holder next to the chair and tapping his hand gently to guide it to the handle. She nodded to Kalyna. "Milk or sugar?"

Kalyna smiled. "Black is fine, thank you." She wanted him to go on. "Tell me about the daily life, how did the men spend their days?"

"It was a work camp and the men like your father, they were the work horses behind building the roads, the parks, the gardens." He paused. "Your father worked hard, Miss Federchuk, perhaps hardest of all, believing that his hard work might get him out earlier. We told the men that to make them work harder. Your father believed it with his heart and soul. It was my job to make him, all of them, believe that. It was my job." He reached down beside the chair locating a small box bound with string, bringing it to his lap.

"I've kept this to remember. Elise has read it to me so many times now, I've memorized every word. You see, Miss Federchuk, we didn't want to be in those camps any more than the men like your father did. They were forced..." his voice trailed off. "We were all forced to be there and we made the best of it."

He caressed the top of the box finding the knotted string. "Elise?"

"Right here, dear."

"It is time."

Mrs. Davis took the box and handed it to Kalyna. "He wants you to have it."

Kalyna felt the weight of the moment as she took the box. It was an old tool box, made of grey metal with a little padlock, unlatched for the last time.

"It's my diary in there. It's for you. To build your case. Daily life, the good and the bad, details nobody knew unless they were there at Castle."

Mrs. Davis nodded encouragingly and Kalyna removed the tiny padlock, her fingers quivering, and opened the hinged lid. The worn string, tied and untied multiple times, unlaced easily and fell to the sides of the journal as if sighing from relief. Kalyna opened the yellowed pages of the diary, feeling the weight of the information held within its covers. Soft graphite curled over the pages: dates, sketches, and weather reports. Captain Davis' dated entries filled the leather-bound notebook. Kalyna felt an overwhelming sense of gratitude.

"Thank you, Sir. This is exactly what I need. To make things right."

Captain Davis wiped his eyes. "Some say you can see clearer when…oh just make it right, Miss Federchuk, so people can understand and forgive."

He stood up then and reached out to her.

Kalyna nodded. "Yes, Captain Davis, I will." She set down the box on her chair and stood up to take his hands in hers.

"I'll see you out," Mrs. Davis said.

When he heard the safety lock go back on, Captain Davis held his face in his hands and wept. It was done.

Kalyna held the silver box in her lap on the plane not daring to let it out of her sight. "Thank you for dreaming with me, dreaming of what can be possible with forgiveness and understanding. Now, it is the right time."

Acknowledgements

I would like to thank my family for their support throughout the writing process, including listening to the first oral version as we trekked the trails of Kananaskis, Alberta. As an adult, I asked my grandma Olga to tell me stories of her childhood in Edna-Star and about her meeting my grandpa, Carl. Their stories and their journeys have made their way into Kalyna. I also want to acknowledge the strength of my mom who, like Katja, was steadfast and true in her belief that life goes on and we must keep the past in the past. I have been very inspired by my mother-in-law, Joan Clark, who encouraged me to write this story as we crossed the bridge in Banff en route to Cave and Basin many years ago.

Many people provided feedback to the story in its many stages including: Tony Clark, Joan Clark, Lorraine Sanborn, Gloria Lawrence, and Sara Clark. I am grateful for all your feedback and support.

I would like to acknowledge the research and work of Lubomyr Luciuk entitled, "*In Fear of the Barbed Wire Fence - Canada's First National Internment Operations of Ukrainian Canadians 1914-1920*", published in 2001. This was the same year Inky Mark brought forth Bill C - 331 to Parliament. Kalyna is told to "wait for the right time" and in 2008, Prime Minister Harper acknowledged this event in our history and recognized the need to fund the Internment Museum and other educational initiatives across Canada. All of the characters in Kalyna are fictional although the events are based on facts that have occurred and the people that have lived through these events.

Our collective history is what strengthens us and binds us in one great community and gives us hope for our future. Kalyna is part of that hope.

I would like to thank Simon Lee for taking the promo pictures.

Oi Khodyt Son Kolo Vikon-The Dream Passes By the Window
English Translation

The Dream passes by the window,
And Sleep by the fence.
The Dream asks Sleep:
"Where should we rest tonight?"

Where the house is warm,
Where the child is small,
There we will go,
And rock the child to sleep.

There we will sleep,
and will rock the child:
Sleep, sleep, my little falcon,
Sleep, sleep, my little dove.

When You Are Old by William Butler Yeats

When you are old and gray and full of sleep,
And nodding by the fire, take down this book,
And slowly read, and dream of the soft look
Your eyes had once, and of their shadows deep;

How many loved your moments of glad grace,
And loved your beauty with love false or true,
But one man loved the pilgrim soul in you,
And loved the sorrows of your changing face;

And bending down beside the glowing bars,
Murmur, a little sadly, how Love fled
And paced upon the mountains overhead
And hid his face among a crowd of stars.

Translations

Sviata Vecheria.................................. dinner holidays

vsi peryadky seyallorder .... in this manner

vy smilyvi.. you are brave

ya doviryaayutobi .... I trusted you

spasybi..thank you

troisti muzyki ....folk music trio

kutia and kolach ....loaves of bread

dudkh...spirit

About the Author

PAM CLARK grew up in Edmonton, Alberta close to Edna-Star and lived with the story of Wasyl, Katja and Kalyna inside of her for many years. Kalyna is her first novel and is a tribute to her Ukrainian Canadian heritage and prairie home. She now lives in Calgary with her family.